BONE LAKE

BONE LAKE

DRUSILLA CAMPBELL

MADISON
PARK
PRESS™

NEW YORK

Published by Madison Park Press, 15 East 26th Street, New York, NY 10010. Madison Park Press is a trademark of Bookspan.

Book design by Christos Peterson

ISBN: 978-1-58288-268-0

Printed in the United States of America

For Art

Acknowledgments

Since 1981, the Southern Poverty Law Center in Montgomery, Alabama, has been teaching tolerance and speaking out against all forms of discrimination. In the last decade they have been particularly fearless about exposing white supremacist organizations and hate groups of all kinds. The SPLC's quarterly magazine, the *Intelligence Report*, was a source of inspiration and reliable information throughout the writing of *Bone Lake*.

I am grateful for the patience and support of my family and friends. You forgave me for not returning your calls and for missing our appointments. The months wore on and you did not abandon me.

Rocky Campbell urged me to write *Bone Lake* and knew what it was about before I did. Matt abandoned his wife and child to keep my computer running. Nicki and Isabelle, I love you both.

To Guru Judy Reeves, to Carole and Sharon and all the ladies of the Arrowhead Association, thank you for your wisdom and ready humor.

Thank you, Carole Baron, for taking a risk with this book, and Christine Zika for being a talented, inspirational editor. Always my appreciation to my agent, Angela Rinaldi, who returns my calls and does not nag.

Finally, Art Campbell deserves public recognition for his patience, love and loyalty. What a guy!

one

ISABELLE CALCULATED that there were roughly seven hundred and twelve highway miles between San Diego and Santa Rosa, and the only stoplights were on the road between the ranch and I94, which meant that except for LA, where anything was possible, it would be fast driving all the way north. She divided the distance by eighty miles an hour and came up with a minimum trip of eight and a half nerve-shredding hours.

But they had to go. Immediately, even if it was the middle of the night. FBI agent Billy Horne had been her husband's friend for years, but the tone of his call was peremptory, leaving no room for argument.

"You stay home," Eli said, dropping toiletries into his dopp kit. "I'll be okay. I've got a book to listen to."

A bitchy corner of her heart thought this was a fine idea. He had lied to her and deserved to be alone, brooding on his mistake. She watched him bend over and dig around under the bathroom sink. She knew he was looking for a small tube of toothpaste, and she knew where there were several, but at that moment his frustration gratified her.

He found the toothpaste, and she saw him wince as he straightened up, holding the tube hard in his hand like a relay runner with the baton. The long drive would be hard on his back.

She blurted what was on her mind. "You told me your brother was dead. You told me you had no family."

"Hurting you was never my intention."

"Did I say I was hurt? Did you hear me say that?"

"Okay, I get it; you're pissed."

More like mean as snakes, but confused too. It was not like Eli to deceive her, and if he had lied about having a brother, maybe he had been keeping other secrets.

"We promised to be honest with each other." She tried not to sound whiny.

"I didn't lie. I never mentioned him."

"He's your family."

"No, he's not. You're my family. I left him behind a long time ago."

"You can't just leave a brother behind."

"He was my half brother. My mother got together with his father after my dad left. I've told you, Isabelle, we weren't a Norman Rockwell family. When I met you I wanted to forget it all. My life began with you, with my work and the ranch and the horses. All that time before . . ." He shrugged. "Don't blame me for this, Izzy. I'm talking survival here."

Eli was a great writer and respected the power of words. If he said survival, he meant precisely that.

"That settles it. I'm coming with you. If this brother was so important you had to pretend he didn't exist, then you can't go through this alone. Whatever happened between you two, whatever he did—"

"Darren," Eli said. "His name is Darren."

⌒

"He's dead. And so is his wife."

Eli felt relief.

Behind federal agent Billy Horne a square of window framed Santa Rosa's modest skyline under a heavy sky; flags whiplashed in a cold wind, and an ominous cloud bank crept over the foothills between the town and the Pacific.

He felt no grief, no regret. And now maybe he wouldn't have to feel guilty either.

"What did Darren have to do with the FBI?"

Horne pinched his nose between his thumb and forefinger. Though he was roughly Eli's age, a man in his early fifties, his face was deeply lined.

A young woman came in with a tray of coffee and sweet rolls and placed them on the desk. Horne waited a moment after the door closed behind her.

"When's the last time you saw your brother?"

"He was in high school."

"And you never saw him after that?"

The memory of their last meeting still stung.

"Well, let me tell you a little bit about him." Horne took a swallow of coffee. "After your last visit to Great Falls, he stuck around town for a year or so. Turned out he was a gifted mechanic, and he made out okay fixing cars and motorcycles."

In Great Falls, Darren had worked at a Harley dealership called Hog Heaven; when he could, he bought a bike of his own and took off, driving from one small western town to another, stopping to work only long enough to stake his next ride.

"Eventually he landed in the hospital after a spinout in a place called Red Bird, in Idaho. Broke his collarbone, so he was stuck there through the winter. Two things happened to him in Red Bird. First off, he met a girl named Barbara who worked nights at the hospital as a nurse's aide. Days she helped out at a day-care center in exchange for a room."

Eli listened, and with his writer's imagination he saw his brother, scrawny and long boned with pouting James Dean good looks, blond and blue-eyed like his father, riding a motorcycle, lying in a hospital bed, making love to a girl.

"He fell pretty hard for her, and right away she was pregnant. They got married by a justice of the peace. The other person he met in Red Bird was Edgar Barrett. Barrett was a witness at the wedding and so was his daughter, Andrea. Called Andy."

Horne did not have to remind Eli and Isabelle who Barrett was. A few years back he had made headlines when federal agents found firearms, ammunition and bomb-making supplies hidden in an underground bunker behind his house in a small town in eastern Oregon. Eli remembered a news photo of a snarly old man with a bad set of false teeth.

"He died in prison four years ago. But not before he wrote something called 'The True Word Manifesto.' "

"I've never heard of it," Eli said.

"The True Word Brethren are militant white suprema-cists. Cockeyed, so-called Christians whose declared goal is to bring down the government of the United States," Horne said. "Their brand of Christianity isn't like anything you'll en-counter in your friendly neighborhood church. They believe that when the Bible says, in Genesis, that God created the an-imals first, it means dogs and cats and birds and bugs *plus* all the nonwhite races. Adam was the first Aryan, and he was created to be master over everything that came before. If you're not an Aryan, the Brethren say, you don't have a soul and you're an animal, a mud."

When True Word Brethren talked about animals, they meant people like Eli's beautiful dark-eyed wife, Irish on one side and Mexican on the other.

"The Brethren especially hate the Jews. It's the usual Christ-killer garbage, and they deny the Holocaust, of course. Jews don't even count as animals in their mythology. They're the offspring of Eve and Satan, and they get blamed for everything bad that ever happened in the world. The Brethren call the government ZOG, for Zionist-Occupied Government. And their stated goal is to bring it down."

The atmosphere in the room was stale, and the coffee had

left a foul taste in Eli's mouth. He wished he were home, riding Zarahas up the mountain behind the ranch in the clean morning air.

"Barrett's daughter, Andy, is even worse than her old man. He was a talker, but she's a doer. And she's smart. If she were mainstream, she'd be president of some big corporation."

With her father in prison, Andy Barrett had organized the scattered groups of True Word Brethren in the West. There were a few Brethren groups in the upper Midwest and the South, a few in Texas, but the majority were in the small towns west of the Rocky Mountains.

"Normally the Brethren wouldn't like it, a woman in charge. But Andy is Edgar's anointed and tough as any man."

"Okay," Eli said. "There's this group—a group of groups—and they want to overthrow the government. Because they're Aryans and everyone else is an animal."

"That's pretty much it."

The conversation was hard to take seriously. "Are you guys running out of work? Not enough kidnappings and bank heists to keep you busy?"

Horne stood up, shoved his hands into his pants pockets and turned to stare at the raindrops slipping down the window behind his desk. To the west, where the clouds and the summit of the coast range met, a bolt of lightning illuminated a fortress of clouds. Eli felt the prickle of anticipation that real weather always brought. It had been the same when he was a kid in Great Falls, standing in the vacant lot next door to the duplex, shivering and smelling snow on the wind from Canada.

After a moment Horne again sank into his desk chair. Through the continuing silence the only sounds were the clicking of the heater and the beat of rain on window glass.

"What I'm going to tell you is classified, and I'm only doing it because we go back a way and I want you to know what you're getting into."

"I didn't know we were getting into anything," Isabelle said.

"Just hear me out. Okay?"

A flash of lightning illuminated the window. The ceiling fixture dimmed and brightened. Later, Eli would remember the lightning as a portent. He and Isabelle could have stood up right then and made it clear they wanted no part of whatever Horne had in mind for them. Instead, they let their curiosity rule the moment—curiosity and, for Eli, a peculiar excitement akin to what he had felt as a kid waiting for a storm.

Perhaps to give himself time to order his thoughts, Horne collected their empty coffee cups and the napkins covered with flakes of pastry and dropped it all into a gray plastic wastebasket.

"For a long time the Bureau dismissed the Brethren as a bunch of harmless malcontents. Around here, in the mountains north to Oregon, there's lots of weirdos. You can get lost in northern California, and that's what most of these people want, to drop off the map. But after Barrett went to prison,

Aryan Nation guys started coming out, talking about this Manifesto like it really mattered. They took it seriously, so we decided we should too." He shook his head as if for a moment even he thought the story was too wild to believe. "What we found was a wake-up call, let me tell you. The True Word philosophy may be crazy, but the men and women who believe it aren't. Thanks to Andy Barrett and the inspiration of 9/11, they are confident and organized and committed to their cause. Willing to die for it, if necessary."

"Even so," Eli said, "you're still talking about a small group—"

"The core group is maybe no more than ten or fifteen. But small's good. Barrett says in the Manifesto that the bigger the group, the more vulnerable it is. He favored many small groups, scattered around the country."

"Like Communist cells," Isabelle said.

"That's right. Andy Barrett's the only one who knows how they link up. But we know how they work. They move into small towns, and right off they establish themselves as good, quiet neighbors and hard workers. According to the Manifesto you can't be a full member of the Brethren unless you've got a trade. They want nothing to do with welfare. It says somewhere that if you can't earn your living—preferably with your hands or your strong back—you're either a child or an animal.

"These people make ideal neighbors. They work hard and they don't disturb the peace. Their kids are well behaved. If they attract attention, it's the good kind. In every town they pick up a few converts, and if these people stick long enough, they maybe hear about the Manifesto; and if they like what they hear, it makes them feel powerful. That's roughly what happened to Darren in Red Bird."

Eli had virtually raised his younger half brother, and he supposed the clannish Brethren had felt like family to him. But so what? Eli was impatient and had to remind himself that Billy Horne would not have called them to Santa Rosa to waste their time.

"One of the big mistakes we make in this country is believing that people who don't think like us are stupid," Horne said. "That's why we're always getting caught with our pants down, looking dumb as dirt. The True Word Brethren know how *not* to be noticed. With them it's practically an art form. They don't stay put for more than a couple of years at a stretch, and when a group moves, it breaks up, scatters to other towns. They start all over. New names, new identification."

"That must cost a bundle," Eli said. "Where's the money coming from?"

"I'm getting to that." Horne put his elbows on his desk, steepling his hands. "But first, I want you to know you can back out. It's not too late."

"Shit, Billy, we don't even know what you're talking about."

"What I say can't go outside this room. We clear on that?"

Eli looked at Isabelle. "Okay."

"If it does get out, the Bureau will take away my gun and bounce me up to Deadhorse, Alaska."

Eli, still irritated but interested now, held up three fingers. "Scout's honor."

Horne chewed his lower lip.

"You remember the bombing up in Olympia? Washington?"

Someone never identified had planted explosives in the underground garage where state employees parked their cars. The wife of a state senator had been killed, several million dollars worth of vehicles and structure destroyed and the city thrown into a crisis that now, eighteen months after the event, still reverberated.

"They tried the same thing in Sacramento six months ago, but a parking attendant got suspicious and called the bomb squad in time."

"I never heard that."

"Eli, my man, there's lots you never hear."

⟵

Horne rolled his chair back, put his feet on his desk then put them back on the floor. Isabelle didn't think she'd ever seen anyone wound so tight.

"The Manifesto says the stability of this country, any country, isn't about government and human rights. What really matters to people is predictability: knowing that when they flip the switch, the lights go on; that there's water in the tap; that the phones and electricity work and that the mail gets delivered on time. You take away predictability, and this country's closer to the edge than any of us want to believe."

From her own experience Isabelle knew this was true.

A few months back someone had shot out the stoplights along Pico, Santa Monica and Wilshire boulevards. LA police later claimed it was a gang event and nothing to worry about. But no one driving in the city that day would forget the jam caused by the vandalism. She and Eli had just come from an exhibit at the Los Angeles County Museum of Art and were caught in traffic on Wilshire for four and a half hours. Since then, whenever she saw a traffic light out of service, she felt a frisson of anxiety.

"Edgar Barrett believed that if the True Word Brethren can create a mood of distrust and fear in the country, the people will happily give up their rights and liberty to whoever promises to restore order."

"How does this connect with my brother?"

"Darren was good at engines—brilliant, actually. And a certain kind of bomb—it's like an engine. You fit the parts together and bang, it works."

"Darren killed that woman in Olympia? He made bombs? I don't believe it."

"The thing about bomb makers is that most have big egos, and they're real proud of their work; and when they're successful, they get pissed because no one knows who they are. They don't like being anonymous, so they can't resist leaving a signature. Kind of a gotcha thing to the cops or the feds.

What Darren did was scrape some of the label off every battery he used. They look striped.

"The first time Darren came on our radar was when a couple of kids were seen hiding something in the bushes around the playground equipment at a Jewish school in Shasta. Police were called in and disarmed a small bomb. Inside were these batteries with striped labels like we'd found on the device in Sacramento. We knew there was a True Word cell in a little burg called Codyville in the Siskiyou Mountains, and it's not far from Shasta. Right off we suspected them and put an agent in the big thrift shop in Yreka where the women shopped. Our agent was an Indian guy. All the Brethren women except Barbara treated him like he had Ebola. Barbara, though, she was curious and started asking questions about India."

Isabelle gave half her attention to Horne, the rest to Eli. He had a death grip on the arm of the chair.

Over a period of several months, as Barbara came to trust Agent Singh, she confided some of her unhappiness with the True Word Brethren. She said Darren had a hobby, explosives, and it bothered her. He spent too much time in a basement room behind a locked door. Singh asked about the Olympia bombing, but Barbara didn't know anything. She might have been lying, but Singh said her shock was real. She was never part of the inner circle. Darren was, but apparently Andy didn't trust Barbara, which meant no one in the Brethren did. Singh asked her why she didn't just leave, and she said she was afraid. She would never go without her daughter, and Darren would kill her rather than let the child go.

Isabelle straightened. "There's a child?"

"Singh told Barbara that the government would protect them."

"And now she's dead," Isabelle said.

Horne took his feet off the desk and leaned forward. "The girl, Callen, had a special relationship with Andy Barrett. That was one of the things that bothered Barbara most. She wanted to get her away from Andy's influence."

A child, Isabelle thought. This is all about a little girl. She held her hands in her lap and pretended she was calm.

"We don't know exactly what happened. Apparently, Andy's suspicion of Barbara extended to Darren too. There was a fire and they were both killed. We believe they were shot first."

"And the daughter? How did she get away?"

"Luck and guts." Horne chuckled. "She's a formidable kid. If it's true Andy wanted a protégé, Callen was a great choice."

It was quarter after two. They had been in Billy Horne's office since before nine that morning. Off and on throughout the day someone had brought them coffee, sodas and sandwiches. Isabelle could not remember what she'd eaten.

"Barbara told Singh—let it slip, actually—that Andy took Callen with her to meet whoever bankrolls the Brethren. We want Andy, but even more we want her patron."

"Without cash, the True Word Brethren are harmless," Eli said.

"Pretty much," Horne said. "For the last month we've had Callen in custody, but she won't tell us anything. She thinks she's a soldier in the war against ZOG. Keeps repeating the Fourteen Words over and over—like name, rank and serial number."

"What are the Fourteen Words?" Isabelle asked.

"I will secure the existence of our people and a future for white children. Basic True Word bullshit. We could break her down, but to do it we'd have to screw with her head, and I really don't want to do that."

Isabelle glanced at a credenza under the window behind Horne. There was a picture of his family, a gang of children and a pretty, pudgy wife.

"She doesn't even believe her parents are dead. She says the fire was a cover-up and they're really off on assignment."

"What kind of assignment?"

"She doesn't know. Close as she was to Andy, our shrink doesn't think she knew anything about Olympia or Sacramento. And right now her mind's shut down around the trauma of the fire."

Isabelle understood where Horne's story was going and why they had driven all night to hear it.

Horne said, "I'd never ask you this if I didn't believe you two have what it takes to turn this kid."

Eli looked incredulous.

"Listen, all I want is for you to soften her up, bring her around so she doubts the Brethren, begins to question the shit she was taught. Next step is to have her believe that her parents are dead. If she accepts that the Brethren killed them, she'll answer all our questions."

"No," Eli said. "It's too dangerous. I don't want Isabelle or me involved."

"They won't know she's with you."

Eli waved his words away. "They'll find me. All they need to do is a reasonably sophisticated Internet search. I'm famous, Billy, remember?"

"Right, but here's the thing. No one knows Darren had a brother. Even Barbara didn't."

Isabelle looked at Eli and Billy Horne facing off across the gun-metal-gray desk, two big men with miles on them, friends brought together at this time by coincidence and necessity, discomfited by conflict. The tension between them made her neck and back ache.

She said, "We need to be alone to talk about this."

"There's nothing to talk about." Eli's face had gone white with determination.

"I don't think we should dismiss the idea without at least considering it. After all, we've come all this way—"

"Jesus, Isabelle, you can't be serious."

Horne said, "Give it six months, Eli."

"I won't give it six days."

Isabelle turned in her chair so their knees were almost touching. Looking into his eyes, she said, "We have everything. She has nothing. Can't we take a chance?"

"She won't be our baby, Izzy." His expression twisted with the memory of their daughter born dead ten years before. "That chance is gone."

The doctor had told Isabelle she would never have children, and after a long time she had accepted the truth and turned her energies to the ranch and the animals they rescued. She had made her peace with fate, or so she thought. Now the possibility of a child on the ranch—even a difficult one—thrilled her. She would consider the negatives later.

two

S HE HEARS her mother's voice.

Stay here, Callen, you'll be safe. Take this pill. See how small it is? You don't even need water. You'll sleep, and when you wake up, we'll go on a trip. Just you and me.

Callen tugged up the yellow blanket and dug her shoulder deeper into the pillow.

She is in the blanket basket, buried beneath quilts and blankets; her mouth is full of screams, but her jaws are frozen shut and the screams multiply, trapped inside her, filling her chest and throat and blocking her breath. She feels her eyeballs swell against her eyelids, and her legs won't move. She imagines she is a beam of light and focuses her energy up through the top of the wicker basket. Slowly it begins to rise, but she isn't doing it. Someone bad is lifting it, a person without a face. But she sees a necklace, a long chain with an iron cross at the end swinging inches from her face. She tries to burrow deeper into the blanket basket, but the more she digs, the closer to the top she is, and then the lid floats up like a sheet pinned to the clothes line, a windy day, sunshine pouring down, a yellow and white sheet, a field of daisies . . .

⟿

An angry voice from outside woke Callen. She threw back the flowered sheet and ran to a window, believing the Brethren had finally come for her. A beat-up truck idled in the graveled yard between the house and barn. An old man with sparse, springy gray hair, shirtless, in overalls and shit-kicker boots, stood by the truck's open door. The slope of roof hid her uncle Eli, but Callen heard him speak in a firm voice.

"Jubal Spry, if you can't be a good neighbor, I don't want you on my property."

A rock of disappointment dropped to the bottom of Callen's stomach.

The old man said, "I'm tellin' you, there's a big cat around and it's gonna get my goats. Best you help me kill it 'fore it does serious damage. You got a nice couple of colts out there on your back paddock. Make a good meal for a—"

"First off, Jubal, it's illegal to hunt mountain lions. You catch one after your goats, that's one thing, but you can't just go off like a big game hunter. And second," Eli moved out from under the roof's overhang, and Callen saw the top of his soft-brimmed hat. "I've moved my colts in close for the summer, and there's plenty dogs around. Protect your goats and the cat'll move on. No cat'll mess with your pit bulls."

Jubal Spry sneered and climbed back into his truck and slammed the door. "You got more money than sense, Browne." He shifted into gear, and the vehicle rattled to life and chuggered off, digging its tires into the gravel. Across the rear window he had a rifle in a gun rack, like Callen's father and Andy and Sarge, like all men in the Brethren who cared about protecting America and were prepared for any emergency. After about fifty feet, Spry braked and backed up. He leaned across the front seat and stuck his frizzled gray head out the window.

"I seen that girl of yours out at night, nosing around. Hate to see her mauled, maybe worse."

"I'll take care of my family, Jubal."

Callen did not want to be a part of Eli Browne's family.

"You tell her to stay off my property. If my dogs're loose—"

"Keep those brutes penned up or I'm calling the county. You know the law."

When Eli was angry, his voice was quiet, but with an edge like the knife Callen's father, Darren, used to clean fish. He kept it in the shed, hanging by a bit of rawhide strung through a hole drilled in the handle. In his dark moods he sat on his stool by the shed door, facing the woods, whetting the blade on a round stone the color of gunpowder. He said it helped him think.

Callen tugged on jeans, pulled a T-shirt over her wild red hair and laced up her shoes, the kind of fancy athletic shoes no one in the Brethren could afford. Eli Browne was a rich man. He could buy Callen a thousand pairs of fancy shoes, but he couldn't keep her prisoner forever.

In the wide and sunlit upstairs hall a cordless phone sat on an old-fashioned dresser next to a vase of purple irises. There were always flowers in this house. Isabelle had a garden bigger than the house in Codyville, and even last winter there had always been something in bloom. Callen looked at the phone, and the number of the Brethren safe house flashed through her mind as it had every day since she'd come to the ranch. She lifted the receiver and listened for the dial tone. She was certain she heard a click. She didn't know for sure that the line was bugged, but it made sense. The FBI thought she was a kid too dumb to be suspicious.

She had just gotten out of bed and already her stomach hurt. Isabelle said the pain was stress, but Callen did not believe her. She was a soldier of the True Word, too brave to feel stress.

At the end of the hall she stopped at the top of the stairs, listening to the conversation coming from the kitchen below.

"Might be a bobcat," Cholly said. He was Eli's mud foreman. "Old man like Spry don't see so good."

"I doubt he could tell the difference between a mountain lion and a golden retriever unless it barked at him," Isabelle said.

She was a mud too, a breed, half American, half Mexican, and Eli was a race traitor for marrying her. After the Aryan takeover, the Zionist-Occupied Government and all the race traitors would be shot or run out of the country along with the other subhuman garbage. The Brethren would make America safe and white again, the way it was meant to be.

She did not like to think of her uncle being shot, and hoped he was one of those who would be exiled instead. He was definitely a race traitor for marrying Isabelle, and as a writer he must be in league with all kinds of Zionists, but he had been good to Callen. Or tried to be. He didn't seem to understand that she didn't want his kindness.

"I've lived here all my life, and a cat's never come in so close."

Callen liked Isabelle too, even if she was an animal without a soul. Isabelle had taught her how to ride horses, and now Callen would rather ride than eat.

"A young male lion maybe," Cholly said. "Spry is right. He might be dangerous."

Eli sighed. "Let's just be clear. We don't want him killed."

That figured. Callen had watched Eli and Isabelle with their dogs and horses, the ones they bred themselves and those they rescued. They cared for animals as if they were humans when everyone knew they were like niggers and muds and Jews and did not have souls or feel pain much, not like the sons and daughters of Adam.

"Better nothin' happens to them goats." Ixsky, Cholly's wife, was from Guatemala. She spoke with a thick accent, and her skin was dark and creased like a walnut. She gave Callen the creeping willies. "Spry loves them goats 'cuz they smell like him."

Everyone laughed and Callen felt shut out. She had no
desire to be part of her aunt and uncle's strange family, but
neither did she like being outside, looking in. She had often
felt like an outsider in Codyville, but never as much as now.
Barbara said it was always hard for smart people to fit in. And
no doubt about it, Callen was smart, the smartest kid in
Codyville. Her home teacher, Marilu, said she was too smart
for her own good. Barbara said Marilu had the brain of a cau-
liflower.

Now Eli was talking about her. "We have to figure out a
way to keep her in the house at night."

Ixsky muttered, "Lock her door."

"If she's going to run away, she would have done it
months ago," Isabelle said. "And there's nothing wrong with
her being out at night. She's a country girl. When I was her
age, I loved being out alone in the dark. It made me feel powerful."

Ixsky harrumphed.

"I asked her if she wanted to drive out to Horse Haven
with me."

"I don't think that's safe."

"Eli, she's desperate for a change of scene. She's hardly
been off the property since she came."

"Watch she don't run off," Ixsky said.

"She's not going to do that. She likes it here."

"She's got a peculiar way of showing it."

"Callen's proud, Eli. And loyal. I admire her loyalty."

At the foot of the stairs Eli's German shepherd, Zacky,

lifted his gray muzzle from his paws and looked up at her. He was mostly blind and deaf and about twenty years old.

"I hear you, Callen," Isabelle said. "Come down and have your breakfast. I want us out of here in thirty minutes."

In the great room of the ranch house, the wood surfaces—the cedar walls and oak floors, the oak breakfast bar and long walnut sideboard and pine chests—glowed like butter and honey in the sunlight streaming through the windows over the sink. It was a nice house, the nicest Callen had ever lived in. She wished she could live in this house with her mother.

Ixsky laid a plate of scrambled eggs and tortillas before her on the breakfast bar.

"Can't we have toast? Can't we eat American food?"

"Tortillas are good food," Isabelle said. "I've eaten them all my life."

"I make you toast," Ixsky said. "I make you anything. Just ask nice."

Callen wasn't going to take orders from a mud.

"Toast." She kept her eyes fixed on her plate. "Please."

A moment later Ixsky handed her two pieces of browned sourdough bread. Callen looked at Eli. "I can't eat this; it's practically burned."

Ixsky leaned back against the counter next to the sink and folded her arms across her chest, her eyes full of black secrets.

Callen stared at the toast on her plate. It was the same

color as Ixsky's skin. "This is pig food. We're all gonna die eating it." In Patriot Camp she'd learned that muds carried Chagas' disease, TB and other ailments doctors couldn't cure.

"Eat it or go without," Eli said.

"We've got a long drive ahead of us."

"I don't want to go."

"Of course you do."

Isabelle was right, but Callen was not going to let on. She stirred her fork in the scrambled eggs flecked with bits of green onion and red pepper. "I can't eat this. What'd the mud put in it?" She glanced across the counter at her uncle, pleased to see she'd made him mad.

"Eat it or go without."

She recognized the sour smell of anger and saw that the skin around Eli's tightly pressed lips had faded to white. He hated it when she called anyone a mud, but in six months she'd never known him to lose his temper. At her or anyone else. Eli was plugged down tight, not ready to blow like her father. She felt compelled to get under Eli's skin, sharp as a blade, testing him.

Isabelle folded her napkin and fitted it into its napkin ring. She stood and pushed her chair under the lip of the breakfast bar. Laying her hand on the back of Callen's neck, she said, "Some of the horses we rescue, they're hard cases and it takes a lot to bring them around, but mostly Eli and I can outlast the worst of them."

Callen hated this part. After she had done her best to make them angry, Isabelle's kindness was somehow worse than a slap. Callen wasn't a horse needing to be rescued. The back of Callen's throat ached.

"I'm going out to check the trailer. Be ready in fifteen minutes?"

Callen stared down at the whorls in the grain of the breakfast bar, imagining she saw patterns like the pictures of galaxies Eli had shown her in books. All that science shit the Jews made up.

three

A S ISABELLE knelt beside the horse trailer checking the
tire pressure, she wondered what had set off Callen at
breakfast. Eruptions like that morning's had become the ex-
ception when once they had been the rule. She had buried
her memory of what happened on the night of the fire, buried
it deep, but Isabelle sensed she was on the brink of trust and
tremblingly close to excavating the truth. That talk of food
and disease was just a smokescreen.

Obstreperous as she could be, stubborn and irrational,
Callen had made great progress at Pasatiempo. On the second day Isabelle had given her a tour of Pasatiempo's barns
and paddocks and corrals, introduced her to the horses and
offered to teach her to ride. The half-mystical chemistry that
exists between some girls and horses was immediate. Callen
took to riding as though born to it and had the patience to
work with horses that was completely absent in her relations
with humans. When it came to horses, Callen was as much

like Isabelle as her own daughter might have been. On good days they were that much in synch. She saw through the girl's strut and attitude to a twisted image of herself at the same age. Isabelle, too, had been a loner scrambling to the summit by the steepest trail while everyone else seemed content to helicopter in.

Callen could not go back to the FBI now, not when Isabelle knew she was close to a breakthrough. Callen listened differently now, with more intention and focus, and she asked questions about the world that proved she was weighing what she'd been taught against what she was learning at Pasatiempo.

But the six months Eli had agreed to were almost up, and she knew he would refuse to ask Billy Horne for more time. She did not understand why he couldn't just admit he liked Callen. It was obvious he did. He gave his true feelings away all the time.

Two nights earlier Callen and Eli had watched the movie *Schindler's List* together, and throughout it she had continually pressed the pause button to ask questions and dispute what she'd seen. Isabelle, across the room paying bills online, heard their conversation, their squabbling. When Eli had a response to all her objections, Callen had finally stormed off to bed, announcing over her squared shoulders that the movie was the dumbest thing she'd ever watched.

Afterward Eli laughed and shook his head and said to Isabelle, "When she shapes up, she's going to be one hell of a girl."

And for a man who claimed he didn't want her around, he had great patience with Callen—too much, in fact. There had been times in the last six months when Isabelle wanted him to rear out of his chair and grab the girl by the scruff of her neck to shake the nastiness out of her. Instead, he'd held himself back, fooling no one about what his true feelings were. The change had not begun with Callen. He had never been an outwardly emotional man, but in the last year he had grown even less expressive. He smothered his anger, and his joy too.

He'd had a rough night, another in a long string, and that meant Isabelle had not slept well either. If she had not promised to do the pickup at Horse Haven today, she would go back to bed, sleep an hour and start the day all over again.

A dozen times she'd tried to get him to tell her what was wrong, and he always smiled and said the same thing. The new book was giving him a little trouble, nothing serious. He wouldn't say anything more about it.

Just a little trouble with the book.

A week ago she had done the unthinkable, opened his computer and read what was written in the file labeled "Current."

He had been working for almost a year on his new novel and had written fewer than one hundred pages.

four

IN THE kitchen, Callen lifted a banana from the fruit bowl in the center of the table and pulled down the peel. She knew Eli was watching her. Like everyone else on the ranch, he had brown eyes, and brown eyes gave her the creeps, like murky water in which something might be hiding, waiting to get her.

"Can I trust you not to give Isabelle a hard time today? Would you give me your word? Or maybe your word doesn't mean anything."

"I don't lie." Except when it mattered, except when she had to lie for the True Word's sake.

"Do you get how lucky you are to be living here? If you were with the FBI, they'd never let you out of their sight."

Callen knew what the FBI wanted. Agent Horne had tried to make her talk about the old bat Andy had introduced her to in Shasta City. Horne thought it was a man, and Callen didn't tell him otherwise. Andy had called her Mrs. Smith, and had been so fawningly respectful Callen felt embarrassed for her. Smith wasn't her real name. The FBI could lock Callen up for the rest of her life, and she'd still never tell them anything.

She bit into the banana. She liked bananas. They were a very sanitary fruit.

"We keep you on the ranch because you're in danger almost anywhere else."

"Bullshit." Her mother would never let anything bad happen to her.

"Don't cuss."

"You can't tell me what to do. You're not my father. He's gonna come and rescue me, and then you'll be sorry."

She saw a flare of temper in her uncle's eyes, but as quickly as the fire sparked, he smothered it. "You know your parents are dead, Callen. You know they died in the fire."

"That was a cover-up." And it worked, she thought. Even the FBI had fallen for it.

He changed the subject, throwing her off balance, confusing her.

"I heard you dreaming again last night. You were crying. And talking to someone."

"You spy on me? You come in my room at night? That's so bent!" She had heard the slang on a TV show. It made her feel powerful to use it.

"I don't sleep at night," Eli said. "You know that. And you were making quite a lot of noise."

"It is so weird, you walking around the house in the mid—"

"I gave you dream books."

How was she supposed to keep up with him if he never stayed on one subject?

"Did you read them?"

She lied. "Too hard." Some of the words were big, but she wasn't an idiot; she knew how to use the dictionary.

"I think you're afraid what you might learn."

"I'm not afraid of anything."

At school she was the smartest. At Patriot Camp she was the bravest. She was a crack shot with the .22 pistol Darren had given her for her birthday. A born soldier, Sarge said. She wasn't chicken to pick up a rattlesnake or climb to the top of a tree or jump off a rock into a fishing hole too deep and dark to see the bottom. Buddy said the crawdaddies under the rocks were big as lobsters, and there was an old trout about two feet long with teeth like vampire fangs. He dared Callen to dive right to the bottom with her eyes open, and she did it. All she saw was murky brown water, but on her way back up, the trout's scales scraped the back of her legs. Afterward Sarge washed the scrape with vinegar. Buddy said she smelled like a salad.

"I don't like you sneaking out at night."

"I can take care of myself."

Only city people thought it was too dark to see at night. In the country the stars were bright, and she and her friends from Patriot Camp had wandered freely, looking in windows to see their neighbors sleeping. They had stolen loose change from unlocked cars and gone swimming in the river in the moonlight. In Bone Lake the starlight was even brighter because there were not so many trees.

"It's not safe. You're eleven years old—"

She gave the base of the breakfast bar a strong kick.

"That book you read to me about Tom and Huck, those guys were always going out at night."

"That's different." A smile twinkled at the corner of his mouth. "Tom and Huck were a long time ago."

She kicked the base of the breakfast bar again.

"Stop," Ixsky said. Her long plaited hair was navy blue in the morning sun. She wore a suede bag the size of a golf ball around her neck on a length of rawhide. Callen didn't even want to imagine what was in that bag.

She kicked a third time. "I don't take orders from muds."

"Don't use that word," Eli said.

"What if it rains? What if there's puddles all over? Can I say mud then?"

"Ixsky's a full-blooded Mayan, and her name means 'mother of a king.' "

"So? Mother of muds."

Oops, she might have done it this time. His jaw muscles rolled, and the tendons in his neck quivered like a bow strung too tightly. Just like Darren, Eli wanted to whack her, raise a welt from her eye to the corner of her mouth. She wished he would. It would be worth it to prove he wasn't as good as he thought he was.

"Ixsky's been at Pasatiempo Ranch longer than I have." He had to work to control his voice. "Ixsky raised Isabelle and she's our family. How many times do I have to tell you? I don't want to hear that racist stuff in this house."

They'd had this conversation about a thousand times. Though the truth was she had grown used to Ixsky and the other Mexicans on the ranch, and none of them seemed too bad to her—not like when she'd first got there. But it was still fun to challenge Eli and make him rise to the bait like that wily old trout.

"I just believe what it says in the Bible."

"The Bible isn't racist."

"So? I'm not either. True Word Brethren are racial purists. We're Aryans, and we don't want our blood contaminated by animals."

"I gave you a Bible, Callen. Have you actually read it?"

His Bible was full of Jew lies.

"When are you going to start using your brain?"

Callen sat on her hands to keep from fidgeting. Sarge said that stillness was a sign of strength.

"You're a logical girl when you take the time to think. You're too smart to fall for this—"

She stood up. "Can I go now?"

"Sit down."

"My stomach hurts."

"I said sit down."

He'd used his command voice, and she did as she was told without thinking.

"The Brethren aren't really Christians. They're cowards, afraid of the real world. Afraid of anything they don't understand."

"You calling your own brother a coward?"

"Yes, Callen." She saw his Adam's apple move when he swallowed. "I am calling Darren a coward."

She stood up again.

"Sit. Now."

She threw herself down and folded her arms across her chest.

"The nighttime excursions have got to stop." She opened her mouth to speak, but Eli held up his hand like a stop sign. "I get that you're eleven years old and you want to be out doing things, making friends—"

"I already have friends."

"No, you don't. The Brethren might have been your friends once, but no more."

Her stomach squirmed like a bucket of night crawlers. Maybe she had gotten Chagas' disease from Ixsky's food and she was going to get sick and die. She thought of never seeing her mother again and her eyes stung.

"I'll never lie to you, Callen."

That was the biggest lie of all.

"And I'm telling you now that if I have to, I'll lock you in your room to keep you home."

She almost laughed. This wasn't her home, and her uncle was so dishonest he didn't even know when he was lying. Bone Lake would fill up and freeze solid before he let himself get mad enough to lock her up.

"Are you keeping a diary like I told you to?"

She rolled her eyes.

"Write about how angry you are, how much you hate me. Write down what you remember and what you feel. Write about your dreams."

"You told me this about a zillion times."

The corner of Eli's mouth twitched again.

"Can I go now?"

"I'm not going to read it, Callen. I value your privacy, and a diary is something you write for yourself. To help get your thoughts in order."

"There's nothing wrong with my thoughts."

He sighed and shook his head. He waved his hand in the direction of the stairs.

She wondered what she would have to do to make him really mad, so mad he'd pop the cork.

five

ISABELLE WATCHED Eli cross the ranch yard to the truck. He reached through the cab window and smoothed her hair away from her forehead, tucking it behind her ears.

"Penny for your thoughts."

His mouth was still a boy's, tender and expressive. She loved his dark eyes and the way he looked right at her, as if she were a code he could decipher if he concentrated hard enough.

"I don't think you should go today."

"I promised Ellen."

"Then let Cholly make the drive. The kid's in a real snit today."

"It's only pride makes her act up."

"Six months and she's still giving us that True Word crap. I think it's time you stopped fooling yourself. Callen's never going to come around, Isabelle. Not far enough."

"For whom? Billy Horne? All he cares about is getting

the name of the patron, Mr. Money Bag. That's the only reason he wanted us to take her. He's using her and he's using
us." Isabelle felt herself winding up, but she let it happen.
"She's a little girl without a family, a little girl without anything to hold on to. A soul, Eli. A human soul. And she needs
us even if she despises us."

"I know, Izzy. I know."

"Don't be dishonest and don't use that tone that says you
pity me. Like there's something wrong with me because I
care what happens to her."

"She calls you a mud; she calls you a breed. Am I supposed to sit back and let that happen?"

"Yes, I wish you would. It's all for show. She wants us to
think she's exactly the same tough little girl who came here six
months ago."

"Ah, Izzy, my girl, my girl. I knew this would hurt you—"

"You're doing it again, goddammit." Nothing riled her
like that paternalistic tone. "And incidentally, you're no help
at all."

The hash marks between his eyes deepened.

"You confuse her because no matter what she says or how
much of a monster she is, there are never any consequences.
She needs a stronger hand. You never even let on that you're
mad. That's lying because she and I and everyone else in
Southern California can tell you're hiding your real feelings
behind this . . . Mr. Calm. She doesn't understand why you
don't blow."

"You want me to hit her? I won't hit her."

"Did you hear me say to hit her? She needs to be disciplined, not beaten. And it has to come from you because in her world women are weak. If I punish her, it barely makes a dent. I know she likes me; I even think she halfway respects me. But at the bottom of it all, I'm still a mud, Eli. A breed. But you're a man and an extension of her father."

Eli made a face.

"A kinder, gentler father."

"You just said you wanted me to be tougher."

"My exact words were 'she needs a stronger hand.' You can be strong and kind at the same time. And fair. My father was."

There had always been a clear chain of causality connecting her childhood misdemeanors and the old man's punishments. He found her smoking stolen cigarettes with Myrrh Watson's son, both of them aged eight, and slapped the cigarette out of her hand so hard her palm stung for an hour. At thirteen she called him a "goddamn Fascist," and he hit her across the backside, humiliation that at thirteen was much worse than pain.

"I am who I am, Isabelle."

The way he said it, the rut-stuck certainty, she wanted to scream in his face, but she managed to sound reasonable. "If a horse bites, you let it know you're pissed."

"If Callen were a horse, this'd be a whole lot easier."

"She won't break if you show her you're human, that you've got a temper. She'll respect you."

"I'm through talking about this; I'm done."

A dismissal, one subject closed and another left gaping wide, questions hanging.

"I'll call Horne and she won't be our problem anymore."

"You do that and I'll never speak to you again. I want every hour we bargained for."

"She's dangerous."

"To what? Your almighty self-control?" She saw what she knew Callen saw too: the quick dilation of his pupils, the taut sinews of his neck. "Two more weeks, Eli. It's what we agreed on."

He drew a ragged breath. "I can't talk about this any-more. I'm under a lot of stress. When this book is done I'll be able—"

"Don't hide behind the book. I don't call seventy-two pages a book!"

He looked stunned. "How do you know how many pages I've written?"

"You're using the book as an excuse."

"You went into my computer. You know how I feel about my first drafts."

He had never forbidden her access to his computer to read his work. But it had been *assumed,* known without words, that she would not trespass any more than he would open up and read the journal she erratically wrote on her laptop. She could leave the file open with print on the screen and trust he would never stop to read it.

"I was worried: I've been worried about you for a long time." It wasn't easy, but she could bite back her anger as well as he could. To contain this argument she would measure words as carefully as a pharmacist with a controlled substance. "I believe everything's connected, Eli. The kid, the anger and the discipline, the reason you can't write . . . If you could get to the root of one—"

"This from the woman who doesn't believe in psychology?"

"Your insides have been hog-tied since before Callen came." She wondered why her presence had made it worse.

"I can't believe you read—"

"Seventy-two pages is not a book, Eli. In over a year that's what you've written. What was going on during all those dawn hours and the late nights, all the agonizing?"

"The book's my business. When Callen's gone and we've got out life back—"

"You were having trouble before she came."

"She's just made it worse."

She wanted to know why, but there was no reasoning with him. He wasn't even trying to be honest. He was writing life and making up the truth as he went along. As if their lives were a plot he could change with a press of a key.

"If someone had asked me yesterday, I would have sworn you understood what a writer goes through. What it's like to have a hundred stories and a thousand characters in your head and all of them beating on your skull, trying to get out, and how—"

She struck her fists against the steering wheel. "Stop it, Eli. I've heard all this before."

"Okay. You're right. Repetition is boring, and God forbid I should ever bore anyone."

"You're not boring me. It's just that we've been over this—"

He stepped back from the truck. "Take care, cowgirl. Call if you run into trouble."

"That's it?"

"You've heard it all before."

"You're punishing me for saying what's on my mind. You want me to be honest, and then you—"

"You can't have it both ways, Isabelle."

"What's that supposed to mean?"

"You, me and her."

He would use whatever he could for distraction. He was making up dialogue now, and it didn't have to make sense.

"Eli, whatever's got us fighting, it isn't just the book. And it's not Callen. She's a lot of things, including obnoxious, but there's more going on here. Just talk to me, Eli. Please."

The screen door slammed, and Callen jumped down the veranda stairs and loped across the yard to the truck. Red-orange was the perfect hair color for a girl with the personality of a blowtorch. She climbed into the front seat and closed the door.

"I'm here. Let's go."

six

HALFWAY DOWN the driveway, Callen coughed and gagged dramatically. "This truck stinks of horses."

"Open a window." Isabelle had paid one hundred and fifty dollars to have the truck detailed three days earlier. Besides, she liked the smell of horses.

"I'll freeze."

"Wear your jacket."

⟸

When she was Callen's age, Isabelle had become a student at the Bishop's School in La Jolla at a time when enrollment was restricted to girls. She had been sent to live with her father's sister, who was happy for company in her run-down beachfront cottage. Isabelle would have been happy without an education, but her mother had attended Bishop's; and though he missed his daughter's company, her father saw that she was running wild and needed Bishop's civilizing influence.

He was also loyal to the memory of his Mexican bride, the seventeen-year-old for whom he had borrowed on everything he owned and a chunk of his future to buy the ranch property in Bone Lake. Isabelle's grandfather, a rich Mexican businessman, had sent his only daughter to the Bishop's School, hoping to marry her off to an even richer American. Instead, she fell in love with a poor rancher possessed of nothing except a few dry acres.

From her first day at Bishop's, Isabelle set about making herself obnoxious to everyone she met, hoping the school would declare her incorrigible and send her home. She made few friends, and her teachers declared her bright but unmotivated. She lived for Fridays when her father picked her up and took her home to the horses and the mountains where for forty-eight hours she felt like herself again.

In high school she was mad for horses and barely noticed boys. Perversely, the less interest she showed in them, the more the boys from La Jolla High and Country Day came after her. Dark and doe-eyed like her mother, with her father's fair Irish skin, Isabelle had been an exotic. On Saturdays and Sundays the bleached-blond boys with expensive teeth and triangular torsos and long thigh muscles strutted past her aunt's cottage with their surfboards under their arms.

"They break my heart." Her aunt could not comprehend Isabelle's disinterest. "I never saw a horse as pretty as those boys. Everything's horses with you."

In particular there was a stallion named Jack, a gift from her father when she was younger than Callen, a skinny, hang-headed quarter horse mix penned in a paddock beside a bus stop in Jamul. She fed him an apple and he bit her fingers. She reached to stroke his nose, and his ears flattened, his nostrils flared and he beat his hooves into the mucky ground. She thought he was wonderful and knew she could tame him.

⟵

The road to the Anza Valley twisted through the San Diego back country. Cool, clean air rushed into the truck through Callen's open window, stinging Isabelle's cheeks like February. She and Eli agreed on most matters, and when they didn't, they could almost always talk out their differences. Arguments were all the more devastating for being rare, and they threw her into melancholy afterward, a gray mood that could take days to lift. Fragments of sad songs played in her mind. Songs about parties being over and cautions not to smoke in bed. The songs went around in her head on a continuous loop, and she knew she was letting the words make her unhappier. She didn't stop.

In a marriage there had to be boundaries, niches of individual privacy that were sacrosanct. Looking in Eli's private files had not seemed so bad when she'd done it, but now it felt like infidelity. Add to that the problem of Callen, and the gulf between them felt oceanic.

She vowed they would talk it out tonight, and she would be convincingly contrite. She imagined what he would say and what her replies would be, back and forth until she ended up making herself defensive and then angry again. If Eli would only stop protecting himself for one minute, he would see that she had opened his computer because she loved and worried about him.

And then they would talk about Callen, and Isabelle would insist on two more weeks, the full six months.

In Riverside County it was obvious that Los Angeles had discovered the undeveloped backcountry. Behind walls and ornate iron gates rose mansions of flagstone and timber, hybridized by way of colonial Spain, the Loire Valley crossed with Merry Old England with detours into Kentucky—minus the bluegrass. Isabelle resented the interlopers. Except for one semester at U.C. Davis in a failed effort to become a large-animal veterinarian, she had lived among the rocks and arid canyons all her life. The city people in their ostentatious piles were an invasive species crowding out the native growth and sucking up the precious water.

Everywhere she saw horses, so many of them expensive and beautiful: Thoroughbreds, quarter horses, Arabs, none like the animals awaiting them at Horse Haven.

She warned Callen, "You won't like what you see. Ellen rescues some of the worst cases."

"How come we're going if the horses are already rescued?"

"Ellen can't afford to keep the ranch, so we'll take as many as we can off her hands." There was never any shortage of horses needing rescue. "We'll make room for them at Pasatiempo."

A few people were cruel by nature, so low down in the pecking order that they took pleasure from the suffering of helpless animals. Isabelle understood this as an emotional deformity, and though she despised such people, she found a space in her heart to pity them as she did all blighted creatures. But most of her rescued horses had not been damaged by such people. They were simply neglected to the edge of death by owners too self-absorbed to care about anything except themselves. Isabelle had no forgiveness for them.

"My dad says if an animal can't do something useful, it's no good." Callen didn't look at Isabelle. "We had this cat named Tiger who kept having kittens. There were these wild yowlers outside and Tiger inside, and we still had mice and rats; so my dad caught all the strays and Tiger and put 'em in this canvas bag and sent me and Billy to the river."

Isabelle watched the road, but she felt Callen studying her response.

"We drowned 'em."

And this was Eli's brother. "When was this?" she asked. "How old were you?"

Callen shrugged, still watching out the window.

"You get how awful that is, don't you, Callen? You were just a kid and those were your pets. What your father did was ignorant and cruel."

She shrugged again, elaborately disinterested. "I'm just saying what happened."

The fight with Eli had left Isabelle argumentative and

perverse. "Lucky we don't have to drown horses to get rid of them. There's a big market in horsemeat. I've been thinking maybe it's time to sell some of ours to one of the killers."

"What killers?"

"That's what we call the guys who buy up horses no one wants and kill them for horsemeat." Isabelle slowed behind a Mercedes turning into the driveway of a pink stucco hacienda. "Timing's important. Even the European dog food companies won't buy a horse if it's too scrawny."

"That sucks."

"Actually," Isabelle said, pleased that for once she had upset Callen instead of the reverse, "it might be good to clean out our corrals and make room for stronger animals."

"Who eats horsemeat anyway?"

"Europeans. In Japan it sells for almost twenty dollars a pound."

Callen muttered, "Slopes."

"Don't use that word."

"You defend them?"

"I don't think they should eat horsemeat, if that's what you mean. But no matter what they eat, you don't get to use race words."

"I think it's ignorant to eat horses."

"So do I."

"Why'd you say it then?"

"I was curious what your reaction would be."

Callen glared at her. "You are so bent."

"Race words are a sign of ignorance, Callen. Have you ever even met an Asian?"

Callen chewed on her lower lip. "Is an Indian an Asian?"

"You mean a Native American?"

"From India."

"I don't know. I think they're sort of Asian, sort of Middle Eastern. It's a good question."

"A guy from India ran the big thrift store in Yreka. Him and Mom talked a lot, and I had to watch the door in case anyone saw them."

"What did they talk about?"

"How should I know? He was gross. An animal."

"We're all animals. We're mammals just the same as horses and dogs."

Callen snorted again. "It says in the Bible that first God created the animals and then Adam. He was the first human and he was an Aryan. He had blond hair and blue eyes."

Here we go again. The True Word Brethren theory of Creation.

"Jews are the worst. God didn't even create them. They started when Eve and Satan did it. Eve and Satan had sex and their son was Cain."

Her confidence chilled Isabelle and made her wonder if Eli was right. Maybe nothing said or done by them in six months had changed Callen's contaminated view of the world. She was incorrigible.

"The first murderer and the first Jew."

Isabelle didn't know much about the Bible, but she knew Jesus had been a Jew, and she said so.

Callen looked at her sourly. "You only believe that because the Jews want you to. Jesus was a Gentile. If he was a Jew, then we would be too." Callen grinned as if she'd just won a debate for a big cash prize.

Isabelle braked late on a curve and felt the big trailer swung wide.

"I've got to watch the road. I can't listen to that crap."

"Don't blame me. That's just the way God set the world up." Callen slid down in the seat, planting her feet on the dashboard. "It's all in the Bible."

"Not in my Bible."

"What do you expect? The Jews wrote *your* Bible."

⟿

At four thousand feet, pocketed between the desolate Cahuilla, San Jacinto and Santa Rosa mountains, the Anza Valley community had grown without design. It sprouted along California Route 371, a careless mixture of the shabby and crassly new: real estate and doctors' offices side by side with motorcycle repair shops, a tack and feed store, weedy vacant lots, a Mexican restaurant and a VFW Post flying a supersized Stars and Stripes. There was one very large gas station and a food mart in stucco as white and shiny as Mecca under a high-desert blue sky.

A half mile east of the gas station Isabelle took a sharp

right turn and drove south for three miles into the Buckshorn Mountains. Her heart sank when she saw Horse Haven ranch more derelict than it had been just a few months earlier. The vegetable garden and yard were overgrown with weeds. The chilly wind had blown a roller of tumbleweed half under the front porch, and bits and pieces of shingle littered the yard in front of the house.

"What a dump," Callen said, curling her lip.

Isabelle flushed in defense of her old friend. "Ellen uses every penny for the animals. People donate, but never enough."

Ellen and a man came out of the barn, and Isabelle saw her old friend as she was sure Callen did: a sloppy, beaten-down country woman in boots split along the sides, a baggy sweater in need of a wash and Wrangler jeans stretched across a broad butt. Her salt-and-pepper hair was stuffed up under a cowboy hat that hadn't been blocked in years.

The man with her wore pressed Levi's and a clean white hat with a turquoise patch on the band. Ellen introduced him as Emmett Fleming, a Realtor from Los Angeles.

"He's buying the ranch," Ellen said, looking caught. "Stock too."

Fleming handed Isabelle a business card. "It's going to be a great development. Top-of-the-line equestrian community, smallest lot five acres, big houses and lots of trails. You know, on a clear day you can see downtown LA from up that hill."

"What happens to the horses?" Callen asked.

"We'll find homes for every one of them," Fleming said with grating assurance.

"And how," Isabelle asked, "will you manage that?"

"Advertise. They'll sell. I've already had offers."

"Really? There's a big market for plugs?"

Ellen said, "It'll be okay, Isabelle."

seven

ISABELLE WALKED away, ignoring the realtor, who was saying how glad he was to meet her. When she was out of sight behind the barn, she leaned against the weathered gray planks, stabbed by a headache that made her see double.

"Are you sick?"

"Let me alone a minute."

"Are you going to throw up?"

"I have a headache. I'll be okay."

"You're mad 'cause that man is buying the horses."

"He doesn't give a shit about them."

"What'll he do? Sell 'em for horsemeat?"

Isabelle shook her head. "I don't know."

"That's what you said you'd do."

"I told you, I wanted to see how you'd react."

"Don't you care if he sells them?"

"Of course I care."

"You and Eli are rich; you could buy them."

Isabelle straightened her back and smoothed her hair away from her forehead. One argument per morning was enough.

"Let's see what Ellen's given us."

"You could buy the whole ranch."

In a sagging pipe corral were eight woebegone horses: five swaybacked mares, two ribby geldings and a raw foal. Isabelle guessed Ellen had been shorting feed to save a few dollars.

"That one looks like a skeleton." Callen pointed at the foal, precariously balanced on its skinny legs. "Is it dying?"

"Probably. Poor little guy."

Sometimes a careful diet could bring a young horse like this one back from the brink, but Isabelle had seen it happen that an animal so far gone became disheartened and would not eat no matter how hungry he was. This little guy had been weaned too early. He had a vacant and bewildered look in his eyes; his ears drooped; and when Isabelle rested her hand on his bony flank, he flinched as if his skin hurt.

"If he dies, will you sell him to the horsemeat man? He's awful young. No meat on him at all."

"I wouldn't sell any horse and you know it."

"But you said—"

"I don't want to talk about this anymore."

Callen smiled, not bothering to hide that she was pleased with herself.

"So what do you do if they're sick and you can't make 'em better?"

Isabelle put her index finger to the middle of Callen's

forehead, half way between the bridge of her nose and her hairline. "If you know where to put the bullet, it's the best way."

"Do you do it?"

Isabelle shook her head.

"How come?"

"It would break my heart."

"Who does then?"

"Eli."

"I don't believe you. He'd never."

He suffered for days afterward.

Ellen came around the barn saying, "Jesus, I'm sorry about that. I thought he'd be gone by the time you got here."

"I bet you did."

"I don't need you to beat me up about this, Isabelle."

"Selling's your choice."

"Bullshit. It's my *necessity.*"

"He'll sell 'em to the killers," Callen said.

"He says he'll find homes."

"And you believe him?" Isabelle asked.

"Why wouldn't I?"

"For starters, you've been rescuing animals for almost twenty years, and you know the way it works."

"I don't need a lecture from you, Iz. You're married to the great and famous author, but I'm alone and I've got to think about myself. No one else does." Ellen sighed and cranked her neck, wincing. "I don't even have health insurance. If one of these buggers kicked me, I'd be up shit creek."

"Have you talked to your accountant? We could do a fund-raiser. Eli'd be willing to sign books and talk. He always gets a big crowd."

"And then what happens? Next month, next year when more bills come due?"

Isabelle took Ellen's rough hands in hers. "My father told me how they die."

Ellen ripped her hands away. "Don't you think I know?"

Isabelle turned to Callen. "The horses know what's happening; they smell the blood and the fear, and that terrorizes them and they try to get away. Some of them are just babies, and the mares from the estrogen farms usually have foals. He said their screams were like—"

"Stop it," Callen cried, pressing her hands over her ears.

"You're a dilettante, Isabelle," Ellen said, ignoring the outburst. "Don't mistake me, you do good work and I'm grateful for your help, but you've never had to choose between paying the electric and feeding your horses."

"But you're giving up too soon. I'm sure there's a way—"

"There is!" Callen yelled. "I told you! Take them all. We've got lots of room on the ranch." She turned to Ellen. "How many horses are there?"

Ellen looked at Isabelle.

"Go ahead, tell her."

"Around thirty, give or take. People know about the Haven and just abandon their animals off in a paddock, and I don't even know I got 'em till I do a count."

Callen looked at Isabelle expectantly.

"Honey, we don't have that kind of room."

"You do. You told me yourself there's all the room in the world at Pasatiempo."

"That's an expression. I didn't mean it literally."

"You said you love horses. You'd never let them go for horsemeat." Callen's face was bright pink. "You didn't mean that either?"

Callen was right. There was plenty of room at Pasatiempo, and she and Eli weren't going to run out of money in this lifetime even if he never wrote another book. Mostly she made her decision because Callen wanted her to.

"Okay, I'll take a bunch. I'll send Cholly back with the big trailer. It'll take him a couple of trips. But, Ellen, I only want those who're in really bad shape. Pregnant mares too, of course. If Fleming's keeping count, tell him to call me." To Callen she added, "We'll leave him the ones he can sell to riders."

"The foal?"

"He'd be lucky to survive the ride back to Pasatiempo."

"But he's beautiful."

He was far from this. Besides his knobby and malnourished body, his coat was so dull it was almost colorless.

"He's not going to make it, honey."

"We could give him medicine."

"He's too far gone."

"But that's not fair. He's only a baby. He can't help being sick."

In spite of everything that was racist and deceitful in

Callen, there was a deep well of innocence too. She talked tough, talked smart, but she had no idea how the world ran. At eleven wasn't she entitled to her ignorance? And an occasional grace?

"You'll have to care for him. He'll be your responsibility."

Callen flung her arms around her and immediately jumped back as if burned.

"Whatever."

eight

CALLEN DID not like the way Isabelle looked at her, as if all of a sudden they were blood sisters. And she did not know why she wanted the foal. She didn't care about horses all *that* much. It was the talk about horsemeat that had done it. Once she'd heard about people eating horses, she could not shake the images of hamburgers and barbecued ribs.

"Can I use your bathroom?"

"Callen, there's work here."

"I'm gonna puke."

"Go ahead," Ellen said, "but I'm warning you, the place's a mess."

"And make it fast. We need your help out here."

Ellen's front screen door had a big tear in it, and the house was full of flies. In the cigarette-smelly front room, magazines and newspapers lay scattered on the couch and floor. Callen thought what her mother would think of such a dump; automatically she made a tsk-tsk sound with her tongue against the roof of her mouth.

All the Brethren knew that Barbara Norgaard kept the cleanest house in Codyville. She could sew things so that they looked store bought, and she was the best cook; all the men said they envied Darren. But Callen knew that in other ways the Brethren disapproved of Barbara. They said she didn't deserve her brave and committed husband; she was too inclined to ask questions and express opinions that differed from the majority.

Callen had been her mother's only true friend, and she must be missing her right now and doing some serious, down-on-her-knees praying that she was safe. The stink of Ellen's house made Callen's eyes burn, and she rubbed them with the back of her hand.

Looking for the bathroom, she picked her way into the kitchen reeking of garbage spilling from a can by the back door, orbited by flies that were iridescent in the bright light. On the windowsill she saw a cell phone the size of a deck of cards and stopped where she stood, not breathing.

At Patriot Camp they had to memorize the number of the safe house. The number was burned into her memory.

She grabbed the phone and looked at the keys. She pressed the one that said Power. And nothing happened. She pressed Start and Call, and still nothing happened. She tilted the phone's screen away from the light, but there was nothing written there. Furious, she threw the phone across the kitchen. The batteries were dead, or there was a trick to getting it started, or Ellen hadn't paid her bill. It didn't matter why the cell phone was useless; it just was.

At Patriot Camp, Sarge had taught her how to make a bow and arrow and start a fire without matches, and maybe those were useful skills if it was 1950. In the twenty-first century a mud who couldn't even speak American would know better than her how to make a call. The sense of being powerless and ignorant bit at her insides. How could she fight the Zionist conspiracy if she didn't know how to make a telephone call?

Twice she had tried the pay phone in Bone Lake. The first time, in the middle of the night, it had been out of service. She had had a second opportunity one morning when she'd accompanied Eli to the feed store. While he was occupied choosing a new halter for his favorite horse, she had put her coins in the slot and a mechanical voice told her to deposit another forty-five cents—which she didn't have. Eli came out of the feed store as she was hanging up the phone. He never asked what she was doing, but after that day she was never alone near a working phone except the ones at the ranch, and they were useless because she knew the FBI had bugs on them. Isabelle and Eli both had cell phones, but reception was erratic and staticky in the bowl of Cat Canyon. Maybe that was the problem at Horse Haven too.

She did not think Ellen would live alone so far from town without any phone at all. There had to be another one somewhere.

In Ellen's bedroom the plastic blinds were pulled tight,

shutting out the sun's sharp light as if a vampire slept in the unmade bed that occupied most of the floor space. The room smelled like the rest of the house. Clothes were piled on one side of the bed and on a chair; a litter of envelopes and bills and documents covered the top of a bureau, its drawers hanging open. There could be three or four telephones hidden in the mess, but she would never find them in time. And then a miracle. She glimpsed something blue and plastic in a pile of clothes half in the bathroom, half out. Her pulse quickened in her ears.

She picked up the blue cordless, held the receiver to her ear and heard the sweet music of a steady dial tone. She rubbed her palms down the front of her jeans and told herself to calm down. She could not make a mistake this time.

Her trembling fingers jittered on the keys as she entered the number of the safe house.

After one ring the phone was answered by a muffled male voice she did not recognize.

"It's me. Callen." No response. "Is this the safe house?"

"You got ten seconds. Talk."

"Come and get me."

"Where are you?"

"Some ranch called Horse—" Horse Haven wasn't important. She was wasting time. "No, forget that."

"How'd you get this number?"

"Sarge told me. At Patriot—"

A hand pinched the back of her neck.

"No!" Callen yelled as Isabelle knocked the phone from

her hand and the blue receiver flew into the bathroom, where it landed with a crack and skidded to a stop at the base of the toilet.

Without thinking, Callen whirled and slammed her elbow into Isabelle's midsection, punching the air out of her. Isabelle grunted and fell, twisting and striking her temple and cheek against the edge of the bed frame. Callen dived toward the bathroom, screaming.

"I'm in Bone Lake! I'm a prisoner!"

nine

HIGHWAY 99 runs down the middle of California's Central Valley, four divided lanes connecting the minicities of Stockton, Fresno and Bakersfield and the large agricultural towns like Visalia and Delano. Highway 99 is an old-style highway with two lanes on either side of a dry and weedy median strip; the asphalt is rough and the on and off ramps too closely spaced, so traffic moves in bursts and crawls. For Andy Barrett DeWitt, in a hurry to reach Los Angeles and then get back, every slowdown was that much more time to mull over Callen's call to the safe house.

She was alive and wanted to be rescued, but Andy would have guessed that without the phone call. She mentioned horses, which probably meant the FBI had placed her in witness protection in some rural area. In California that could mean any of thousands of places.

Andy had never abandoned her belief that Callen survived the fire and would call when she could. But maintain-

ing the patience of her small band of Brethren had grown in-
creasingly difficult, though they had adhered to all the proce-
dures set down in the Manifesto. After the fire the group split
up, some going east into Idaho and Montana, others to
Brethren communities in Oregon and Washington. Her
group of insiders had moved to Bakersfield, where she directed them to live like the sheeple and blend into the land-
scape. This was easily done. They had the kinds of jobs for
which there was always a need. Thanks to the generosity of
Mrs. Smith, they all had new identification, so they could not
be connected with the men and women who had lived in
Codyville.

If necessary, they could stay in Bakersfield for years. But
they were restless, and word of Callen's call had only exacer-
bated their anxiety. The disposable phone in the safe house
could not be traced, but the Brethren were uneasy and dis-
trusted all electronic technology.

A rattletrap truck passed her with a mud family in the
back: parents and too many black-haired children. The Central Valley was more brown than white, and living in contin-
ual disgust had exhausted her. She had fought ZOG and its
minions her whole life, and the weight of responsibility had
grown much heavier since her father's death.

She had never loved anyone deeply and eternally except
her father. She had obeyed him even when her heart and soul
cried out for something different. Edgar Barrett had advised
her to marry Dor DeWitt because he wasn't very smart and
wouldn't interfere with what she had to do. He had told her

to feed him well and give him enough sex; set him in front of the TV, and he would be too fat and satisfied to interfere with her work.

Until recently that had been true; but lately Dor had grown antsy and pestered her to forget Callen, leave Bakersfield and go back to the country. If she did not soon find some action to occupy the group, it would fracture.

Even Sarge was urging her to leave Bakersfield. Each evening he and Ansel and Dor and some of the other men sat at the Formica table in the apartment and studied maps of the West, looking for the perfect small town. But Andy insisted no one was going anywhere until Callen had been rescued. She had confidence in the girl's ingenuity. She would find another phone; and wherever she was, Andy intended to go after her.

Within the culture of the Brethren, Callen had always been too curious, too ingenious, too much a thinker and calculator. She knew more than she should, and the longer she was in FBI custody, the more vulnerable Andy felt. With so much at stake, Andy was willing to take some risks to get her back. When the time came, she would enlist Darren's help. The FBI may have managed to turn Callen, but she would flip right back when she saw her father.

No matter how it was done, when or by whom, retrieving Callen was a dangerous business. Before Andy could do anything, Mrs. Smith had to approve a mission of such importance. It galled Andy to admit it, but Mrs. Smith controlled the money, which meant she controlled the Brethren.

Her real name wasn't Mrs. Smith, though Andy had only known her by this name. She swam in money inherited from her husband, who had been a Hollywood producer of some kind. He had grown up outside Tacoma in the house beside Edgar Barrett's, the son of German immigrants and her father's great good friend. As a young man, Mr. Smith had gone to Los Angeles and made a fortune in the entertainment business, first as a blond and blue-eyed actor playing Luftwaffe pilots and SS officers and then as a director and producer. Throughout his life his values had remained the same as when he was a boy speaking German and broken English, playing war games with Edgar Barrett, rewriting history with the Germans victorious. When Mr. Smith died, he left instructions with his wife that a portion of his estate was to be funneled to the True Word Brethren and their cause.

The night before, Andy had lain awake beside Dor, dreading the long drive and difficult meeting ahead, listening to the sounds of the busy street that ran beside the apartment complex. Trucks and cars and motorcycles, buses and a screaming cop car. The racket was worse than Dor's muttering and snoring. One thing she knew: It was the Jews and the muds who had created the great ugly cities of America, the Jews and the dark races who wanted to live crowded into ghettos. As much as any of the other Brethren, Andy longed to be back in the country where she could breathe again, but Callen had to be dealt with first.

Near UCLA she stopped at a Jack in the Box for a soda and a review of directions scratched on a sheet of yellow paper. She did not want to be stopped by a security cop suspicious of a 1985 Ford truck chugging aimlessly around the manicured streets of Beverly Glen.

She drank her soda and admitted to herself that she was stalling because Mrs. Smith made her nervous. Her hands sweated on the steering wheel, and her thumb was bleeding where she had chewed off a strip of cuticle. Edgar Barrett had told his daughter there was nothing wrong with being nervous so long as she kept the feeling to herself. No one must ever suspect she felt less than confident. Andy hoped food would settle the bubbles in her stomach, so she ordered two burgers and a large order of fries. As she waited for her order, she counted her pulse; it was twenty beats too fast.

Every one of the teenagers behind the counter at Jack in the Box was a mud and taking food from their hands disgusted her. Returning to her car, she rubbed an alcohol sanitizer into the lines on her palm, between her fingers and under her nails. Chagas', tuberculosis, AIDs—she wasn't even sure the sanitizer would eliminate these germs.

She turned the radio dial, listening for some wholesome white music and heard half a dozen languages she could not identify. Los Angeles was the True Word Brethren's nightmare, a stew of races and colors. In Los Angeles it was hard not to be daunted by the immensity of Satan's army.

Sometimes Andy thought God asked too much.

She finished her meal, tipped the seat back and closed

her eyes. She still had the jimjams, but it always steadied her to imagine an Aryan America. She pictured orderly streets safe for women and children; in clean parks she heard the laughter of fair-haired children. On the busy sidewalks there would be girls and boys courting, husbands and wives and families and no muds or queers or coloreds, no outsized noses and lips, no kinky hair. The stores would be filled with goods manufactured by white hands, and in the churches True Word preachers would proclaim the new world order. This was the vision Edgar Barrett had shown Andy. It lifted her up, gave strength to her will and meaning to life.

ten

CALLEN LAY in her secret place on the roof and stared at the fading stars. Eli had given her an astronomy book to read, and the ideas in it—the science of black holes and dust nebulae, white dwarves, red giants and quarks—had impressed her with their ingenuity. She believed Eli that these things were confirmed by a science written in a language of numbers only scientists and mathematicians understood. She saw in his eyes when he lied about his feelings but never about information.

The Brethren would never let her go to college and learn the language of mathematics. Back with the Brethren she would argue with Andy, but she knew she didn't have a chance.

Sometimes she thought her brain would burst with all the new ideas she was learning from the books at Pasatiempo. She could read from sunup until after dark for the rest of her life and never get through all the books. In the last six months she had probably read more than Sarge and Andy and Darren had in all their lives combined. The most disturbing thing she had learned was that the more she read, the less sure she was about anything. She wished her mother were on the ranch with her so they could talk about black holes and quarks and make some sense of what was real and what was not.

Rimming the mountains, the dawn sky was a pale yellow-green. She wondered where her mother was and if she was awake, maybe looking up at the same sky as she was or in a kitchen somewhere, sitting at a table with her head on her folded arms. Weeping. Fearing that her daughter, her only child in the world, was dead or in danger.

Callen whispered to the sky, "Don't forget me, I'll find you, I'll never stop looking."

She felt the words and feelings leave her body and move out into the sky. It wasn't logical, but she believed her messages flew on and on until they found Barbara, then swooped down a chimney or through an open window and into her thoughts. She'd been stopped from finishing her call in Ellen's bedroom, but there had to be another phone somewhere.

"I'm coming back, I promise."

She liked the roof in the afternoon when it was shady and cool, and sometimes she went there to draw the things she remembered. Eli and Isabelle promised never to nose about in her room, but she did not completely trust them and kept these pictures in a tube at the back of her closet. She liked drawing horses and had already done several likenesses of the foal from Horse Haven. These pictures too she rolled and hid in the closet. Her pictures were private, no one's business but her own.

⌖

Callen had discovered the flat spot behind the chimney not long after Christmas when she woke from a dream that was the first in a series of nightmares. The dreams were like connect-the-dot puzzles without enough dots and missing half their numbers. After the first one she woke in a state of burning terror that leaped and turned in her like a flock of birds with wings afire. She pounded out of bed and dressed in a rush, and though it was after midnight, she threw open her bedroom window and crawled out on the roof, drawing the cool air deep into her burning lungs as if her life depended on it.

Behind the chimney made of river stones, she discovered a flat space just big enough to stretch out on and press her bare soles against the comfortingly warm stones. That night in January she had lain on her back just breathing and staring at the stars, listening to a screech owl mark its passage across Cat Valley and come to light in the pepper tree beside her bedroom window. Its shining eyes had stared at her from the branches and drawn her to the roof's edge. She cast away her bad dream, grabbed a rough-barked tree limb and swung to the ground. Under a moon as bright as a flipped half dollar she had explored Pasatiempo alone for the first time.

The ranch occupied thousands of acres in Cat Valley and the surrounding hills and canyons of the mountains southeast of San Diego. In many places it bordered on wild and empty land belonging to the Department of Fish and Game and so seemed literally boundless. The canyons were deep and the stone-hearted mountains sparsely treed, bouldered and sliced by escarpments, scored by the eroded remnants of the area's ancient and violent history, strewn with chaparral in many places too dense to walk through.

Eli Browne's acres spread across grasslands, bottomlands and oak meadows. On their rides together he talked about his land as if it were a living thing with a history and personality. Callen liked to listen, though she told herself it was probably all nonsense invented by ZOG scientists.

Eli believed in Darwin's Big Lie, and in the beginning Callen had been afraid to listen when he told her that a jillion years before there were humans on earth, Cat Mountain had been part of a towering volcanic range extending down the west coast of the continent from Alaska to Mexico. Marilu said evolution was a godless theory and a sin, but Callen could no longer remember exactly how or why a thought, a theory or an idea by itself could be sinful. Eli said that over thousands of millions of years the great mountain range had worn down and the valleys lifted up. Proof of the region's history was right there in the rocks, he said, exposed like the bones of old monsters gnawed on by time. It was just like him to describe something that way.

Where whole mountains had worn away, all that remained were roundish, bouldery outcrops like big kernels of caramelized popcorn. Elsewhere angry fingers of granite shoved up through the ground, and she imagined fortresses built along the mountain contours. Other hills had eroded away to their granite bones, leaving rock faces of pale yellow stone streaked with white and pink and gray, and isolated rocks in shapes Eli called tors and monoliths and hoodoos.

Callen loved that word: *hoodoo.*

It seemed like Eli knew every word in the American language.

When she came to Bone Lake back before November, she had thought it the ugliest place in the world, dry as stale bread. But in February, rain had transformed Cat Valley miraculously, and everywhere she looked there was green. Eli showed her how the small, hard leaves of the lemonade berry relaxed and opened out of their protective twists, and after just one good soaking the blue flowers of the Cleveland sage filled the air with their sharp-sweet fragrance. The yarrow shot up parasols of pink and white and yellow, and the mountain lilac bloomed in blue and white on all the hillsides. California poppies waved at Callen, and the yellow bursts of mustard grass tossed clouds of pollen that made her nose itch and drip.

All around Callen the world seemed to be opening up, showing her its true beauty.

One morning Eli had taken her out early to see the dens of foxes and coyotes; they watched for mountain lions and bobcats, and the musk of skunk hung in the damp dawn air.

Prairie dogs owned the underground world, and above them jittery cottontails, their ears translucent as silk, gorged on new grass. Eli showed her rattlesnakes and king snakes and black snakes and taught her the difference between a red-tailed hawk and a peregrine, and a sparrow and a mockingbird.

His teaching emboldened her. On her own and under the cover of night, she explored the nearby ranches, including Jubal Spry's dump, and Sunny Hills, a nudist resort owned and operated by someone called Myrrh, who was Isabelle's friend. She had ventured as far as the dry lake where archaeologists and their students sifted the fine dirt for remains of ancient cultures that Eli claimed had lived beside the lake thousands of years ago when it was full of water.

She had sneaked through the campground and the town and crept between houses and trailers, her pockets jammed with hot dogs to quiet the dogs she met. Now Spry's pit bulls wagged their behinds when they saw her coming. She had stolen money from open cars and hidden behind boulders to watch the muds from across the border less than a mile from town. Buddy and his pals in Codyville would have thrown rocks at them. Callen thought about doing this, but her mother's voice told her not to.

Andy said America was filling up with muds, and one day soon white people would be extinct unless the Brethren stopped it. This was a hard job but an honor handed to them by the Almighty, who had created the world by His own hand and for the pleasure and dominion of the Aryan people.

She told Eli this, and he asked why God had chosen the Brethren particularly. Among all the fair-skinned people in the world, why had the Creator of the universe chosen them? The question made her angry; but when she thought about it later, she wondered why no one had asked and answered it at Patriot Camp, in prayer meetings, or in Marilu's home school.

On one of her early morning explorations, Callen had discovered the tree house in the oak meadow a mile from the ranch. Fifteen feet above the ground in the arms of a huge oak tree, it had been a wreck without a ladder, its floor and sides warped or broken or blown off. It was a great discovery, but it made her feel more intensely lonely than at any time since the fire in Codyville. She wanted to show the tree house to Buddy. He would act like it was nothing special because he could never let on that he admired or envied anyone, especially not a girl. But he would be impressed.

She remembered a time the summer before, the final night of Patriot Camp, when the parents came to get their kids. Callen and Buddy had used a bowie knife to take a blood oath of loyalty in front of everyone. Callen did not cry even when the cut bled like crazy.

Going home that night, she had sat between her parents and they did not speak. The cut on her wrist ached, and she felt proud and angry at the same time. Ahead and to the east the moon cast its light on Shasta's snowcap as if the mountain had a lantern buried in its crater. She knew the Indians said it was a holy mountain. This was redskin superstition, but she wished it could be true. Headlights coming north strobed the cab, and she watched her mother's hands knitting fast, tight little stitches in the dark. Her father didn't say a word and smoked so many cigarettes Callen could have blown smoke rings if she'd wanted to.

⟻

The morning after the trip to Horse Haven, Callen lay on the roof behind the chimney, watching the stars fade, remembering Patriot Camp and the Brethren and wondering where they'd gone and how she would ever get to them if she didn't find another safe phone. They were nowhere near Codyville now. Callen would bet on that. There must be a HELP WANTED sign in the window of the garage where Darren had worked, and Mr. Crocker at the Quick Stop Mart would be grousing because his night clerk had left town without giving notice. When it was time to move on, the Brethren drifted out to the highway a few at a time. It might take a week or two and then someone in town would need a drain unclogged or an axle fixed, but the plumber would be gone, the mechanic and his tools vanished.

Callen had to call the safe house again, or they might just give up on her. If only Isabelle had come a moment later, the call would have been made, and she would not have been hurt.

Callen never meant to hurt Isabelle. She liked Isabelle. What Sarge had taught in Patriot Camp—that breeds and muds had small and inferior brains—it just plain wasn't true.

Callen was sure Sarge hadn't actually lived with breeds and muds as she had.

Callen was sorry she had hurt Isabelle, but maybe now she and Eli would understand that it didn't matter if she liked them and the horses and the ranch and just about everything except Ixsky's food, she would do anything to get back with the Brethren.

eleven

ISABELLE OPENED her eyes, and the events of the day before hurtled into her consciousness like a bowling strike.
She hurt all over, especially her ribs and throbbing head. She
reached for the vial of pain killers next to the bed. She laid a
tablet on her tongue and took several swallows of bottled water. She lay back, closing her eyes again.

Despite her aching ribs and face Isabelle had driven the
truck home. Ellen had given her aspirin, which helped a little, and patched her with disinfectant and tape. Alone she
had disengaged the horse trailer, leaving it for Cholly to bring
back later. On the drive home Isabelle's eye and cheek had
swelled. Her upper lip had swollen too, and now she felt like
a duck.

She told Eli she had been headbutt by a mean old mare.
She could not tell him the truth because he would never understand what she had realized almost immediately: It was an
accident. Callen had attacked without thinking, protecting

what was at that instant her most valuable possession: the telephone. In the same circumstances anyone might have done the same thing.

Isabelle fell asleep for another hour and was awakened near seven by Eli bearing coffee and a plate of Ixsky's *pan dulce,* which they took onto the balcony. Sometime during the night clouds had come in and brought a few drops of rain. With a towel Eli wiped the chairs dry. Her ribs hurt and she sat down gingerly.

"We both know you didn't get headbutt," Eli said. "Even when you're distracted, you're still careful."

"It was an accident, Eli. Let it go."

"I'm ready to kill that girl."

"It had nothing to do with her. A mare—"

"Forget the mare. Whatever happened had everything to do with Callen. You're protecting her. You would never lie otherwise."

"She's a good girl."

"She's not. You want her to be, but believe me, I know things about her."

"Things? What things?"

"Just tell me. What happened?"

"First you tell me about these *things* you say you know."

"Forget I said it, Iz."

"You're doing it again, changing the subject like you did yesterday." Anger made her head throb even more. "When you don't want to talk about something, you can't just say forget it. Whatever's bothering you must be important, Eli, or you'd just tell me."

"It's nothing new."

"I think it's new to me." The pulse points at her cheekbones pounded, but if she got up for an aspirin, he would get up too and pretend they'd never started this conversation. "Whatever's going on, whatever it is you don't want to talk about—it's not so hard, Eli. Just open your mouth and let the words out."

The sorrow in his eyes silenced her.

━━➤

Eli knew he had to talk.

As well as anyone he knew that the past was a boneyard he had to travel through to get to whatever was on the other side. It did not matter whether he wanted to. He had to give words to his history, or he and Isabelle would continue to have these truncated conversations—and every day it would be harder to say anything that mattered.

Isabelle already knew his mother had been a drunk. As Callen had the power to bring out the worst in him, "She brought out the worst in my father."

To keep Wanda from drinking, George Browne locked her in their bedroom, leaving her whatever was in the cupboard—a bag of peanuts or half a box of Ritz crackers—water in a bottle, and a bucket to use as a toilet.

"Sometimes he called the bedroom the drunk tank."

One Thanksgiving weekend he nailed the windows shut, and he and Eli drove away. In a Denny's restaurant near the highway he and Eli ate turkey and gravy-soaked mashed potatoes for which neither of them had an appetite. They took a room on the second floor of the Best Western motel next door. All night the big rigs went by, and their air brakes laid down a bed of sound too hard to sleep on. George Browne smoked Pall Malls and played the television; Eli stayed awake, though he closed his eyes for long stretches of time, making up stories about going to sea, being a great captain like Hornblower or a lone sailor crossing the Pacific with dolphin and flying fish for company.

They went home on Friday; and when George Browne opened the bedroom door, she went for him with the face of a wild animal, a broken bottle dripping almond-scented lotion tearing bloody stripes down his cheek and neck. Eli remembered white cream and blood and the cry of sirens.

Isabelle said, "That explains one thing: I always wondered why you hated the smell of almonds."

The police took Wanda away, and she was gone for several weeks. She came back quiet and did nothing but pace the duplex and lie on the couch smoking and watching television until she couldn't stand it anymore and drank the mouthwash in the bathroom cabinet and then went out. She didn't come back for a day and a half.

Drunk or sober, Wanda Browne had been no kind of mother. He told Isabelle of the beatings, of being locked outside in the wintertime as punishment for making too much noise. He had seen Wanda strike Darren across the face with a slipper before he was two years old and been too afraid to intervene.

"You were only a boy," Isabelle said.

"Knowing what she was like, I still left him. And I wasn't a boy anymore."

No decent man would leave his brother with a woman like Wanda. Not for the sea and the sky, not for air to breathe, not for anything.

The only good memories from Eli's childhood were those in which his father figured.

"And then one day he went to work and never came back." George Browne had abandoned Eli, and years later Eli had abandoned Darren.

"What does this have to do with Callen?" Isabelle asked.

"She reminds me of my mother."

"Is that so strange? Wanda was her grandmother."

Inside he shuddered, hearing it put so directly.

"Anyway, what does it matter? I know you like Callen. All the time you've spent with her? You didn't have to do that. You like her."

"Liking her can't change the facts."

"What facts?"

"She's violent, Izzy. Like my mother. You don't want to admit it; you want to protect her. But I know she hurt you."

"You weren't there; you don't understand."

"That's the problem. I *do* understand. There's a kind of anger that's genetic. You can't get rid of it; you can't get psychoanalyzed out of it. You have to learn to control it or it'll control you. This kid, she's spent eleven years with the Brethren. They've probably encouraged her anger; they probably thought it made her tough. A good little soldier. Callen's going to fight until she wins, and hurting you is just part of it."

"Callen is not like your mother." She spoke to him in the soothing tones she would use with a half-wild horse. "This is your imagination, making up a story where there isn't one."

"We've got to give her back to Horne. The longer she's here, the more danger we're in."

Isabelle didn't raise her voice or point her finger, but she might as well have. "We are not giving her back, and that's that. We are going to keep her here for every day of the six months agreed on. If you take her to Horne, I'll never forgive you. I'm not exaggerating, and you know that. I won't forgive you for as long as we live."

twelve

LATER THAT morning when Eli knocked on Callen's bed-room door she was sure he was going to lay into her. In-stead, he stood in the doorway and spoke with his jaw so tight the words barely squeezed out.

He told her he didn't know how Isabelle had been hurt. "But I know you're responsible."

The crampy sound of his voice made her tense all over. She wished he would come right out and blow; it couldn't be worse than feeling the rage seep out through his pores.

"She's lying to protect you."

Isabelle was protecting her? And lying to Eli to do it? Surprise knocked Callen's thoughts sideways.

"I want you to know that if anything like this happens again, I will personally give you the thrashing of your life."

And that was that.

Two more days she waited for the scene that had to come, the scene that would light up Cat Valley and set the chaparral afire. She wanted it and stayed awake at night planning her response. They would come into her room together, a united front. First, they would say how bad she was and lay down rules. She would say they weren't her parents; she'd get angrier and scream her rights and watch their faces contort. Finally, Eli's self-control would vanish, and he'd grab her by the hair the way Darren always did, slam her face into the wall and beat the back of her legs with whatever was at hand—a wooden spoon, a rolled-up magazine or, failing those, his hand.

Was waiting part of the punishment, some new technique to break her spirit?

It wasn't going to work, and it wouldn't stop her from calling the safe house again, the first chance she got.

Cholly finished his last round of trips to Horse Haven, bringing home a total of seventeen horses. Isabelle put the little foal in a corral across from the ranch office, where he would be sure to get plenty of attention. She showed Callen how to fix a special soft mash that would be easy for him to digest.

"It's loaded with calcium," she said as they waited for him to show some interest in eating. "But he's really not ready for it. He should still be nursing. Cholly tried him with a bottle this morning, but he wouldn't take it."

"I'll try."

"He's very weak, Callen."

"He's gonna get strong."

"I hope so. What are you going to call him?"

Callen laid her hand on the foal's dull, woolly winter coat. It was warmer in Bone Lake than in the Anza Valley, and he'd soon lose the shaggy coat. She liked the way he looked.

"His name's Bear."

"You want to call a horse Bear?"

"He's all hairy like one."

Isabelle nodded. "Bear he is." They watched him nose the mash and turn his head away.

"Could I feed him by hand?"

When Isabelle smiled, she had a lopsided face.

Callen spoke without thinking. "Does it hurt?"

"Not much now. Mostly it looks worse than it is."

Barbara would say that hurting Isabelle was a terrible thing and make her apologize. Even knowing this, Callen couldn't do it. She held her hand to Bear with a mouthful of mash on it. He wobbled away from her.

"Go slow, Callen; stand up straight and be calm. Act like you know what you're doing."

Eventually she was able to lay her hand lightly on the slope of his back. There was no fat on him, no muscle either, and his bones were like kindling. She held her hand under his nose and saw the nostrils flutter, then he jerked away to the other side of the corral, all twisted up in his own legs.

It took several tries, but eventually, by sticking her finger in the mash and then up under his lip where he automatically rolled his tongue, he took a little food from her.

"It's a start," Isabelle said. "And make sure he gets water. We don't want him colicky."

✐

At dinner the third night after Horse Haven, Isabelle told her about her own first horse.

"He was a stallion, a light bay with a black mane and tail and a blaze like a lightning bolt."

Ixsky laid a platter of roast chicken and a bowl of salad on the table. "Plain gringo food," she said to Callen and then laughed as if she'd made a great joke.

"Before I went to the Bishop's School, I went to grade school in Lemon Grove. I used to see this horse every day when I caught the school bus, and I started bringing him apples and carrots from home."

"Did he bite you? You told me stallions are dangerous."

"I was careful. Of course, these days—"

"You still have him?"

"He's in the paddock that borders the Ore-Mex Trail."

"He must be old."

"Dr. Blank says he's thirty at least."

Callen thought of Barbara making her own birthday cake in the kitchen in Codyville, laughing and saying she was thirty, an old woman.

"How come I can't go to school?"

"I imagine you'll go in September," Isabelle said.

"I'll be back with my mom and dad then." She looked at Eli, but he had opened the paper and was reading the sports page, pretending not to listen. She still felt his anger, zapping her through the paper.

Isabelle went on about Jack. "He was so beat up. His ribs and hip bones stuck out so much they looked like they'd break through the skin."

"Like Bear," Callen said.

"Worse, Callen. Jack had been abused, beaten. My dad asked around, and apparently the owner thought he'd make a good race horse, but he didn't; the guy lost money, so he took it out on Jack. He was so beaten up by the time I got him, he only had two moods: miserable and mean. Took me more than a year to get him trained, but eventually he got to be a fair trail horse."

"When can I ride Bear?" Callen asked.

"Not for a couple of years. Don't worry, you'll have plenty to do training him."

While Bear grew tall and strong Callen would be back with the Brethren, learning to cook and clean and sew and knit like a good Aryan woman. She would not waste her breath asking Darren to get her a horse.

That night, just when Callen had stopped worrying about punishment, Isabelle came into her bedroom as she was getting ready to turn off her light. Somewhere in the hills a coyote serenade had begun. It would be noisiest around three or four in the morning, when they were on the hunt and yapping like puppies in a box. Sometimes the sound mixed in with Callen's dreams, and she woke up frightened and crying for her mother.

Isabelle sat on the edge of the bed. "I cracked a rib when I fell. It only hurts when I breathe."

It wasn't *human* not to blame Callen. She *deserved* to be blamed.

"I understand that the phone was all that mattered to you. I get that. But what you've got to understand is that all *I* cared about was taking it away from you. If they know you're in Bone Lake, they'll come and get you."

That was the whole point.

"Nevertheless, all that being true . . ." Isabelle sighed. "Actions have consequences, but I can't figure out what yours should be."

"I want to go home; I want to see my mother."

"But you can't do that, sweetheart. Never again." She stopped and seemed to listen to the coyotes.

Even coyotes have homes, Callen thought. They have mothers.

"You just have to let me go. It's so easy." Callen went on, excited. "No one has to know except you and me. Not even Eli. I can walk down to Jamul and call and they'll come and pick me up."

It was miles and miles down a winding road to Jamul, and it wasn't really a town; she didn't think there was a motel where she could wait until the Brethren came. Even so, nothing was impossible when the will was strong. That's what it said in the Manifesto.

"Or I could go into town and use the pay phone and then hide somewhere. You can tell the FBI that I escaped at night. They wouldn't send you to jail."

Callen looked down at the border of the yellow flowered

bedsheet held in her fist. In Codyville their sheets had come from the thrift shop, and they never stopped smelling old and used. She would give anything to smell them again and feel her mother tuck them up around her chin on a winter night. Isabelle's face was familiar now, not strange or foreign anymore, but it would never be the face she wanted to see.

"Believe me, Callen, I know how much you're hurting. Maybe you've already paid enough, and you don't need any consequences."

"I know how to hide out. I know how to make a fire with a flint."

Isabelle started to smile but stopped herself.

"You know a lot of things, and some of them can hurt the Brethren. Suppose you do hide out, and they come and get you. Use your head, Callen; use it for your own good. You know they'll never accept you back. You've been with the FBI. The Brethren can't trust you."

"Andy really likes me. And my mom really misses me."

"They couldn't trust your mother. That's why they killed her."

"She's not dead!" Callen cried and slammed her palms over her ears. "She's waiting for me, and she's worried all the time."

Isabelle's shoulders sank, and her eyes filled with tears. "She's gone, Callen. She was trapped in the fire. Let yourself remember, honey. Just let it happen."

thirteen

AFTER ISABELLE left, Callen was more tired than she'd ever been in her life, and she fell asleep almost instantly. She slept the night through, and when she woke up, she was still tired. At least she hadn't had a dream. Eli's dream book said people dreamed all night long, every night. It said forgotten dreams held images that were too terrible to be remembered in the daylight.

Callen thought you had to be an idiot to believe in dream analysis.

After breakfast Isabelle told her to put a saddle on Sweet Pea. She wouldn't say where they were going.

Behind the barn on the far side of Isabelle's flower garden and Ixsky's vegetables, where the Ore-Mex Trail crossed ranch property, Isabelle and Callen turned to the north and rode their horses along the trail, passing red, white and blue flags set up to mark the final miles of the Oregon to Mexico endurance race that would finish in Bone Lake that weekend. A man and woman in shorts and tanks were setting up a water stop.

Isabelle halted her horse and asked the man, "How far out are they?"

"They'll be in by the weekend, but there's no clear winner yet."

The woman said, "Hey, have you got room for a few campers? There's no space left in town."

"Not this year," Isabelle said, waving good-bye. "Come see me next time."

They walked their horses in silence up a narrow trail marked by small, conical stone mounds. At the top of a rise the hill flattened out, and the trail ran along the crest and down onto the other side where there was a narrow steep-sided valley with a spring and windmill. The horses drank at a cistern, and afterward they went on, following another trail to the head of the little valley where a grove of pepper trees grew on a hillock overlooking a rocky streamlet. In front of the trees, in a space surrounded by a rock wall, there was a little graveyard.

They tied their horses to a metal ring on a post.

"My father wanted to bury my mother near the ranch. She loved it here. She came from Mexico, from a big rancho west of Tecate, but she loved Pasatiempo the best."

Isabelle opened an iron gate and entered the enclosure.

"Back then it wasn't legal, but when my father died, we

went to the county and got permission to have a graveyard on the ranch."

At the stone marking her mother's grave, she knelt and made the sign of the cross.

"Are you a Catholic?" Callen asked, vaguely horrified.

"I'm not anything in particular."

"Catholics aren't Christians. They say they are but not really."

"I didn't bring you here to talk about religion."

Callen felt uneasy standing near the graves. They made her think about death, and when she thought about death, her stomach felt stuffed and heavy, as if she had just eaten three or four of Ixsky's breakfast burritos.

"This is my father's grave. He died when we had just finished building the ranch house. It made him happy to know we weren't going to sell Pasatiempo and move away."

She moved on to the third site marked by a sparkling gray stone with a smooth, polished face in which were cut words and numbers Callen was too far away to read.

"This is my daughter's grave," Isabelle said. "Her name was Lourdes. Same as my mother. She died a few moments after she was born."

Callen took a step toward the gravestone and then back.

"Can we go now?"

"I would have liked having a daughter," Isabelle said. "Actually, I wanted a whole gang of kids, but after Lourdes died, the doctor said we shouldn't try again."

"I think I ate too much breakfast."

"We could have adopted; we always said we would. But we got busy with the ranch, and Eli was writing up a storm . . . And then it just seemed to be too late."

Callen thought of the baby lying under the ground near her feet. She thought of her small bones, and she hoped her coffin was strong and tightly made.

"Why did you bring me here?"

Isabelle touched her fingertips to her lips and then to the top of the gravestone. Callen followed her back to the horses.

"I try to make it up here every day," she said.

"Are we going home now?"

Isabelle looked at Callen, her brown eyes full of hidden things like graves and babies who only breathed a breath or two.

"I wanted you to know me," Isabelle said.

Callen stared at the line of ants following each other into the crater of an anthill. She jammed her boot toe into the light soil and the line broke and the ants reeled off in confused circles.

"I know you," she said.

"No, I don't believe you do. If you knew me, you'd trust me."

⌒

At the Ore-Mex they turned right, away from the ranch, and after a hundred yards they left the trail again and rode cross-country down into the oak meadows. The meadows were rolling, dusty lowlands where sprawling coastal oaks grew. In the early spring the long silky grass came up to Callen's knees and was as green as the pictures she'd seen of the English countryside. But in April it was already looking parched, and the cantering horses threw up dust clouds behind them.

Callen didn't ask where they were going. She was afraid she knew the answer.

Under an oak Isabelle halted her horse and looked up. Callen stared dead ahead, not even blinking. She heard Isabelle's sharp intake of breath and then the leathery squeak as she shifted in the saddle.

"You've been here?" Isabelle didn't wait for Callen's answer. "This is my tree house. I built it when I was ten."

Callen laid her hands on her stomach and wondered what Sweet Pea would do if she threw up all over her.

"You've put broken glass and barbed wire along the top. Where's the ladder? Go get the ladder. I want to see what you've done. What are you waiting for? Just go. Now."

"I don't know what you're talking about."

"Don't be ridiculous, Callen. This is your work. You really have to believe the world is out to get you to put broken bottles on a tree house. You're amazing. You take my breath away."

It sounded a little bit like admiration.

"I want to see everything."

In silence Callen dismounted and retrieved the climbing rope she had stashed behind a boulder a few paces from the tree. After several tries she was successful looping it around the branch above the tree house. She hoped Isabelle might be afraid or not strong enough to climb a knotted rope, but she went up as fast as Sarge would have. As Callen followed her, the thought passed through her mind that if Isabelle were one of the Brethren, they'd have fun at Patriot Camp. She wouldn't be stuck hanging out with Buddy and his gang.

In the tree house Isabelle turned slowly, looking at everything. Below, the horses moved off to a patch of grass a few yards from the tree. It was so quiet in the oak meadow that Callen could hear them tugging and chewing the tender shoots.

Isabelle sat on the stool Callen had stolen one night from outside Jubal Spry's washhouse. Callen hunkered on the plank floor, her knees pulled up to her chin, her stomach doing flip-flops.

Isabelle handled the slingshot Callen had made from a bit of oak kindling. She pulled back the thick rubber band taken from around a bunch of broccoli.

"You need something more elastic."

Callen had others. She indicated several glass jars filled with various sizes of rubber bands, tacks and nails, and stones.

"What about this?" Isabelle held out one of the discarded spray containers Callen had dug out of the Dumpster behind the Bone Lake Motel. She sniffed the kerosene-soaked rag wrapped around it. "Is this supposed to be like a grenade?"

Callen shrugged and stared between her knees at the tree house's weathered floor, embarrassed in case it was a stupid idea, and Isabelle would know the scientific reason why.

She said, "Might not work." Sarge had encouraged them to experiment with weapons.

Isabelle gasped. The silence that followed was what Callen imagined it would be like waiting for a bomb blast.

"I thought it was real. It looks so real." Isabelle shook her head and began to laugh.

This was Callen's most recent fabrication, her third attempt to model the .22 handgun Darren had given her for her tenth birthday. She had fashioned it from plastic piping, paper clips and clay, aluminum foil and toothpicks, shoe polish and black paint. A week ago she had been satisfied with her work the way a counterfeiter would be after producing a good twenty-dollar bill. But real as it looked to her, she wasn't sure it would convince anyone else.

"I apologize, Callen," Isabelle said, still laughing. "I've underestimated you."

Callen was not sure if this was meant as insult or praise, and if the latter, what exactly was she being praised for? Did Isabelle approve of making guns?

"From a little distance you could have fooled me, and I've been around guns all my life. You too, right? Of course you have. The Brethren would make sure you could shoot straight. Or are girls meant to stay home and be good mommies and wives?"

"Some."

"But not you, I bet."

Most of the tree house and its contents, its arsenal, had been constructed from stolen materials gathered on her midnight excursions. Apparently, Isabelle didn't mind. She seemed interested and amused when she should have been angry.

It was like after the day at Horse Haven. Isabelle should have been mad, but she wasn't.

All Callen's life her behavior had been based on the expectation of specific adult reactions: anger, approval and indifference being most common. In that way, living with the Brethren had felt predictable and safe. Callen knew to an absolute certainty that she would be beaten if Darren caught her listening at the door of the meeting room in the basement. She risked a beating and listened anyway. She and Buddy once stole a boom box from a car belonging to one of the sheeple in Codyville. When they were found out, they had to return the radio—they sneaked out at night and put it on the owner's back stairs—and then Sarge had beaten them both with a willow stick in front of all the Brethren gathered for a holiness meeting. In Codyville, Callen knew all about actions and consequences. In Bone Lake the consequences were never what she expected.

"Why'd we come here?" she asked, feeling sullen.

"Same reason as I took you to see Lourdes."

It was warm in the tree house and a swarm of half-pint flies buzzed around Callen's ears. Her temper flared.

"I don't get you. I hurt you and you say you understand. I took your tree house. I fixed it up without permission. That's same as stealing. Why are you being so nice to me?" If Callen could know the answer to these questions, she might also know Isabelle, but she was never going to figure out the answer on her own.

"In some ways you and I are alike. I'm not talking about the mud stuff because that's all bullshit and doesn't mean anything. But when I was your age, I was on my own a lot. I didn't have a mother—"

"I have a mother."

Isabelle looked as if she were going to object, but she didn't. "Okay. I still think you're like me."

Even if it were true (which it wasn't), even if they were Siamese twins joined at the hips, it did not matter because Callen still couldn't wait to get away. She pressed the heels of her hands against her eyes, and in the star-filled blackness she saw the kitchen in Codyville.

Suddenly she remembered her forgotten dream of the night before. Her mother was making wild cherry fudge and singing the hymn about a rugged cross.

"Maybe your mom and dad are alive, and eventually they'll figure out you're here and come and get you." Callen heard Isabelle's voice as a faraway buzz, a chain saw cutting wood half a mile down the road. "But the FBI says they're dead and I believe them. Deep inside where you're afraid to look, you believe them too."

An old rugged cross and Christian soldiers, songs of sin and salvation. Callen knew them by heart, though she had never been inside a church. In Codyville they had holiness meetings three times a week, and Andy talked about what it meant to be an Aryan and one of the Brethren. In the dream

Barbara was in the kitchen singing as she mixed chocolate and sugar, and Callen was watching and thinking about the treat that was coming.

Isabelle said, "My mother died when I was little. Ixsky came to raise me when I was six years old. I had a happy childhood. I don't want to say I wasn't happy. But I know that a girl without a mother . . . she goes through life with a hole in her heart. There's nothing anyone can do about it."

Callen had picked the cherries from an old and forgotten orchard in the woods a mile from Codyville. She climbed the cherry trees and shook the fruit down when they were fat and so darkly red they hung like ruby earrings among the branches.

"This may surprise you, but I really do want your mother to be alive. I'd miss you terribly, but I'd be happy if you were able to go home with her and have a wonderful life."

At home Callen and Barbara pitted the cherries and laid them out on old pizza boxes ransacked from Dumpsters and carefully cleaned for the purpose. She closed the boxes and let the cherries dry out on a shelf above the stove.

"I'd welcome you here on the ranch, Callen. Eli and I both. We can't ever be your mom and dad; we don't want to be. We want to be what we are, your aunt and uncle. Your good friends. Eli's ticked off right now, but he'll get over it. He wasn't at Horse Haven, and what he imagines happened is probably much worse than it was."

In the kitchen they sang the hymns while Barbara made double batches of fudge, one for Darren and one with extra cherries and walnuts for Callen and her; and when it was firm, she poured glasses of milk and they went into the front room and curled together on the couch and ate all the fudge, a whole pan of wild cherry fudge.

She had not remembered the dream because it hurt too much. A tear ran down the crease beside her nose, coming to rest on her upper lip.

She said, "I'm sorry I hurt you. I didn't mean to do it. Tell Eli I didn't mean to do it."

"I think he knows already, Callen. He just can't say so."

Callen stretched her legs out straight and stared at the pointed toes of her cowboy boots.

Crying was for babies.

fourteen

E LI HAD built Pasatiempo's horse barn with royalties
from his second book, the one that put him on the best-
seller list for almost two years. Since then, and for all his
books, the royalties had come as reliably as junk mail.

Though distinctly Western in style and downscale from
some millionaire horse barns with chandeliers and carpets,
central heating and air-conditioning, the barn at Pasatiempo
had plenty of smart extras. There were huge circling fans in
the rafters, a pair of rubber-floored showers with cross ties,
heated water and dryers, four hot walkers and skylighted ceil-
ings; and on either side of two wide alleys, cedar stalls opened
out to spacious individual corrals. The rug on the floor of the
barn office had once belonged to a desert shcik who brought
his Arabians into the tent at night to sleep with his family.

Long ago and fresh from the merchant marine, Eli had
bought two acres in Lakeside near the river and gone south a
few miles to buy his first horse from Pasatiempo ranch.

Though the old man and his pretty daughter had some excellent horses and charged him plenty, the ranch was a shabby two-bedroom bungalow, a tin-roofed feed barn and a vast barren space of mountains, rocks and sky. Today Pasatiempo was what he and Isabel had created together. First they had planted trees: dozens of peppers and cottonwoods, sycamores and eucalypti; the expansive log house came next and then this barn he loved and a big comfortable bunkhouse. There were pipe corrals and wide paddocks kept green and grassy by irrigation and divided by white-washed fences as traditional as Kentucky's. Over the years he had managed to buy up thousands of acres of adjacent land so that now he and the government were the major land owners in the southwest corner of California. Eli's agent accused him of wanting to create his own private country so he wouldn't have to talk to anyone unless he chose to.

His agent knew him well.

Almost any day but today he loved the solitude of his ranch. Today he would have welcomed a few interruptions so he wouldn't have to think about Callen and Isabelle.

Eli was an expert on the subject of anger. It woke him up at night and ruined his digestion, but he didn't need to be an expert to know that day after day of teeth-grinding anger was unhealthy and could burn a hole in your reason. Maybe Isabelle was right and he was overreacting to everything. He didn't trust his own judgment. He wasn't sure about anything, not absolutely. Except that he couldn't get past his anger.

And it was coming between Isabelle and him like nothing before. She was right; he did like Callen, though just now it galled him to admit it, and if Isabelle wasn't furious about whatever had happened at Horse Haven, why should he be? In two weeks Callen would be gone. This should have given him comfort, but it didn't.

The morning air had quickened the barn horses. Impatient for their breakfast, they snorted and beat their hooves on the floors of their stalls. They twitched their ears and flicked their tails and nickered back and forth at each other, and when they heard him load the cart with feed, they whinnied and some butted the gates of their stalls. Most hung their heads over the gates and fixed him with unblinking eyes.

He had paid high prices for a few of these horses, seduced by their strength and beauty. But most in the barn were rescued animals, old and deserving of a little comfort or spooky or so badly bred that no one wanted them. Each bore the genetic inheritance of its forebears as well as the imprint of its former owners, riders and trainers, all their anger, abuse and irrationality. The horses in Eli's barn had survived the worst that people could give them and been gentled back to tractability. A few times Eli had encountered a horse that could not be rehabilitated. Scarred by experience or inheritance, such a horse was too dangerous to have around and had to be put down.

Though mostly blind and deaf, Zacky knew the geography of the barn as well as he did the house. The dog tired of following Eli around and hopped up on a bale of hay to nap.

Each animal in the barn got its morning quota of timothy grass, alfalfa or hay, oats and vitamins and supplements and worming medicine; and the barn filled with the sound of their big teeth grinding. The morning warmed and the air grew rich with the aromas of feed and manure and urine and the strong, hot, dusty scent of the horses themselves.

Zarahas, an Arab cut late but still with a stallion's heart, lifted his head from the feed bin and eyed Eli. He huffled in a friendly way and continued to eat. Fond of the easy life, Zarahas was Eli's favorite.

At sea and only dreaming of a ranch, Eli had read that the eyes of an Arab are larger and more prominent than those of other breeds. A well-fed Arab, exercised and relaxed, softens its eyes; and as it does, the wide, almost rectangular pupils enlarge. Sometimes it seemed to Eli that Zarahas's gaze was an embrace of sorts.

The first time Eli brought Callen into the barn, the horses, even the shy and cautious ones, came to her hand. Rescued horses, rescued girls—they recognized each other. He had thought it a hopeful sign, but now Callen scared him. Anger had clouded his reason, and his judgment might be off a little, but he could not ignore the foreboding he felt in his gut.

fifteen

A FTER THE ride to the cemetery and the tree house, Callen untacked the horses and groomed them. On the way to the house for lunch, she stopped at Bear's corral and was happy to see that he had eaten his mash. She mixed up another batch and tried unsuccessfully to give him milk from a bottle. He leaned his bony shoulder against her as if he were tired, and out of nowhere she wanted to cry again.

Andy and Darren would despise her if they knew how soft she had become.

She couldn't wait around the ranch any longer. She would do what she should have done months ago but was too afraid: hike down the mountain to Jamul and call the safe house from there. She did not know where the Brethren were, and it might take days for them to rescue her. She needed money for food. There was always cash lying around the house—ten dollars in change on the kitchen counter, a big glass piggy bank jammed with coins on the shelf over the washing machine—but she did not want to steal from Isabelle and Eli. She did not know why she had this scruple. Buddy would call her a pussy.

She would stay until the day of the Ore-Mex Race and after the excitement was over, hitch a ride out of Bone Lake. She had seen television trucks in the parking lot at the trailhead. The campground was full, and already RVs and SUVs and trucks with trailers fitted on their beds were parked on the dry lake bed, with ranks of portable toilets set up every fifty feet or so. She had seen an old yellow school bus fixed up like a house on wheels with curtains and a window box on the back. The sign at the Bone Lake Motel said there were no more vacancies, and every parking space in the lot next door was filled. By the end of the weekend she might be able to steal twenty or thirty dollars, more if she found a wallet or purse. Adding that to what she already had hidden in her bedroom, she thought she could feed herself until the Brethren came for her.

Sarge said it was not a crime to steal from muds and the sheeple dumb enough to leave their cars open. Sometimes, he said, the True Word Brethren had a moral duty to break the law. "ZOG law is bad law." Andy's father, Edgar Barrett, had written those words in the Manifesto after he went to jail for hiding illegal guns in a bunker on his own property in Oregon. He was a hero because he had broken the law.

"The future belongs to the man with a plan." That was another one of Edgar Barrett's sayings. He'd made his daughter the boss of all the True Word Brethren. He should have said, ". . . the *person* with a plan."

She bounded across the yard and took the porch steps in one leap. In the kitchen a pot of something savory simmered on the stove, and Callen realized she was starving. She opened the refrigerator and pulled out the plastic bag of sliced ham she knew Ixsky must have touched. Sarge said germs were ground deep into mud pores. There were a lot of things Sarge said about muds that were wrong. Ixsky's clothes and hair were always clean, and she washed her hands a lot. Now that she had been at the ranch six months and never gotten sick once, Callen had stopped worrying about Ixsky and germs. But she still didn't like her.

She bit into her sandwich and it tasted wonderful, though not nearly as delicious as Barbara's. Her mother knew how to make a really good ham and cheese sandwich with white bread and mayonnaise and iceberg lettuce. Darren said Barbara spoiled Callen, but she never felt spoiled. She wondered what it would be like to be spoiled, to get everything she wanted and more than she needed. Darren said she should learn to do without because a good soldier welcomed deprivation. It made him strong. Even Barbara agreed with that. She said new things were a waste of money when so many people threw away perfectly good clothes and furniture. She said it, but Callen learned she didn't really mean it. The first time Barbara talked to Mr. Singh in the thrift shop, she told him that some day she was going to walk into a fancy shop in the mall outside town and buy something brand-new. She spent so long talking to the man that Callen got mad at her and that night told Darren, "Mommy's got a boyfriend at the thrift shop." The next morning Barbara's jaw was bruised, and Callen knew it was her fault. She was ashamed and grateful she hadn't made it worse by saying he was a mud.

Ixsky came into the kitchen carrying laundry. She put the basket on the counter and fixed her black eyes on Callen as if she didn't have a right to eat. Callen headed for the stairs.

"You stay here. Eat in kitchen. We got ants."

Callen thought about ignoring Ixsky's request but decided it was too much trouble. Ixsky would almost certainly follow her upstairs, nagging and wiping up after her. She pulled out a stool, sat at the breakfast bar, took a huge bite of sandwich and chewed at Ixsky with her mouth wide open.

"You tell me something." Ixsky smiled, revealing her red gums and small irregular teeth. "Why you hate me so much?"

"I don't hate you." It was a surprise when she heard herself say this, but she was being honest. She didn't like Ixsky, but it wasn't her fault she was a mud. If the woman had a choice, she would have preferred being an Aryan. "I just want you to go back where you come from. This country belongs to white people."

Ixsky's eyes became narrow slits, and she shook her head, the smile still playing on her lips.

"What?"

"You not so white as you think."

"What do you mean? Of course I'm white. You're crazy.

Look at this." Callen grabbed a handful of her red hair and shook it at Ixsky.

Humming, Ixsky went to the pantry and brought out a bag of yellow-skinned potatoes. Callen stood in the middle of the kitchen, staring at her back as she washed them in the sink.

"I'm Norwegian and Irish and English. My father told me so."

Ixsky chuckled, and her shoulders moved up and down.

Callen was across the room before she had time to think. She grabbed a handful of Ixsky's blue-black braid and pulled hard. Ixsky squawked and wheeled on her, showing the whites of her eyes.

Ixsky stalked her. "You don' touch me, little not-quite-white girl. You understand? You never touch me."

Callen backed away until her hip pressed against the breakfast bar. Ixsky was close enough for Callen to smell toothpaste on her breath.

"You ask Eli what I mean. You tell him I said so."

sixteen

I N THE Bone Lake Motel and Café, Eli sat opposite Agent Billy Horne in the red vinyl booth farthest from the entrance. Through the plate glass window at his elbow, Eli had a view up and down the busy main street. He enjoyed race weekend when, for a few shining hours, the town became a place on the map, a destination of choice not chance. Pickups and SUVs and a dusty, ICE van with a red, white and blue ribbon decal on its back bumper crawled along the main street where vendors had begun setting up their stands, choosing positions midway between the diner and the IGA market where there would be plenty of foot traffic all weekend. By Friday the street would be lined, east and west, with men and women selling running gear, books, jewelry, hiking and camping equipment and food for every diet from macrobiotic to supercarnivore, including buffalo, and venison jerky so tough it made Eli's jaw ache.

Horne had said they had to meet; it was an emergency. He leaned into the back of the vinyl-upholstered booth and pressed his chin down onto his collar bone. When Jenna brought their coffee, he did not look up from contemplating the discolored tabletop in miserable silence. When she was out of earshot, he said, "We lost 'em. About ten days ago."

For an instant Eli's mind went blank, and then he remembered Horne promising with absolute confidence that the FBI was watching the Brethren all the time, never letting them out of sight.

"Whatever you're thinking, Eli, you can keep it to yourself. Just because you write about this stuff doesn't mean you know fuck-all about it."

"But you said—"

"Forget what I said. We were with 'em in King City, and then they were gone. Don't ask me how. The Brethren aren't your typical, homegrown survival outfit. They've got a talent for not being noticed, for fading into the population."

Eli gulped his coffee, burning his throat.

"LA County's the best place there is to get lost in. If they're that close, we've got to figure they'll find her here. It's time for her to come in."

"That doesn't make sense. You don't know where they are, and they don't know she's with me."

Horne's complexion grayed, and the acne craters in his nose deepened and filled with shadows like the escarpment behind Pasatiempo.

"How many people in this town know she's staying with you?"

"They think she's my niece."

"And you know everyone in town, do you? Know their politics? Where they were before they holed up in Bone Lake? What they listen to on the radio after midnight?"

"You're paranoid."

"Maybe. But Bone Lake's the kind of wide spot in the road the True Word Brethren go for." He jerked his head toward the diner kitchen. "The cook in there, how well do you know him? What's his name?"

"He's a relief guy, only comes in when he's needed."

"Right," Horne said. "Towns like this are full of folks way off the map politically."

"But I don't know them and they don't know me."

"I hope that's true, but I'm not going to bet the store."

"If they knew she was here, they'd have come by now."

Horne played with his coffee spoon, tapping the bowl against the tabletop. "I've been working the Domestic Terror Task Force since before 9/11, and I've seen all kinds. What scares me about the Brethren is how slippery they are. Maybe you're right, maybe I'm paranoid, but I sometimes get the willies trying to guess who's really with us and who'd as soon see us dead."

The coffee in Eli's cup looked thick as oil. He pushed it away.

"Of course, that plays right into their plans. They know if

they keep the government guessing, if they get us so we don't trust our neighbors, they're winning the war. They want folks to think there's no safe place, that you can't trust the police, fire, not even your neighbor."

The face of Jubal Spry crossed Eli's thoughts. He blinked and it was gone. He told Horne that Callen had made a call from Horse Haven.

"You should have called me right away." Horne scowled. "We'll check the records." He wrote down Ellen's name. "Prob'ly won't help. If she called a safe house, they'll have a throwaway."

Eli said nothing about whatever had happened between Isabelle and Callen at Horse Haven. He was ashamed that he had not been able to protect his wife, that Callen was his own blood relation, that his anger persisted like a stubborn cold.

The bell over the café entrance rang.

Horne glanced over his shoulder.

"Who's this?"

"Wim Conner. Sort of the unofficial mayor of Bone Lake."

Assisted by a handsomely carved walking stick, Wim walked with the stiff lurch of an over-the-hill athlete. His features were small and even, his face tanned a well-done shade under a white straw cowboy hat. He stopped at the booth and touched Eli's shoulder in greeting.

"Good day, citizen. Another beautiful day in paradise, eh?"

Billy Horne snorted.

"A day for being at home writing a novel," Wim said, adding slying, "not drinking coffee with strangers wearing suits."

"You ready for the race?" Eli asked.

"Pretty near, pretty near. I'm told there's a clutch of runners all within an hour of each other, and the women aren't that far behind, considering their delicate constitutions." He guffawed. "No disasters in sight, so I guess your property's safe again this year."

A few years before, a freak storm had washed out the trail below Pasatiempo, so the race was detoured through the ranch, between the flower and vegetable gardens, past the horses, between the barn and the house and down the driveway to Wild Horse Road.

Wim told Horne, "Made for colorful television, to be sure, and we had a little real estate boom afterward." He dropped a business card on the table. "If you're interested in property, give me a call."

Wim tipped his hat and took a seat at the counter opposite the pass-through where Jenna stood sorting cutlery.

Horne whispered, "How well do you know him?"

"I told you. He's a friend. He's brokered land deals—"

"What've you told him about Callen?"

"I already said—"

"Answer my question."

"He knows she's my niece."

"How long's he been in town?"

"Jesus, Billy, I don't know. A few years."

Horne removed a notebook from the inside pocket of his suit coat and wrote down Wim's name. He stood up.

"Go home, pack her up. I'm taking her in."

Here at last was the opportunity Eli had been waiting for. Horne was the excuse he needed to get rid of Callen before the full six months were up. But he remembered Isabelle's words and knew she meant them; she would never threaten him unless she meant to follow through. She would not forgive him.

He needed another two or three days to convince her they would all be safer when Callen was back in FBI custody.

"Give us through the weekend."

"Eli, I've known you a long time, and it's been a gas, but friendship doesn't change who I work for. Heard of the Patriot Act maybe? Did nine-eleven or Madrid or London light up your screen? This kid called the Brethren once, and she'll find a way to do it again."

Horne cut his eyes to Wim and Jenna and then leaned so far across the table it was ridiculously obvious he was telling secrets. "If it were just the girl, it might not matter so much, but she can identify the Brethren's patron, the guy who makes it all happen. We have to get that name before the Brethren get to Callen." Horne kneaded his cheek with the heel of his hand as if something hurt under the skin. "It won't matter a goddamn if she's got amnesia, they'll still take her out."

"Another few days. After the race."

"Have you been listening to me?"

He was not going to tell him about Isabelle's threat. Like his anger, it was a family matter.

"Why are you fighting me on this?"

The question hooked its talon into Eli's mind and hung there. That first night in Santa Rosa, he had agreed to take Callen back to the ranch partly because she was Darren's daughter, his only niece. Gradually his motivation had morphed into a desire to give her a second chance at life. Perhaps he would not feel so guilty about abandoning Darren if he helped his daughter find a life. And Isabelle was right, after six months and in spite of his anger, he had grown to like the wretched girl.

"If it were just you, Billy, and you were taking her home and she would sleep on the top bunk with one of your girls, even Isabelle wouldn't object to that. But we both know she'll get shipped off to some protected location; they'll put her through hypnotism and interrogation and God knows what else you guys have got going. It'll be all about getting information, and no one will care that she's just an eleven-year-old kid, parents gone, and scared to death."

If FBI methods damaged Callen's mind and destroyed her life, the results would be called collateral damage.

Horne leaned back and stared at the ceiling for a long time. "If you don't give her to me today, I'm gonna have to send a load of agents into this town. Your property's gonna be crawling until you hand her over. You've got to see my side of it, Eli. I've gone so far out on a limb for this kid, I might not have a job next week."

"I don't want you to lose your job. You're my friend, but Isabelle's got feelings for Callen—"

"And you do too. I can see it all over your face."

Horne held his wrist inches from Eli's eyes, forcing him to stare into the scratched face of an old Timex. "This is wartime, Eli. High noon. And the folks gunning for us aren't just Arabs or Muslims or whatever. This country's had a free ride the last hundred years, but the barbarians are now officially at the gate and inside the gate and up on our front lawns. And guess what? They look just like everyone else."

He sat back. "This is about your brother, isn't it? The son of a bitch is a terrorist, but this is his daughter, so you owe him—"

"All I'm asking for is a few days. Monday, after the race, she's all yours."

"Why not Tuesday? Why not Sunday?"

"I need the time to make Isabelle understand."

"You're fooling yourself, my man." Horne rubbed his cheek again. "I should have known you'd get emotional about her. I never should have got you and Isabelle involved in the first place."

"Well, we are." The recognition of truth, of incontrovertible fact, for some reason it made Eli want to laugh.

Horne said, "Darren was a murdering scumbag. You don't owe him piss in a pot."

"Maybe he didn't have to be that way."

"Every killer's someone's son or brother, Eli."

Eli drove the Silverado past his own driveway, up Wild Horse Road to where it dead-ended a quarter mile beyond the Sunny Hills Natural Resort. The road stopped at a plot of leveled land Myrrh's late husband had bulldozed a few years after they opened the resort. Wim had been trying to get her to sell it since he came to town. Eli got out of the truck and picked his way across the uneven red dirt until he stood with a view of all of Cat Valley, from Mexico to the south to where a mountain blocked Highway 94 as it wound down to sea level. To the right, his ranch was spread out like a feast. He thought of how his life and Isabelle's were part of everything within Pasatiempo's borders. He could not give up Callen without Isabelle's agreement. Before he'd take the chance of losing Isabelle, he would risk his life protecting Callen if it came to that.

He felt relieved, lightened.

He stared at the red dust that coated the toes of his boots and tried to remember if he'd paid Jenna when he left the Bone Lake Café. There was a chocolate bar softening in the pocket of his shirt, but he didn't remember buying it. He'd been sidetracked ever since Horne had said that every terrorist was someone's brother.

He had told Isabelle what his childhood was like; he had said aloud that he should not have abandoned Darren. But there was more he had not had the courage to say because as long as he was the only one who knew the truth, he could pretend it had never happened.

He had begun with the best of intentions, renting a car and driving straight back to Great Falls the day after he got his discharge papers. On the lonely stretches of highway between San Francisco and Montana he had anticipated seeing his little brother again, grabbing him in a bear hug and calling him Maggot, a terrible name that meant "I love you." Nights at sea had given him time and space to regret. Guilt had moved in and set up housekeeping.

He should never have left him. He swore to himself that from then on he would take good care of Darren. Eli had no idea where he was going after Great Falls and no clue what he would do when he got there except that Darren and horses and books would be his future. The years at sea had deepened his need for solitude, and he believed he would be happy as a rancher.

He felt his heart shrivel when he stopped his rental car in front of the duplex in which he had been raised. He saw the scrawny fir tree, the dirt yard dug up by dogs and maybe, a long time ago, a little brother building roads and tunnels for toy cars. A coffee-colored stain of damp and rot grew up from the foundation, and some of the windows were covered with plywood and sheets of heavy plastic. Eli had seen poverty in Asia and South America and Africa; and it was always squalid, always depressing. But he'd never feared it as he did walking up to the door of the duplex and raising his fist to knock.

He forced himself to spend an hour with his mother and

the man she called her husband, though Eli knew it was doubtful she had ever actually divorced Browne for Norgaard. Maybe she'd never married either of them. The niceties of the law were lost on his mother. She and Darren's father were drinking wine from a round, green bottle with a screw top, and a movie played on a huge television set. The volume was set high, so the gunfire and shouting happened right there in the front room. A brown metal wall register struggled to heat the place, but the wind off Canada's plains came in through the chinks in the wood and stucco. Eli drank a glass of sour wine, hoping for a little warmth. He waited for Darren to come home, waited until he thought he'd jump out of his skin when Norgaard raised his voice over the noise of the television to rant against the government, the niggers and queers and rich kikes.

His mother named a half dozen street corners, parking lots and convenience stores where Darren might be, and Eli drove around Great Falls until the gray twilight fell and the temperature dropped another ten degrees. He spotted a group of young men and women clustered around a primered 1970 Firebird in the parking lot of a 7-Eleven, passing around a bottle of Jim Beam. He recognized Darren immediately. He had not outgrown the rawboned look of his childhood, but his alarmed chipmunk eyes had lost their wide innocence. They narrowed suspiciously when Eli got out of his rented car and walked toward the group. His friends were a scarred and tattooed crew with sallow skin and bad teeth. The girls, their faces pale and thin, their bodies dressed in parkas, short skirts and boots topped with fake fur, lolled against the hood of the car, looking like arctic hookers.

The bottle of Jim Beam came around to Eli, and he took a swallow to be friendly, not from any desire for alcohol. The conversation moved from cars and engines to guns and back to cars. Looking around at the faces of the boys and girls gathered in the parking lot, Eli realized that whatever he had imagined Darren's future would be if he stayed in Great Falls, he had underestimated its mind-killing pointlessness and never considered that it might be contagious.

In the car, Eli had maps of the West so new they had never been unfolded. He had imagined that he and Darren would examine them together and drive from town to town until they found one pleasing to both. It was time to open the door and hold out his hand. Time to say, "Come on, Maggot. Let's get out of here."

Instead, he refused a hit off the joint and said good-bye, got in the car alone and drove away down the dark street. He turned the heat to high and put a tape in the player. He decided to drive somewhere warm and never think of Great Falls again.

seventeen

ANDY DEWITT closed the copy of *People* magazine she had been scanning and set it on the table beside the chaise longue. She had forced herself to read the articles about whoring movie stars and fashionistas. Someone among the True Word Brethren had to know what was going on in the country.

Half an hour ago she had moved into the shade some distance from Mrs. Smith's gold-bottomed swimming pool. Now the sun was inching up her leg again. She reached into the bag beside the chaise and pulled out a squeeze bottle of number forty-five sunscreen. She had started the day with five, moved up to fifteen and now it was time for the high-powered stuff. It was a science, tanning her pink-and-white Aryan skin in a world without ozone. If, in fact, it was true that the globe was warming up. She suspected it was more ZOG lies, but it was too easy to blame everything unpleasant on Jew propaganda. The challenge lay in maintaining a balance between credulity and complete cynicism.

From where she lay she had a view of Los Angeles, especially clear this afternoon because the winds were blowing from the west, strong and constant. To the right she could see the deep blue of the Pacific and far to the left the peaks of the San Gabriel Mountains. Andy imagined what such a view was worth in real estate terms, and she told herself that it did not matter whether Mrs. Smith kept her waiting another forty-eight hours. This view gave her that right.

The cell phone on the table beside her rang. She frowned and answered.

"You shouldn't call me here. If anyone gets suspicious—"

Sarge interrupted her, something he would never dare do if they were face-to-face. If Mrs. Smith cancelled their appointment again, she might have to go back to Bakersfield anyway. In an organization like the Brethren, respect for authority was essential, and every day she was gone the group's discipline and cohesion grew more ragged.

Sarge told her that the night before, Ansel and Quentin had drunk too much beer and gotten noisy; a neighbor had banged on the door, warning that she would call the police if they didn't shut up. All their apartments were full of guns, and police were the last thing the Brethren wanted poking around on some flimsy excuse.

"I got to give them a date. Friday. Next week. They gotta know when they're getting out of here." Sarge had spent twenty years in the marines. He could get the job done, but he needed leadership.

"A week," she said.

"What about Monday?"

"A week," she said again and broke the connection.

Though she had spoken to Sarge in tones of complete assurance, she was wracked with uncertainty. If Callen did not call, what then? Like the rest of her group, she wanted to disappear into anonymity, lie low, lull the authorities into complacency; but Callen Norgaard was a loose end that had to be dealt with.

Andy knew Mrs. Smith would want to terminate her, but she was determined not to let that happen. To a true conservative, the waste of Callen's intelligence and courage was an offense. Especially when Andy knew her own children would never be more than soldiers and not very good ones at that. Reluctantly and in private Andy admired the Muslim radicals for their ability to focus the energy of their men and women. It took only the roar of a Harley to lure the young away from the True Word. And forget heavenly rewards. Buddy and his pals wanted their virgins now, in a Motel 6 down the highway.

Behind her she heard the French doors open and the Mexican maid padding toward her with snacks and a pitcher of margaritas. According to Mrs. Smith, a person of influence in the entertainment business could not live without servants, and immigrants were the only ones available. Every penny she gave the Brethren was mud and Jew stained. Andy appreciated the irony.

Andy poured another margarita. She lit a cigarette and exhaled with slow pleasure. Her father had instilled in her the importance of maintaining the Aryan body as a holy temple, so she would have to give up these sheeple vices when she got back to Bakersfield. But in Los Angeles everyone smoked and ate and drank with no apparent concern for the sanctity of their bodies, and she didn't want to draw attention to herself by behaving otherwise. In the Manifesto her father had written a long chapter on camouflage.

When she was very young, her father had shown her a photo of a lioness in wait for an antelope. At first she could not make out the body of the cat hidden in the tawny grass. Camouflage, protective coloring that blended into the surroundings, had been the great lesson learned from her father. To destroy ZOG, the Brethren must be indistinguishable from the tall grass, moving toward their prey with slow patience. This was what soldiers like Ansel and Dor and that great lummox Quentin could not grasp. With their love of guns and having little control over their impulses, they would always make too much noise and move too fast unless she was there to keep them in line.

✐

That night Mrs. Smith kept Andy waiting thirty minutes, perched on the edge of a honey-colored brocade couch. A barefoot Hispanic girl brought her wine in a glass as thin as paper. The room had a view of Los Angeles and was larger than her whole apartment in Bakersfield.

Across the room a door opened. Andy stood and then sat down again, ashamed that she, Edgar Barrett's daughter, should feel subservient in the presence of this woman. Ashamed and also embarrassed, in case Mrs. Smith noticed her ambivalence, which she almost certainly had. She was the kind of woman who noticed everything.

Mrs. Smith, tall and slim, paused a moment in the arched doorway to the hall. A hidden light shone on her from an angle that accentuated her cheekbones. Andy wondered how often she had stood in precisely that spot, like a diva about to burst into song or a politician waiting for the crowd to stop talking. Under a sheer, sequined jacket she wore a black sweater and palazzo pants in a floaty fabric. Her pink-gold hair fell in studied tendrils around her forehead and cheeks, a style more suited to an ingenue than a woman nearing eighty. Around her neck she wore a heavy gold iron cross pendant, which Andy was certain she reserved for private occasions.

"I've kept you waiting a long time, Andy. You must forgive me, though I'm sure you understand."

Andy stood up as Mrs. Smith strode into the room, a powerful energy in every movement. Briefly she laid her perfumed cheek against Andy's before telling her to sit. "The liberals think they own Hollywood, but if they knew the truth, they'd be shocked. Into silence, one could hope." She laughed lightly.

No matter how many times they met, Andy was never quite ready for Mrs. Smith's intimidating presence. Despite her age, in the flattering light of several carefully placed and heavily shaded and tasseled table lamps, she retained a rosy girlishness and an unnerving quality of near innocence.

Before he went to prison, Edgar Barrett had told Andy everything he knew about his late friend's wife. She had come to Hollywood during McCarthy's time intent on being a movie star. She had been a pink-and-blond girl from the upper reaches of Minnesota with little talent and a tenacious hold on her virginity. Doomed to failure in the industry, she had met a powerful man in the Paramount commissary. With both beauty and virtue, she was the wife he had been searching for. She had always approved of his politics, and when he died, she did not begrudge the Brethren their share of his legacy.

"This girl you wrote me about. Callen. She's a great problem. To be frank, it upsets me that you've done nothing about her." She lit a cigarette.

"We don't know where she is," Andy said. "We've been forced into a waiting game."

"You do realize what's at stake here." Mrs. Smith stared at the tip of her cigarette. "You brought her to me, Andy. Your little protégé. And against my better judgment I agreed to meet her."

"I thought you would inspire her, ma'am. She is an amazing kid."

"And was that what happened? Did I inspire her?" She

raised one winged brow but did not wait for an answer. "Looking back, I wonder at your motives."

Andy didn't understand.

"Until now you've never given me the slightest reason to doubt you, but you must understand my position. By invading my privacy that day you threatened my anonymity, put me at risk. Of late certain celebrities have caused a great fuss by speaking their true opinions, and however much I might agree with them, I can't afford to have any negative talk associated with my name."

"No, ma'am." Andy made her voice calm and humbly respectful, but inside she seethed. She had been a faithful soldier in the army of the Word since she was a toddler tagging after her father with a stick pressed against her shoulder like a rifle. She had suffered for the Word: She had married Dor and given birth to dolts; she had risked prison, and her father had died in a cell.

"She doesn't know my real name, but I'm quite sure she could identify me from a picture. I'm not easily forgotten."

Though Mrs. Smith claimed to dislike having her picture taken, it did happen from time to time that her image appeared on the pages of magazines like *People* and *Us Weekly*. Callen might be in a doctor's or dentist's office at this very moment, leafing through an old copy where she might see a picture of the woman she knew as Mrs. Smith.

This woman and her husband had insulated themselves against any hint of scandal or extremism. In the movie and television communities, Mrs. Smith was known to be a conservative of the moderate variety. She drew no particular attention to herself and on occasion even contributed to harmless liberal causes. Every year Mrs. Smith chaired a committee to save something innocuous, bears or birds or the redwood trees.

"Your reputation is flawless, ma'am."

"Yes, of course it is, but the Jews are a cunning people. They have learned to dig below the surface. That's how they maintain their power."

Smoke stung Andy's eyes.

"This girl has been with the government for six months."

"Yes, but her father spoke to her when she called the safe house, and he's convinced they haven't turned her. She wants to come back with us."

"And you understand that's impossible."

"If it were anyone else, I would agree, ma'am, but we need a girl like Callen Norgaard."

"She's compromised."

"Maybe not. She has a very strong will, and I doubt if the government—"

"My dear, you underestimate ZOG."

"ZOG killed my father."

"Yes, yes, but he was foolish. Imagine having all those guns where anyone with a wit could find them."

Outraged, Andy struggled not to be distracted. "I thought we might find a way to test her loyalty. Give her an assignment."

"What did you have in mind?"

Andy had anticipated the question. "She's young but quite mature. I think she's old enough to accompany her father on his next mission. And he can begin to teach her about explosives."

Mrs. Smith tapped the ash off her cigarette into a large glass ashtray. "You are defending her."

"She's done nothing wrong as far as we know."

"You defend her. You protect her. What am I to think, Andy?"

"Ma'am?"

"Let me guess. You have come to regard Callen as rather like a daughter."

Where was the crime in having affection for a child? "She loves the Word; she's committed to our cause and she thinks for herself. But in a good way. She's not a drone, ma'am."

Mrs. Smith laughed. "My dear, the war against ZOG is a war to the death, a war for the heart and soul of America. Do you suppose those raghead boys who blow themselves up in Baghdad are thinkers? They're drones, and what the True Word Brethren need are drones. Drones by the millions."

"If she's remained faithful, it seems wrong—"

"Andy, I have always been grateful for the strength you bring to our cause. My dear husband loved your father as a brother, and so I have been disposed to think of you as a member of our family, a member of whom I am very proud. But now I wonder." She tilted her head to one side. "For the first time I wonder. Can I trust you?"

"Ma'am, no one has ever questioned my loyalty." Andy heard the ripple in her voice.

Again the elegant eyebrow shot up. "You haven't answered my question."

"That's because the question insults me."

"That may be. By all means, be insulted if you wish. But I still want an answer. Can I trust you? Yes or no?"

Andy's cheeks blazed with humiliation. "The Brethren are everything to me."

"I hope that's true, Andy. But words are only words, and I don't feel confident. My husband and I have invested our lives and millions of dollars in the True Word Brethren. And now this brat whom you were supposed to eliminate along with her mother is a threat to everything. She knows who I am. She can identify me. And you are more upset about being 'insulted.' "

Andy looked into Mrs. Smith's unblinking blue eyes and understood for the first time that to this woman she was of no greater worth than the barefoot girl who served her wine.

"You know what you must do."

"Yes, ma'am. I know."

"And I don't want you giving the job to someone else. This time there must be no mistakes." She laughed. "And to prove she's gone, bring me a big handful of her red hair. Like in a fairy tale."

The old witch was enjoying herself. She felt powerful and Andy hated her more and could not hide it.

"Perhaps you don't understand what's at stake here, Andy. I'm going to have to convince you."

She lifted a silver bell from the table beside the couch and rang it. Immediately the barefoot girl entered the room and stood before her, her eyes cast down.

"You've met Milly, haven't you? Milly, look at my guest."

The girl lifted her head, and the stark terror in her eyes made Andy catch her breath.

"Milly isn't her real name, of course, but we don't use mud names in this house. You notice she's barefoot?" Mrs. Smith smiled. "Milly hasn't been with me very long and being barefoot discourages her from leaving."

With her index finger Mrs. Smith lifted Milly's chin.

"Some would say she's pretty though to me her features are gross. You'd agree, wouldn't you, Andy?"

She nodded.

"Milly has a primitive intelligence but she's slowly learning that if she obeys me, nothing too terrible will happen to her. I won't have to call the immigration people." Mrs. Smith looked at Andy. "Or the FBI."

Milly's expression made Andy forget her own fear and brought her back to herself. She was not a feeble-minded mud cowed into slavery. She was Edgar Barrett's daughter, leader of the Brethren and a warrior in God's army of the True Word. She had learned camouflage and concealment from her father and could hide her fear behind her hatred.

For Mrs. Smith there was no satisfaction in being hated.
After a moment a frown line appeared between her pale eyes.

"Milly, hold out your hand." Mrs. Smith took a long drag
off her cigarette. She said to Andy, "These girls can sometimes be stubborn, they don't believe me when I tell them
what will happen if they fail to obey me. They need to be convinced." She placed her left hand under Milly's to steady it.
She flicked an ash from her cigarette into the servant's hand;
and then, smiling at Andy, she drove the coal into Milly's
palm.

"Now we understand each other."

eighteen

OLEANDER BUSHES were poisonous. Eli had told Callen that.

Now she lay on her stomach in the dust under the shrub, inhaling the half-rotten smell of the flowers and wondering if she was inhaling poison. When she stood up, would she keel over dead?

She wished she had the guts to shove a handful of the leaves and raspberry-colored flowers into Ixsky's lying mouth and make her chew until her eyes crossed.

Callen knew she was pure Aryan. She *felt* like a pure Aryan. Even so, she needed something to take her mind off the impossible idea that maybe she *wasn't* pure Aryan. She had run right out of the house and up the hill to spy on the sunbathers at the nudist resort.

From her position in the bushes she had a clear view of Sunny Hill's lawn and patio and swimming pool. Forty feet away from her two men reclined on a pair of lawn chairs. The chairs were made of wood, had solid arms and were angled slightly away from Callen so she couldn't see anything interesting. Both men wore Dodgers baseball caps, one the right way around and the other backward.

She needed to pee, but she wanted to hold on long enough for one of the men to stand up. She couldn't see the point of living down the road from a nudie resort if she never got to see the business.

She judged the men to be pretty old because what she saw of their darkly tanned arms and legs was wrinkled like the carrots she fed the horses. One man had stick-straight, fake, lemon-yellow hair that hung like a girl's to his tanned and oiled shoulders. He had been arguing on his cell phone the whole time she watched, and though she could not hear the conversation, a moron could tell he was angry from the way his hands karate-chopped the air. The shoulders of the other man were covered with a lot of thick, black hair. Like an animal. He was trying to read a book. Once he reached over and yanked his friend's hair. His voice carried and Callen heard him tell the other that he'd promised no business that weekend.

She tried to imagine her father and Sarge sitting side by side, bare-ass naked, pulling each other's hair. These men must be sodomites. She had learned a little about sodomites in camp and gotten the details from Buddy. She knew most of them were Jews or in league with ZOG.

Something poked her in the side. The toe of a boot.

A woman's voice said, "You. Girl."

Callen popped up to her hands and knees. And peed.

"Oh hell, why'd you do that? How old are you anyway? 'Bout two?"

Mortified, Callen crawled out from under the bushes and rose to her feet, brushing dirt and oleander litter from her clothes, staring at the puddle she had left behind.

"You know this is private property?"

She thought about running, but she knew this was Isabelle's friend Myrrh. Isabelle said she was tough.

Myrrh grabbed the back of Callen's T-shirt and shoved her along the path ahead of her. "Get going. Head for the house." Callen squirmed and Myrrh's grip tightened. "I'm calling your uncle. He can come get you."

"Lemme walk back."

"Not on your rosy-tomato life. I want a few words with Eli on the subject of sneaky little girls."

Callen twisted and Myrrh's grip tightened again. The woman had iron hands.

"You're hurting me."

"My heart bleeds. Just walk."

Callen peed again, and this time she did not stop until her bladder was empty.

"Good God, preserve us. Someone needs to take you to the doctor."

Her wet underpants and shorts stuck to her skin. Even her socks were soggy.

"You stink like a cow barn," Myrrh said conversationally as they came around the side and behind the sprawling single-story adobe house, its red-tiled roof overgrown with scarlet and orange vines. "Go in there." Myrrh nudged her toward a separate adobe building, and from within Callen heard the churn of a washing machine and smelled laundry soap and bleach.

She stopped at the threshold and peered into a dark room filled with the shapes of outsized washing machines and a pair of dryers spinning so hard the floor vibrated under her feet. At one end, on the wall beside two large washtubs, she saw a telephone as black and utilitarian as the one that had hung on the wall in Andy's kitchen.

"Take off your clothes."

Callen hesitated.

"Oh, for the love of heaven, don't look at me like that. Your little-girl parts don't interest me. I've seen a thousand twats in my time and not one's ever been as pretty as my own. So just take off the stinkies and wrap your butt in one of those clean towels."

Callen stepped deeper into the laundry room, closer to the phone. There was no point running to it straight off. She'd never finish dialing before Myrrh got her.

"Move your hips now and don't even think about trying to ditch me. I'll be right out here."

Myrrh pulled a cell phone from her pocket and shook it in Callen's face. "And just so you know, little girl, this high up the mountain reception's real clear. Not like down at Pasatiempo. And I've got your uncle's number programmed. All I got to do is press one button."

In the warm shadows of the laundry room Callen kept her eyes on the wall phone as she stripped out of her clothes, her shoes and socks, and left them in a pile on the floor. She wrapped herself in one of the white towels that lay in a warm pile in a basket and walked to the door.

"You need a shower."

Callen shook her head and tried to look ferocious.

Myrrh laughed, not unkindly. "You are certainly a thorny one. Izzy said you were." Her voice trailed off into an annoying chuckle, as if she and Isabelle had a private joke between them.

Behind the house there was a large and carefully tended garden laid out in precisely marked rows. Callen recognized peppers and tomatoes and lettuce all weeded and staked. The paths of trodden dirt that ran between the plants were so tidy they looked as if they'd been swept with a broom. Pea and bean plants climbed wigwam frames, and between the lines of edibles rose bright yellow and gold marigolds swarming with bees. If Barbara had been there, she'd have oohed and aahed and asked what kind of fertilizer Myrrh used and how she got things to grow so early in the season.

"Up the steps. Open the screen."

Just inside and to the right a door stood slightly open, revealing a tiled bathroom.

"Go on in," Myrrh said. "Take a shower. Scrub with the soap. I make it myself."

"You make soap?"

"I do make soap and a lot more besides, so I could really

use a little help around here. If you don't behave yourself, I'll
make you my servant and feed you bread and water."

Inadvertently Callen smiled.

"Think I don't mean it? Just test me, sparrow."

It wasn't truly a bathroom at all. More like a jungle with
potted plants on stands and hanging from the ceiling and
even a ceramic pot on the toilet seat. The air smelled of earth
and plants and felt tropically warm and watery with their res-
piration. From above, sunlight poured through a skylight.
The shower had no curtain, and Callen could not tell where
it stopped and the rest of the room began. The whole room
seemed to be the shower, which explained why the plants
looked so happy. She wished she could show this bathroom to
Barbara. The floor tipped slightly toward a drain and was covered in blue and green and black tiles, unevenly shaped and
bumpy underfoot. The same tiles covered the four walls almost to the ceiling. Here and there among the plain tiles
were others oddly shaped and decorated with drawings that
looked like a child's work: the face of a man with long hair and
another of a woman wearing dangling earrings.

Myrrh pounded on the door. "I don't hear any water. Do
I have to come in there and wash you myself?"

Callen turned on the water and stepped under the
stream. She lathered the soap between her hands and covered herself with suds fragrant with the smell of cherries.
Wild cherries that stained her fingers when she picked them.
Cherries and fudge.

With the suddenness of a match flaring in a dark room,

Callen's tears returned. She leaned against the tiled wall and slid to the floor, and the water showered down on her bent head. Just like in the tree house, once she started crying, she couldn't stop.

She became aware of Myrrh standing at the open door, looking at her.

"You know in fifty years folks'll be fighting wars over water, and they'll cuss the memory of wasteful girls like you."

Callen did not care what happened to anyone now or in the future.

"Oh well, never mind. Way things are going, there's other problems ahead just as big." Myrrh reached over Callen's head and turned the water off. She handed her a fresh towel. "Get yourself dry, sparrow. I found some clothes should fit you good enough. I'll get your other duds washed and send 'em down to the ranch mañana."

Callen wiped her nose with the back of her hand. "What about Uncle Eli?"

"Did I not make myself clear? Stand up, get dry and dressed. We'll talk about him later."

Callen sat where she was.

"Jesus bloody-what-me, I'll turn my back. Okay? Is this okay?"

Tears and warm water and the memory of wild cherries had washed the strength from Callen, and all she really wanted was to curl up on a soft bed and pull the blankets over her head until she heard her mother say she'd better get out of bed before she grew roots.

"Can I turn now? Lord God Almighty, you are a touchy sparrow."

Callen did not like being called a sparrow, but she was too sodden with longing to tell Myrrh she was more the eagle type.

nineteen

"WHERE YOU been?" Ixsky asked Eli.

"In town."

She pointed at his boots. "No red dust in town."

He grunted.

"Where's Callen?"

"Out somewhere."

"Did she say where she was going?"

Ixsky rolled her eyes at Eli and pressed a rolling pin into the ball of pie dough on the butcher block.

"Did she have anything with her? What about her backpack?"

"Her and me," Ixsky pointed to herself with a floury finger, "we're not good friends."

"Wait a minute," Eli said, alarmed. "You must have said something to her."

Ixsky turned the pastry circle and rolled the pin.

"Spit it out, Ixsky."

"Why're you so mad at me?"

"I'm not mad."

"Ha!" Ixsky rolled the pastry into an almost perfect circle, rolled it on the pin and deftly lifted it onto a pie plate. "I know you, Eli Browne. A long time."

"Hey, Ixsky, I'm the guy who pays the bills around here. And I want to know what you said to Callen."

"I just tol' her she isn't as white as she thinks."

"Why the hell did you say that?"

"I was cleaning," Ixsky said. "I saw the papers on your desk."

"Ixsky, you had no right."

"I can't help what my eyes see. You don' want me to see, you shouldn't—"

"She could be half way to San Diego by now."

"Don' think so. She just ran out, didn't take nothing with her." Ixsky's knife whacked an apple in half and then in quarters. Eli stepped back just in case.

"She made me mad." Whack.

"She makes us all mad."

"Not you, Eli. Nothing makes you mad. Right?"

More whacks.

There was no point telling her again that she should have kept her mouth shut. Ixsky—mother of kings—might as well be back in the Guatemalan highlands; she cared that little for Eli's questions and opinions. But she wasn't washing clothes in a stream; she was in his kitchen whacking Granny Smith apples, tossing them into a bowl with sugar and spices as casually as a Dakota farm wife. And she read English as well as he did.

He had taken the papers from the safe two nights ago, wondering when he would tell Callen the truth. He had decided to wait until he wasn't feeling angry anymore. And then he had left them in plain sight on his desk, where Ixsky could read them. Maybe it was Freudian.

He left the kitchen and went upstairs with Zacky padding in his wake. The old dog had slept most of the day, and now, as the afternoon waned and thoughts of supper entered his mind, he had begun to take an interest in the life of the house and wasn't going to let Eli out of his feeble sight. At the door to Callen's room Eli paused a moment, considering, his fingertips resting on the dog's big shepherd head. Ixsky said Callen had stormed out of the house taking nothing with her. He had to be sure. He turned the knob and walked in.

The sun had moved to the western side of the house, leaving the room in shadow. The windows were open, and he smelled the great pepper tree's leaves, which brushed the roof. He rarely entered Callen's sanctuary, and when he did, it was always when she was there. On his previous incursions he hadn't noticed how the room had changed since she'd moved in and how it now bore the imprint of her personality. To the wall over her bed she had tacked two drawings. One was of a woman and a girl, obviously Callen. The pretty woman with sad eyes must be her mother, the woman Darren had married. Callen's self-portrait was eerily accurate. The other picture was a house on a country road surrounded by tall trees. Eli realized that in addition to missing her mother and father, all these months she had been homesick for Codyville and the wild Siskiyou country where she'd grown up.

He and Isabelle should have left her in Santa Rosa. But they hadn't, and now the situation, every part of it, was brain-bendingly confused. As he stared at the pictures, Eli felt the last of his anger fall away.

On the dresser she had arranged a bird's nest, a fossil they had found on one of their rides together and a horseshoe into which she had scratched *Sweet Pea.*

He slid back the closet door and stared at the clothes Isabelle had ordered from catalogs, the skirts and shirts and pants, the row of shoes lined up like books on a shelf. Her backpack lay on the floor, open and empty. He relaxed. If she'd meant to run away, she would have taken that. He saw something white at the back of the closet shelf and brought down a mailing tube. He opened it and discovered a dozen or more line drawings.

Horses, horses and more horses, and the pictures were good, correct in their proportions. He could count the ribs on Bear's chest. There were sketches of the ranch house, the barn and the pepper tree and more pictures of the woman Eli took to be Callen's mother. There was even a wild-eyed drawing of Ixsky. Callen's talent for portraiture startled him.

He rolled the pictures back into the tube and returned it to the closet shelf.

He stood at the center of the room, absorbing Callen's

space as if by doing so he could discover an element of her personality that would give him access to whatever would unlock the puzzle of her. Why would a girl so intelligent and talented want to trade Pasatiempo for the windowless, hallway life of the Brethren world? Looking again at the picture of Callen and her mother, he realized that there was no puzzle at all. It was her mother she missed and wanted; until she believed Barbara was dead, she would continue fighting to get back to the Brethren.

The desk Eli had set up for her with a computer and halogen lamp was a mess of papers and magazines. Automatically he began to tidy it as he would his own, putting the pens and pencils in an old cup, grabbing a handful of papers, stacking them, squaring the edges. A pictorial history of World War II lay face down, open to photos taken when the camps were liberated. She'd drawn a Hitler mustache on one of the GIs. In ink. He slammed the book shut with such force it knocked the papers to the floor. Several fanned out, and one in particular, a portrait, drew his attention. The woman was no one he knew personally, but he had seen her face before, perhaps in a magazine or on television.

In pencil Callen had drawn an old woman with a girlish, curly hairstyle. It was obvious that she had been beautiful once, but Callen had captured a stridency about her efforts to remain youthful. Around her neck she wore a conspicuously oversized pendant, an Iron Cross.

twenty

MYRRH DREW the blinds that faced the swimming pool and turned on the lights. Callen thought about how much her mother would like the Sunny Hills kitchen. All the surfaces shone, there were flowers in vases, and the air smelled of sweet baking. She saw Myrrh filling an electric kettle.

"I don't like tea."

"Good thing, since I'm not planning to waste any on you."

Callen was thirsty, but if Myrrh was going to be so inhospitable, she would rather suffer a dry mouth.

"What's your name?"

"Callen."

"What kind of name is that?"

"It was my mother's before she got married."

"She a red head too? Red hair's good. Reminds me of salsa. Makes you look like you got spunk."

Barbara used to say that Callen thought so hard and fast her hair was permanently on fire.

"Get yourself a Coke out of the fridge."

"*Your* name's weird too." Callen popped the top of her Coke and sat down again.

"Used to be I was Emily Jane. Changed it to Myrrh in the sixties. When me and Frank were first together, we had a cat named Incense. Folks called us Frank, Incense and Myrrh. Funny, huh?"

"Like in the Bible."

"You got it, sparrow."

Myrrh opened the refrigerator and set out bread, lettuce and mayonnaise and tuna fish mixed with hard-boiled eggs and chopped celery. "Bet old Ixsky never makes tuna sandwiches. How many, sparrow? One or two?"

"Two," said Callen so quickly that she and Myrrh both smiled. Lunchtime had been three hours back, and she was hungry again.

"I know your uncle pretty well, and Isabelle's been coming around here since she was a youngster. They both of them told me you aren't supposed to leave Pasatiempo, but I've seen you up here spying on my guests ever since the weather warmed up." Myrrh laid the sandwiches before Callen on a red pottery plate. Callen took a huge bite and her eyes rolled as if she'd gone dizzy.

"So, Callen, what's the scoop, huh? You just a rule breaker by nature?"

Callen opened her mouth to answer, and Myrrh covered her eyes. "Spare me the Mixmaster."

Callen sucked the mayonnaise off her fingers.

"What you have to understand is that folks come to Sunny Hills expecting privacy. They don't want some ten-year-old—"

"I'm almost twelve."

"And I'm the hippie Queen of the May. Your age isn't the point, and I expect you're smart enough to know that. What I care about is keeping you out from under those oleanders. For one thing, it probably isn't healthy, and for another, I don't like sneaks. ¿*Comprende?*"

Callen noticed a tall, coconut-frosted cake under a glass dome.

"I can give you a cookie, but that's it. The cake's for my guests. It's race weekend, and I've got a full house." Myrrh lifted a brown-bear cookie jar off the refrigerator and set it before Callen. "There's no better spot to watch the race finish than Sunny Hills. If you weren't such a patch of crabgrass, I'd give you a job. I could use the help."

On the wall above the coconut cake hung a white phone. Though the FBI had surely put a tap on Eli's telephones, they weren't smart or powerful enough to bug everyone in the neighborhood.

Myrrh waved her hands in front of Callen's face. "Earth to Callen, earth to Callen."

"What kind of job?"

"I don't know. Maybe taking care of the garden while I see to the guests. How long will you be with Iz and Eli?"

Callen said, "Not long."

"Too bad. It's a nice place. You like horses?"

Callen nodded and tried not to look at the phone.

Myrrh put the cookie jar back on top of the refrigerator, and as if she'd gotten some message from Callen's thoughts, she walked to the phone and lifted the receiver. Anxiety pinched Callen in the area of the tuna sandwiches. She'd eaten too fast, and now she felt sick. Isabelle always said her stomach problems were caused by stress and for once Callen thought she probably was right. She felt like a ticking bomb.

"You calling my uncle?"

"No. I'm calling the pope. I hear he's visiting your folks down at the ranch."

"They're not my folks."

"Whoever they are, they want to know where you are."

"You gonna tell him I was . . . you know?"

"Spying? Trespassing? Want me to say you've got the manners of a salami?"

Myrrh laughed as she reached across the counter and patted Callen's hand. "Learn to smile, sparrow. Life's too hard if you don't have a sense of humor." She tapped the receiver against her lower lip. "Stop looking so worried. I'm not going to tell him. When you're on your own and there's no other kids to play with, it's natural to get nosy."

"Sarge says we should always get to know our territory."

"Who's Sarge?"

Callen stuck her hands up under her arms. "No one."

Myrrh nodded. "Okay." She hung up the phone and lifted a basket off a hook by the back door. "I've got some chard I'm going to pick for Isabelle, and then we'll get you back to Pasatiempo."

"Are you really going to give me a job?"

"Maybe. Let me think on it." Myrrh had started down the steps. "By the way, I had some pretty visitors in the garden this a.m. Two of them. Second day in a row."

Callen wanted to push her out into the garden.

"A pair of young lions, male and female."

Lions got her attention. "You saw them?"

"Honeymooners, I expect. Right out there by that big old boulder. Pretty as centerfolds."

"Jubal Spry wants to kill them."

"Jubal would shoot his own kids if the mood took him. The man's got carbolic acid in his veins."

At the edge of the garden Myrrh stood waiting for her. "What's the matter with you? Scared of a couple of pussy cats?"

"I have to go to the bathroom."

"Again? What did you do, rent that Coke? Go on, do your business. I'll be in the garden. And don't touch that cake."

Sometimes Callen's mind and body worked together so quickly and smoothly that the best thing she could do was just let things happen one after the other and not pause for thinking or planning. In this way she crossed the kitchen and lifted the receiver off the wall phone and calmly keyed in the number of the safe house. The dial tone was as loud as an airplane. She looked behind her to see if Myrrh had heard it. But she was clipping chard, paying no attention to Callen.

A man's voice answered, the same she had spoken to from Horse Haven.

She said, "It's me, Callen. Again. Darren and Barbara's girl. I called before, but they caught me."

"What's your last name?"

"Norgaard. I already talked to you."

"How do I know you're not lying?"

"Do you know my mom and dad? They're on assignment, or they were; they're probably back now, and I think they must want to know where I am. The FBI thinks they're dead, but I know the fire was just to throw ZOG off their track. Right? Have you seen my mom?"

"Who told you the fire was a cover-up?"

"I figured it out."

Callen did not blame the man on the phone for being suspicious, but she didn't have much time. "I'm in a neighbor's house, and I've only got a minute."

"Where are you staying? We'll come and get you."

She thought of the Brethren worrying and wanting her back. She imagined the party they would have when she returned. Covered dishes of chicken and chili and potato salad and cherry fudge for dessert. Plain American, Aryan, food.

"Can you get word to my mom? Tell her I'm okay?"

"Where are you, Callen?"

"With my uncle. I didn't even know I had an uncle till he got me in Santa Rosa. He's a really famous writer." The buzz on the line made Callen's palms sweat. "Are you still there?"

"Where's your uncle live?"

"In California, near the Mexican border. In a town called

Bone Lake, way smaller than Codyville. He has a ranch called Pasatiempo." The man asked her to spell it.

"Do I know you? Your voice is sort of familiar."

"Are there agents with your uncle?"

"No, but I think the FBI's in town, watching. There's a big race in Bone Lake this weekend."

A shadow blocked the light from the screen door. Myrrh said, "What the dickens do you think you're doing?"

twenty-one

DARREN NORGAARD whooped and threw the cell phone down the length of the trailer and onto the unmade double bed. Edgar Barrett had sworn that a man in service to the Lord would be rewarded in the Lord's own time, and as always, he was right. The Lord's time was now, and Callen was Darren's reward, his way out of Palm Springs, the wings on his bird.

Darren missed the old man. It was as if he had lost a physical part of himself, an arm or leg that couldn't be replaced and never stopped aching.

Edgar had found Darren working in a garage in Red Bird. Married two days with a baby coming and no prospects, he already felt trapped. Edgar had treated Darren like a son and taught him that the Lord walked beside the True Word Brethren because he loved the Aryan children he had made in his own image and wanted them to cleanse creation, starting with the United States of America. Edgar had told Dar-

ren that his skill with machines and gizmos was a talent from
God, and it was a sin not to use it on the side of righteous-
ness. He taught him simple bomb making, and after that
Darren charged ahead, leaving his teacher behind. In the
days after the old man passed, Darren was inconsolably de-
pressed, but Andy had told him to trust God. At first it was
like blasphemy to hear a woman speak Edgar's words, but
he'd gotten used to it. And when she told him that Callen
would call in the Lord's good time, he had believed her.

He opened the refrigerator and took out the beer he had
been saving for this occasion. Kicking the door shut with his
bare foot, he popped the top, chugged and belched mightily.
He shouldn't drink after taking the pills Andy had given him,
but he deserved this beer. He'd earned it.

Never, not if he'd been given a year to list the possibili-
ties, would he have guessed Callen was hiding out with Eli.
As far as Darren knew or cared, Eli had died in the merchant
marine, wrapped up like a mummy and sleeping with the fish.

Sitting at the kitchen table, rolling the cool beer can
down his cheek and neck, he felt the alcohol and pills fizzing
in him, making him twitchy.

Next door to the safe house trailer, two small boys lived
with their single mother. That morning he had watched them
from the window while he drank a cup of instant coffee.
Joined at the hip, those little bums, running barefoot around
the trailer park yelling and shooting each other with sticks.
Way back, Eli had called Darren Maggot. Back then Darren
didn't know what a maggot was, but it sounded okay. *Hustle*

your heinie, Maggot. Grub time, Maggot. Move your butt oxes, Maggot. He remembered clinging to Eli's hand, feeling safe as they crossed three or four busy intersections to get to the 7-Eleven for dinner. It did not matter what Maggot meant. The way Eli said it made Darren happy.

He downed the beer and heaved the can out the door of the trailer in the direction of the Dumpster. He checked the time and shook his watch to make sure it hadn't stopped, sat down again at the built-in table under the fly specked window, stood up, sat down again. Living alone made a man squirrelly. There was only so much time he could spend sharpening his knife and studying survival manuals. He had no stomach for the Jew media and did not own a television.

Being in the desert made waiting worse; the heat and the wind fucked with his mind. He had lost track of time since he'd come to live in this died-and-gone-to-hell trailer park at the end of a gravel road off a side street northwest of Palm Springs, up against the base of rock mountains that rose right out of the ground, no foothills and pointy as vampire teeth.

Twenty feet from his door a six-foot chain-link fence and a line of tamarisk trees marked the western limit of the trailer park. He looked at that fence and it never failed: He felt like a prisoner. The trailer park had no hot tubs, no tennis courts and no golf course. The "clubhouse" was a twenty-by-twenty-foot room tacked on to the park office and furnished with a couple of recycled video games and a pool table with torn felt mended with duct tape. Sliding glass doors opened on to a cement deck and swimming pool roughly the size of Darren's trailer.

He despised the muds and mestizos who were his neighbors and the lazy white sheeple who cashed their welfare checks so they could lie by the pool getting brown as coons at the same time they thought their white skin was a passport to the easy life. They'd learn something different when ZOG was gone, and welfare and food stamps were history.

He took a long drag off his water bottle and grimaced. The Mexican who cleaned the pool drank designer water, but Darren was so broke he had to refill his plastic bottle from the tap several times a day. Palm Springs water tasted like chemical sewage.

He checked his watch again, thought about calling Andy with the good news, and decided he'd better wait until later and walk up the street to a pay phone. Though he'd been assured the phone bought at the minimart could not be traced, Darren didn't trust technology. You let it into your life and pretty soon ZOG was using it to spy on your family, and you couldn't have a private conversation anymore. He wasn't taking any chances.

He slapped a bongo riff on the table top. He could not wait to see the look on his brother's face. Callen and Eli—it was fucking amazing the surprises God came up with.

On the other side of the chain-link fence, teenaged boys on dirt bikes bounced from hillock to hillock. At the sound of their yelling, laughing voices, his stomach twisted and he wanted to punch something. Where did they get the god-damn energy to ride bikes in this heat?

The trailer's air-conditioning had died the week before, and Darren had no cash for a new one. In the late afternoon, as the thermometer read up near one hundred even though it was not yet summer, he heard the ping of the hot metal expanding when the skin of the trailer was too hot to touch. At night he slept in fifteen- or thirty-minute fits, naked on the sheet and skidding in sweat. During the day he hung wet towels over some of the open windows and doused them with water when he could be bothered, telling himself these makeshift swamp coolers made the interior of the trailer bearable.

After dark Darren would turn on the radio. Away from the sun's glare and protected by the anonymity of night, listeners called Los Angeles from Bismarck and Syracuse, Rapid City and Abilene; and they all told the same story of jobs lost to slant-eyes and Mexicans, children gone to drugs and property stolen by the government to make way for banks or rapid transit or shopping centers. Even when they didn't say it outright, Darren could tell these callers knew that race war was necessary and inevitable.

Darren did not blame these people for their daylight silence. They were frightened and thought they were alone; but when the Brethren came out of their small towns all over the West, the sheeple would realize their power, rise up and take their country back.

In the tiny bathroom he stripped and stepped into the shower. Gradually he turned the tap from warm to cool though it never did get really cold. Without drying himself he carried a bath towel into the bedroom, spread it across the sheets and lay down with his head propped on a sweat-stained pillow. He closed his eyes and imagined the look of dismay and surprise when he shoved the Beretta Cougar in Eli's face.

twenty-two

FROM THE barn, Eli heard Myrrh's old Ford truck come up the driveway and brake to a dusty stop in the yard. He dropped what he was doing, stormed out, and jerked open the passenger door, hauling Callen down from the front seat. Saying nothing, he shoved her ahead of him, across the yard, and up the stairs into the house.

Her arm was soft and small and he held it too tightly, but he was just too angry to care. He remembered being skinny and helpless, and his mother dragging him across the kitchen floor, making him lick up the milk he had spilled. Involuntarily his grip tightened and Callen squealed in protest. He had survived and so would she.

He turned his back on Myrrh, not wanting her to see his expression, knowing it was transparently ugly and ignorant and volatile as gunpowder. But there was nothing he wanted to do about it now. He'd crossed the line, and now he was on a roll, heading into the reaches of rage where he hadn't ventured in decades. He dragged Callen into the great room; Zacky, sensing trouble, found a safe spot around the corner from the fireplace and lay still and watchful.

"You're breaking my bones."

"Shut up."

"You could go to jail for this."

"You're lucky I don't break your neck."

Callen screeched as if he'd tried to do it; stumbling over her feet, she fell against the breakfast bar and to the floor. Eli reached down, but she shoved him aside and raced for the stairs, leaping forward two steps at a time. He went after her, saw her dash down the hall to her bedroom and dart inside. She slammed the door in his face; he thundered, grabbed the knob, and wrenched it open.

Behind him another door opened. "Ixsky? Eli? What's going on?"

Through the booming in his skull he heard Ixsky say something in Spanish, and then Isabelle's reasonable voice telling him to stop, take it easy, take a deep breath. But he'd gone too far now. He'd seen this happen to his mother when inertia outpaced whatever self-control she possessed.

Callen cowered on the floor in the farthest corner of the bedroom, her arms wrapped around her knees, pressing back into the wall and watching as he tugged his belt through the loops of his jeans.

Isabelle grabbed his arm. "You don't want to do this. Stop. Breathe. For God's sake, Eli, breathe."

He shook her off and advanced on Callen, a burning in

his arms and hands. He was gladdened by her terror and elated by the break in her cocky attitude. He had put the fear of God in her, the vengeful, racist god she understood. And he wasn't finished with her yet.

He towered over her, felt his arm go up and back and saw his belt and a flash of light off the buckle, felt the weight of its silver and turquoise buckle.

Callen screamed and begged him not to hit her. Isabelle dragged on his arm and a sound came out of him, a cry and a roar at the same time. The belt flew from his hand and hit a mirror, shattering it.

It was Callen who had broken *him* and not the other way around.

Isabelle's voice, maddeningly calm: "Come back to me, Eli." She stepped between him and Callen and touched his cheek. "You don't have to do this. Please—"

"Get out of my way." His right hand spasmed into a fist.

"No." No.

"He was going to kill me," Callen cried. "I saw it right on his face. If you hadn't come, he'd have killed me. He's as bad as my father."

No.

"I'm warning you," Isabelle said. "Don't say another word."

"But I . . . He . . ."

Eli was breathing again, and his tunnel vision had opened up. He looked at Callen, and the full impact of her phone call hit him anew.

"Ixsky, get me the hammer and some of those long nails with big heads. In my tool box."

"All I did was pick up the phone. I never talked; no one answered." Callen's trembling lie was thin as smoke. "This is child abuse. I'm gonna tell the cops you—"

"You're not telling the police anything." Isabelle jabbed her finger at Callen. "You will keep your mouth shut. And you will . . ." She stopped. Eli saw her hand shaking.

"Dammit, Callen, you've ruined everything. Don't even think about lying. Myrrh told me everything. You told the Brethren where you are. Myrrh heard you. Do you know what this means? Have you thought once about someone beside yourself? Don't you get what'll happen to us, to the ranch if the Brethren find you here?"

Eli's rage had vanished, leaving him as calm as if he'd taken a tranquilizer. He was able to separate himself from the scene and realize the importance of what had just happened to him. With one phone call, this girl had sprung the anger he'd been controlling all his life.

He said, "The people you called on the phone are terrorists. Killers. Your father built a bomb that killed an innocent woman."

"You're making it up. You want me to hate him because you hate him."

"I don't hate my brother. I don't even know my brother."

"Think of the animals," Isabelle said. "Imagine if the Brethren set fire to the barn. Do you think they would take the time to free the horses first? They'd be trapped in their stalls."

"You've put all our lives at risk, Callen."

"That old lady's crazy. She hates me. You all hate me."

It was pointless to continue. "Go in the closet and close the door."

Ixsky handed Eli the hammer and a handful of nails.

Callen's eyes widened, and the fear in them both gratified and appalled him.

"I'm done talking."

Eli's wrath had left him so calm he was weak. Determined to do what he had to before he lost the little energy remaining to him, his teeth clamped down on his tongue. He yelped in startled pain. At the sound, Callen screamed and darted for the closet, and Ixsky laughed, a wildly inappropriate cackle that made them all turn and stare at her.

"Stupid girl," she said. "Ignorant, stupid girl. You are the crazy one."

The hammer in his hands weighed a hundred pounds.

"I told you after Horse Haven that if you made more trouble, I'd lock you in your room and that's what I'm doing. *All* I'm doing."

He closed each of the two sash windows facing the barn and the four on the side of the house where the pepper tree grew. Isabelle sat on the bed, watching him nail them shut.

"I'll suffocate," Callen whined. "I'll starve."

"I want you alive tomorrow."

"Eli? What's happening tomorrow?"

"I'm taking her into town." He didn't look at Isabelle. "I'm through with her."

Afterward he would not talk to Isabelle, would not explain. He went into his office and called Billy Horne, told him he would bring Callen into the San Diego office early the next day. After he hung up, he recalled the picture she had drawn of the oddly familiar woman with the Nazi-like pendant. Whoever she was, the FBI would probably want to see her picture.

At bedtime he took a sleeping pill, but the drug was no competition for his churning thoughts; at four o'clock he was up and dressed and sitting at his desk, staring out the window at the mountains etched against the predawn sky. The moon had risen late and rested on the peak of the barn roof like a pearlescent ornament.

His muscles ached as if he'd run the Ore-Mex trail, and his head hurt. An adrenaline hangover. He circled his head first to the right and then the left, hearing muscles and tendons creak. In Ixsky's chicken yard a cock crowed, and somewhere at the edge of the corrals the guard dogs set up a racket.

With or without Callen on the ranch, the Brethren were coming.

He could ask Cholly to organize the ranch hands and post guards, but the Brethren would as soon kill a Mexican as a cockroach. Billy Horne said he would bring in federal agents, a platoon if necessary. Eli recalled the travesties of Ruby Ridge and Waco and did not like this idea any better.

His office was dark except for a pool of light on his desk illuminating a pad of lined paper. Days earlier he had tried to write by hand, hoping this switch to low tech might lure back his muse. The best he'd managed was a doodle of squares and triangles.

Isabelle spoke from the door. "Have you slept at all, honey?"

"A little." The back of his neck flushed with shame at what she had seen the night before. He avoided her eyes.

"Shall I make coffee?"

"Go back to bed, Isabelle."

"It'll be light soon. I'll get an early start."

She returned with coffee and toast, hard-boiled eggs and sharp cheddar cheese and set the tray on a table in front of the couch by the window. He sat beside her, knowing that she believed all problems could be solved by talk and food in combination. She peeled an egg and gave it to him. For the fraction of an instant, a gust of optimism lifted him and he smiled. Isabelle put a lot of faith in the power of protein.

"I'm sorry you saw that. I lost it, Isabelle. I just couldn't help myself. Now you know the kind of man you married."

"That wasn't you, not any you I've ever known."

"Oh, it was me all right." There was a grim satisfaction in admitting the truth. "You've never seen it, but I've always known . . . She just pushed me too far. I couldn't hold back. This is what I meant about Callen and my mother. It's genetic, this rage. I've got it, Callen and—"

"You've made this up, Eli. I don't know why, and right

now I don't even care. What I do know is that you got to the edge and then you stopped. There's a broken mirror to prove it. You threw the belt away. You did not hit her."

"Don't be nice to me, Izzy. Don't make up excuses. I don't deserve them."

"You're a good man, Eli. The best I've ever known."

"Leave me alone, will you? I need to be alone. I've got a bitch of a day ahead."

She looked at him a moment, took a breath and flipped her hair back off her shoulder, a familiar gesture that meant she was getting ready to be dead serious. "I'm begging you, Eli, please don't take her away. She doesn't really want to go to the Brethren. She just wants her mother."

"I know."

"Tell Horne you've changed your mind."

"He's a federal agent. I can't just tell him—"

"Sure you can. He's so far out of line on this case, we can't make it any worse for him."

"You haven't thought this through."

"And you have? When? Somewhere between flying off the handle and beating yourself up?" She flipped her hair again. "I've been thinking, and I've decided it's maybe not a bad thing she made the call. Now we know they are definitely coming, and we can stop walking on eggshells, worrying about what might happen. We can make a plan and get this thing over and then go back to living like normal people."

Isabelle was being naive. He knew better than she did what the Brethren were capable of.

She leaned toward him, planting her hands on her knees. "Saturday's the race and there'll be thousands of people in town, and you know what Billy said, how the Brethren can disappear in a crowd? I think they'll come Saturday. We'll be ready for them."

"They don't know about the race."

"Yes, they do. Myrrh heard Callen mention it."

"Shit."

"They'll come no matter who's here. They can't let her spend any more time around us or the FBI. They can't take the risk she'll blow the whistle on them. They'll come for her and when that happens—"

"They'll kill her."

"But she won't be here."

"Where's she going?"

"I haven't figured that out yet."

"In that case, why not just give her to the FBI? The safest place she can be is in their custody."

"You're right; I know you're right. But if we give her back to them . . ." Her expression changed and she seemed to go deeper into herself, to a level of seriousness he'd never seen before. What she was feeling now was like his anger of the day before, every bit as intense. "It might be the smartest thing to give her back to Horne. The safest thing. But it would still be wrong because if she goes to the FBI, we'll never see her again. You know that as well as I do."

He wanted to wrap her in his arms and hold her. But he knew better.

"She's a wonderful girl, Eli. Extraordinary. I know she's not easy, and she can be awful sometimes, but it's like that story of the ugly duckling. If we can keep her with us, she'll be a swan some day. I see the changes all the time. Even Ixsky does, she's told me. Callen's beginning to trust me. She doesn't think I'm the enemy anymore."

Light swam in her eyes.

"Oh, Isabelle, Isabelle."

"When the government finishes with her, there won't be anything left of Callen's pride or her courage. God knows she'll never trust anyone again. They'll cut it right out of her to get what they want."

"She knows things."

"True. And if she stays here, it won't be much longer before she's willing to tell us those things. She'll be willing, not tricked by the FBI. But if she goes back to them, all the good we've done will be for nothing."

Neither Eli nor Isabelle knew what methods the government might use to get the information they wanted. It was bad enough that they could imagine them.

"Billy's a good man," Eli said.

"I know he is. And the FBI isn't bad, and I'm glad they're out there doing their job. But Billy's only one of many. And what about Homeland Security? He'll probably have to hand her over to them. It's the individuals that scare me, individuals doing bad things for good reasons. Eli, we can't let anyone do bad things to our Callen. We're the only people on her side. Her future's up to us; it's in our hands."

He didn't disagree with anything she said, and he'd known for a long time how much she wanted and maybe needed for Callen to stay. He, too, had seen the subtle changes in the girl, and if he gave her to the FBI, Isabelle might never forgive him. But keep her on Pasatiempo? The risk was enormous.

twenty-three

IN BILLY Horne's office in San Diego, utilitarian metal furniture sat on a worn gray-green carpet in need of vacuum-
ing. Between her chair and Eli's, Callen counted three paper
clips and a hairpin. To the left of the desk there was an un-
marked door with a dark window set in the wall beside it. To
the right, dingy vertical blinds over square windows clucked
against each other in the draft of the air conditioner.

Locked in her nailed-down room the night before, she
had been afraid there wasn't enough oxygen. Even so and
despite her shrill objections, she didn't blame Eli. Although
she had said he was like Darren, he wasn't. Darren would
not have dropped the belt. He would have whacked her hard
with the buckle end, and afterward he would have locked
her in the closet, not given her a whole room to grumble
around in.

In the morning, before breakfast, Ixsky had packed her
bag; and Isabelle, her eyes red from crying, promised to send

the rest of her things when Horne gave them an address. They had left Pasatiempo in a hurry. There wasn't even time for Callen to say good-bye to Bear.

"You'll feed him?" she had asked Isabelle. "If you give him a little extra molasses, he likes the mash better."

Isabelle promised and hugged her tightly.

"And I read in that horse magazine, maybe he should have this kind of Gatorade for horses. In the summer." Callen's eyelids ached from blinking.

She did not turn around or wave good-bye, despite being sure that Isabelle stood at the edge of the lawn watching. Down 94 and into the city she stared out the window, everything a blur.

Now she was in Agent Horne's office as Eli had promised, and everything Sarge had ever taught about the FBI and interrogations stood front and center of her mind. Sarge had said the enemy would try to make them uncomfortable to wear down their resistance. It would take a lot more than a numb butt on a plastic chair to make her talk.

After hours, when the counselors were asleep, the kids at Patriot Camp played a game called lockup. The person who drew the short straw became the prisoner—the others were the interrogators—and for ten minutes they could do almost anything to make the prisoner obey. When Callen was prisoner, they wanted her to take off her panties. To make her do it they pulled her hair and twisted her toes, and even when Buddy dropped an earwig into her ear and she felt it crawling around, Callen resisted. At the end of camp she told Darren what had happened; he boasted to his friends that she would make a better soldier than any boy in the True Word Brethren.

"How come you don't have any pictures?" she asked Horne. "Don't you have kids or a dog or something?"

Her interruption irritated Eli, but Horne smiled at her.

"Thanks for reminding me; I forgot to put 'em out." He opened a drawer. "I've only been down here a few weeks, so I haven't had time." He set several framed pictures on the desk, facing Callen.

Like she cared about his sheeple family.

Seven kids. The boys were homely like their father, and the girls had straight blond hair like girls in sitcoms. Except one. Three girls had blue eyes and perfect teeth, and their hair was neatly held in place with barrettes and elastic bands. One looked as if she had just run in from an electric storm. Her yellow hair stuck out all around, and she wore braces so big Callen wondered how she closed her mouth. She probably sucked her dinner through a straw.

"Who's that?"

"Polly." Horne's voice softened. "She's going to be president of the United States one of these days."

Callen had to get out of this office before she barfed up her breakfast. "How long are we going to be here?"

Horne told Eli, "I know I'm not supposed to favor one kid over the rest, but I can't help it. Pol's got that something, that special extra, you know? I bet Isabelle had it when she was a kid." He fixed Callen with his pale, beige eyes. She'd win a stare-down with Buddy any day, but Horne's eyes could bore holes in cement.

"You have it too, Callen."

Callen's skin tightened around her; it felt as if she were wearing a T-shirt many sizes too small. She stared over Horne's head at the corner of the room where ceiling and wall met.

"Your mom knew you were special."

She pretended not to hear him.

"She didn't want you to grow up with the Brethren. Especially after Andy took you to see someone, a person very important to the Brethren. Then she started getting scared for you."

Callen ran the Fourteen Words through her mind. *I will secure the existence of white people and a future for our children.*

"We know you met someone. Your mother told our agent. She and your dad had a fight about it, and he broke her tooth. Do you remember that?"

Of course she remembered. She wasn't retarded.

Horne tapped the eraser end of a pencil against the desk blotter. The seconds and minutes limped by.

I will secure the existence of white people and a future for our children.

She hadn't thought about the Fourteen Words in weeks.

"Something's been puzzling me," Horne said. "Back in Santa Rosa you told me you don't remember anything about the fire because you took a sleeping pill. You said everything was a blank until you woke up in the hospital. But when the FBI found you, you were outside. How'd you do that?"

"Do what?"

"Wake up."

"The house was on fire."

"If you were drugged, you sure came out of it fast."

Callen stared at the knee of her jeans, at the threads criss-crossing each other like tic-tac-toe gone wild. She wasn't going to talk any more; they could torture her and she still wouldn't.

"Why do you think she wanted you to take that pill anyway?"

She folded her arms across her chest.

I will secure the existence . . .

"Maybe she knew something bad was going to happen, and she didn't want you to be awake to see it or hear it?"

"She never would've left me if she'd known about the fire."

"No, I don't think so either. But I think she knew she was in trouble and that there was going to be a big fight. She didn't expect to be killed, though. She didn't expect the Brethren to set fire to the house to cover the evidence."

"She's not dead. She's on assignment."

"What kind of assignment?"

"How should I know?"

Andy and the rest had come to the house to talk about the assignment, and Barbara had given her a pill to protect her. If Callen heard where they were going and what they were going to do, someone like Horne could torture her for the truth.

It felt okay to tell Horne that much.

"Did they know you were in the house?"

"Mom told my dad I was up the hill reading to an old lady." She wasn't one of the Brethren, but she was so feeble Darren said it didn't hurt to visit her.

"We know that right after the fire the Brethren looked for you. When they didn't find you, they had to get out of town anyway."

Callen stared up at the spot where two walls and the ceiling met. She imagined she was a spider, a fat, hairy one like the ones in South America.

"The Brethren never stopped believing you were alive, though."

She spun a web and put herself in the middle of it, where she was safe and could do what Sarge had taught them at Patriot Camp. She spun a cocoon of fourteen words to protect herself.

Horne said, "Polly's a little older than you, almost thirteen—"

"Shut up about her."

"Callen!"

"She's a turd."

Eli stood up.

"Easy, Eli," Horne said, his voice so strangely unperturbed it made sweat break out on Callen's forehead. "She's frightened."

"I am not."

"So why did your mother put you in the blanket basket. Why not in a closet or under the bed? Why didn't she actually send you up to see the old woman?"

Because Callen had refused to go. She had put up a fight, and when there wasn't any more time for arguing, Barbara did what she could. Callen liked the basket. The soft blankets smelled good; and she had slept in it when she was little. It didn't hurt to tell Horne that much.

"Pretty big basket."

She had to lie on her side and bend her knees up to her chest, and the snug feeling was part of what she liked.

"Why wouldn't Andy look in the basket?"

"I told you; she didn't know I was there."

She couldn't think the Fourteen Words and talk at the same time.

For extra security Barbara had stacked books on top of the basket. And a radio. Later it was hard for Callen to push up the lid with all that weight on it. She had not meant to tell Horne that. She tried to put herself back in the spider web, tried to think the Fourteen Words; but the more she thought them, the more they sounded like gibberish in her head.

"Did you hear Andy and the others come into the house?"

"I don't know anything. I told you and told you. I was asleep."

"No, you weren't. You didn't take that pill. You pretended to, but you didn't because you knew something big was up and wanted to know what it was."

"I don't remember anything about that."

"Sometimes, Callen, people know things even though they might not remember them. Sounds kind of crazy but it happens. It's called repression and it's a way humans have of protecting themselves. Something bad happened to you, and you're afraid to think about it because a really primitive part of you believes that if you remember, it'll be real all over again. You've shoved the memory way down into a dark corner of your mind, and you'll do just about anything to keep it there." He smiled at her. "It's the same as when you were hidden in the basket with all those things piled on top. You struggled to get out of the basket, and now your memories are struggling to get out too."

With her index finger Callen made a corkscrew motion beside her head.

"The part that's still very small and frightened wants to keep those memories buried down in the basket under all those blankets. But I think the eleven-year-old Callen is brave enough to remember. I actually think she wants to."

Horne used a grandfatherly voice, pretending to be someone who would never hurt her. Or maybe he wasn't pretending. Six months ago Eli and Isabelle were her sworn enemies. Now she liked them a lot. If it were not for Barbara, she might like to stay on the ranch. For a while anyway, and if the FBI would let her, which they wouldn't.

She didn't blame Eli for bringing her here. It was her own fault; she'd made the phone call. She did not regret doing it; she was sorry she hadn't been more careful. It was as Isabelle said, actions have consequences.

In the Brethren days she had been sure about a lot of things; but now most of that certainty was gone, and she knew she would never get it back. The world and the people in it were a lot more complicated than she had been taught. Horne might be telling her the truth; maybe a person could hide bad memories from herself. Maybe the United States really did send men to the moon and the Holocaust happened and evolution wasn't a lie invented by ZOG. She just didn't know anything for sure anymore.

Horne changed the subject again.

"Do you remember the man in the thrift shop? That man, Callen, he was one of us. He was FBI."

"They talked, that's all. They talked."

It had been Callen's job to sit near the entrance and tell Barbara if any of the Brethren came along the street. She didn't mind doing this. She had a pile of magazines to read, the kind Andy called mind pollution. The celebrity magazines had been as fascinatingly forbidden as pornography.

Horne said, "Our agent's name was Ben Singh. He's disappeared. We think he's dead."

"He was a mud."

"We think the True Word Brethren murdered him."

"Good."

"But you see what this means, Callen. If the Brethren knew about Singh, they knew about your mother too."

She let this thought sink in.

"That's why they killed her. She told him things."

She remembered her mother's laugh echoing in the big thrift store. It had been rare to hear it. After their visit Barbara was always in a good mood until they reached home.

"Your mother told Agent Singh that Andy had taken you to see someone very important to the Brethren about a week before the fire. She didn't know the man's name, but I think you do." He leaned toward Callen, resting his forearms on his desk. "What was his name, Callen?"

In the photo, Polly and her homely brothers and perfect sisters posed in a pyramid in front of a set of bunk beds. They wore identical black-and-white striped pajamas. Convicts. The pajamas were a joke.

"Why are you crying?" Eli asked, laying his hand on her shoulder.

"Leave me alone!"

"What was the name of the man you went to see with Andy?"

"It wasn't a man!" Callen cried, fed up. "It was Mrs. Smith."

The office went suddenly quiet.

"A woman? Mrs. Smith?"

"I will secure the existence of our people and a future for white children."

Eli said, "Christ, not this again."

She screamed the Fourteen Words at him. The sound of her voice saying the words stirred a familiar feeling. Emboldened, she stood up, proud of her heritage, her red hair and white skin, her Aryan blue eyes. Ixsky was a lying mud.

"I will secure the existence of—"

The door to the left of Horne's desk opened, and a tall, slender black woman stepped into the room.

"Hello, Callen," she said. "Please come with me."

twenty-four

THROUGH THE observation window Eli had a clear view of Callen's belligerent face and the back of the agent's closely cropped head.

"You want to listen in?"

No. He was afraid of what he might hear and his reaction. That morning he'd been sure that giving Callen back to the FBI was the smart way to protect Isabelle and the ranch. Now he had begun to wonder. Maybe it wasn't really smart; maybe it was just easy.

When it was time to go, he had run out of the house and into the Silverado as if his doubts pursued him. Callen was already strapped in her seat belt and staring straight ahead. In his eagerness to be gone, he had completely forgotten the drawing of the old woman wearing the Germanic necklace.

"I was so damn pissed at Isabelle . . ." Eli felt like a kid with a lame excuse. "It probably wasn't important."

"Call her." Horne handed him the phone. "She can fax it to us."

He called, but no one answered. A shiver of anxiety made sweat break out on his palms.

"If I didn't know better, I'd guess you wanted to sabotage this—"

"You know that's not true!"

"Well, yeah, maybe, but you heard what she said. The Brethren's patron is a woman. That drawing's probably the money shot."

"Okay, okay." Humiliation made Eli bellicose. "You'll get your fucking picture."

Unless Callen had brought it with her. Eli emptied the contents of her backpack and found the rolled drawings of Barbara and Bear. No others.

Horne walked to the window, and drawing the vertical blinds, stared out at the city. Eli and Callen had driven into San Diego under blue skies, but in the last hour the marine layer had moved onshore, turning the sky to pewter.

Horne said, "Even with Callen in custody, you and Isabelle and the ranch are still at risk. The True Word Brethren are still going to converge on Bone Lake. Two of them or twenty. We have no way of knowing for sure, but we can be fairly confident there won't be many of them. That'd be out of character. I'm not sure what'll happen when they figure out she's gone. They might just fade away like they did out of Codyville, and we won't be any closer to getting them than we were two years ago."

Horne's back was to Eli. His voice expressed a mix of bitterness and disgust.

"After this they'll divide up, realign themselves with other groups, blend into the scene, and then one day there'll be another bomb on a plane or at a ball game . . ."

Eli got the picture.

"We have nothing concrete on them." Horne turned. "We need that woman, the patron."

"You have Callen."

"And you think she's going to draw another picture 'cause we ask her? Just like that?"

"Isabelle says she's close."

"Around Isabelle maybe." An almost visible cloud of frustration surrounded Horne. "I can't believe you left that drawing at home. What is it with you? You can make this stuff up in your head, but when it comes to real life—"

"Why did you involve us in the first place?"

"She was your niece. You're my friend."

"Bullshit."

"Because I need my head examined?"

"Why didn't you just do what you had to and leave us out of it?"

Eli watched his friend's expression as he tried to wrestle his thoughts into order. For moments the question hung in the air unanswered.

"Sometimes I think I ought to get out of this business." Horne sat on the window ledge and stared down at his scuffed loafers. "In the beginning you love the job—you're a hotshot federal agent—but God help you if you start seeing both sides of an argument." He picked a paper clip off the carpet and shot it onto his desk, where it landed with a soft ping. "It's complicated."

"Try me."

"You don't have kids—daughters—Eli, so this is probably going to sound crazy to you. I honestly think that if it weren't for Pol, you and I wouldn't be having this conversation. The thing is, the first time I met Callen I knew the kind of girl she was. It was as if I recognized her. Brave girls like Pol and Callen? They stand out."

Eli listened.

"My sons, they just bang along in life, taking risks and dares and never thinking much about anything except being boys. Don't misunderstand me, they're great kids, but they're not really brave. They're just boys acting like boys."

Horne picked up the photo of Polly dressed as a convict. "I worry because no matter what anyone says, the world doesn't like women who are different, and brave women scare the shit out of most people."

"My God, Billy, you're a feminist."

"As soon as these girls hit puberty, everything—the schools, the media, advertising and music, you name it— everything tries to pound them into being tentative and coy and . . . agreeable. Maybe it was worse in the old days, but believe me, it's still bad. Eli, I think I'd do just about anything to keep the system from breaking Polly."

"Doesn't the FBI have personality tests or something to screen out feminists?"

"You want to hear this or not?"

"You surprise me, that's all."

"There's a lot in the world that would surprise you, Eli. You sit out there on your bucolic ranch and you write your terrifying books, but you don't know what it's like here in the jungle, where you can't hide from the bad stuff. I gave Callen to you because I knew you wouldn't break her apart. But if Callen comes with us, I'm going to have to hand her over to HS, and they will break her. One way or another, they'll get the information they want."

It was just about what Isabelle had said.

"They won't hurt her, not physically. But all that fire and spit? You can pretty much kiss it good-bye. And you can most definitely forget about her ever having a normal life."

Eli wanted to talk about something else.

"What makes you think Singh's dead?"

"It was his bones in the fire. They killed him and brought his body to the house."

"I thought Darren—"

"Your brother's still alive somewhere." Horne looked at Eli. "It's a good bet he was in on Barbara's death and the fire both. I don't know what he thought had happened to Callen, but she wasn't with the old lady, like Barbara said."

"So he'll come to get her?"

"Can't say for sure, but if I were going to send someone,

I'd choose him. All Darren has to say is that Barbara's alive and Callen will believe him."

"He'll come to the ranch."

Eli remembered footage he'd seen of Ruby Ridge. The boy about Callen's age was wearing a plaid shirt too short at the wrists when the FBI shot him on the way to feed his dog. Agents had heard the children screaming from the flames of Waco.

Horne dug a loaded key ring out of his trouser pocket and unlocked a desk drawer; he brought out something that looked like a wristwatch with a cheap plastic band.

"This is a panic button. Kind of like the things old folks have if they live alone. Not the latest edition, but it's reliable." He sighed and rolled his shoulders. "Whether you want to fade into the hills or go stay in a hotel this weekend is up to you, but just so you know, if you stay at the ranch, I'm a hundred percent certain you'll meet up with Darren. You're going to want this thing."

Eli held the device in the palm of his hand and stared at it.

"You need us, you press the button. We'll be all over Bone Lake this weekend."

A movement at the corner of Eli's vision turned his attention to the observation window. Slumped in a chair, Callen's eyes were half shut and her hands hung at her side like rags. Suddenly she jerked up straight, her eyes wide. Through the glass Eli felt her fear like a ray of hot light.

twenty-five

CALLEN HAD followed the woman from Horne's office into another featureless room. The only significant difference between the two was the gray light pouring in through the windows, highlighting the stains on the carpet and the pinholes in the drab green walls where pictures and calendars and charts must have hung in the past. The room smelled as if it had been unoccupied for a long time.

The agent said her name was Tara.

Callen had seen a few Negroes in Yreka but never spoken to or even had a chance to observe one closely. She did not bother to hide her curiosity as she compared Tara to the ugly cartoon drawings Sarge had shown them in camp. They were nothing alike. Callen wondered how many colored women Sarge had actually seen. Tara was beautiful, and if anyone said she wasn't, they'd be either blind or lying. Her skin was a milky brown and her cheeks were pink. This had to be makeup because everyone knew only Adamites could blush.

Her hair was cut short, neat and close to her head; she wore long earrings.

"I'm a psychologist, Callen. My job is to help you remember what happened on the night of the fire. I believe Agent Horne has explained repression to you, so you know what we're up against. I can't force you to remember if you don't want to." Her eyes were a startling green. Callen would be willing to bet Sarge had never seen a colored with green eyes. "But I think you *do* want to remember because when you remember, the bad dreams will go away."

"What do you know about my dreams?"

"Bad dreams and repressed memories go together."

"I hardly even dream at all." *So there.*

"But when you do, what do you dream about? Do you hear screams or gunfire or maybe your mother's voice? Some people dream about fires, and they say they can feel the heat." Her earrings were gold with red glass stones hanging from them. "Tell me about the night of the fire. I know the weather was miserable."

Wind tore through the trees, and the house rattled like dry bones. The big pine outside the kitchen scraped its witchy nails across the window.

"Rain was coming," Tara said. "The first really big storm of the season."

Barbara had sent Callen to gather the chickens and put them in the coop. She was upset with Darren because he should have fixed the door to the coop during the summer, but he was always down in the basement doing secret things.

"Home wasn't a happy place."

"You don't know anything about my home."

"Actually, I know a lot." Tara tapped her nails on the top of her desk. They were painted orange, and they could stab out someone's eyes as easily as a bottle opener would do the job.

Gold. Ruby-red and orange. Callen couldn't look at the FBI psychologist without thinking of fire.

"There was a bedroom downstairs off the kitchen, and you slept upstairs in the loft. In the kitchen the tap was broken. You hadn't had hot water for months because your father was too busy to fix it."

"Who told you that?"

"You and your mother managed without it. But she complained a lot."

"True Word Brethren never complain."

"In the living room there was an old moss-green couch with yellow flecks. If you close your eyes, I bet you can see it. There's a big brown stain on one of the cushions where your dad spilled wine. They were having a fight, your mom and dad, and he knocked over the bottle." Tara paused. "Do you think your mom was sitting on the couch when they shot her?"

Callen pressed her fists against her stomach.

"At the last, when your mother knew she was going to die, did you hear her beg them not to kill her? Is that what you dream about, Callen?"

Her mother was a soldier, same as Callen.

"It must be terrible, carrying around those bad memories

every day. Even if they're repressed, they must weigh heavy on your heart."

"I don't believe in—"

"But you don't have to carry them all by yourself, Callen. You know how it is when you've got to haul something big, and it's easier if a friend helps you? Talk to me, Callen; tell me what happened the night of the fire." Her voice softened to velvet. "I can help you carry the load."

"I'm not carrying anything, and I don't want your help, and I don't want you to be my friend. You're just a stupid—" All the words she'd been taught to call black people came and went across her mind.

"What? A stupid what?" Tara wore a look of satisfaction, as if she had been waiting for something to happen and now it had. "Nigger? Is that what you want to call me?"

"It's what you are, isn't it?"

Tara rocked her hand from side to side. "I'm descended from African slaves, that's true enough. But my great-grandma was Native American, and my mother says there's Chinese in there somewhere too. Probably Mexican or Puerto Rican as well."

With all those races mixed up in her, Tara should have been ugly.

"I think I'm about the muddiest mud you'll ever meet."

"You said it, not me."

"If you insult me enough, do you believe I'll either blow up or shut up? Maybe go back to Africa? Am I right?" Tara laughed indulgently and shook her head. "Let me tell you,

Callen. I've been insulted by the big boys. Your little girl stuff doesn't bother me."

Callen had nothing to say, so she sat, chewing on her cuticle and watching the light flicker off Tara's earrings and onto the ceiling. She wondered if it might be true that she was hiding her memories, repressing them. Horne and Tara had put the worm of that idea into her brain, and it would not stop wriggling around in her thoughts.

"Do you dream about the thrift shop?"

"I don't want to talk about my dreams."

"You'll feel better."

"I feel fine. There's nothing wrong with me."

At Patriot Camp, Sarge had taught them that during an interrogation agents of ZOG would ask the same questions over and over in different ways to confuse a person until she became so exhausted she would say anything just to make the questions stop. Sarge had been a marine in Iraq, and he knew all about interrogation.

Two or three nights before, she'd woken up crying, gagging on her tears. The dream was gone before her eyes had opened completely. The ranch and country sounds she normally liked frightened her, especially the coyotes yapping after their prey. She kept thinking how the rabbit or house cat must feel, running for its life.

She stared at the stapler on the desk. "I don't remember what I dream."

"That's another way the mind protects itself." Tara's voice had soft music in it. "And I want to protect you too."

"No, you don't. You're trying to confuse me."

"And you should be confused. It shows how smart you are. You've spent the last six months living with kind and good people. You've learned a whole different way of thinking, and now what you got from the Brethren doesn't make as much sense as it used to."

Tara wanted to trick Callen into believing she was kind and good too, not one of ZOG's trained monkeys.

"You're like a girl standing in the middle of a busy intersection, not knowing which way to turn." She added, softly, "It's enough to make you want to cry."

She wasn't going to cry. She'd rather eat dog scat.

"I want you to listen to something." Tara put a tape recorder on her desk and pressed a button. A wonderful voice filled the office. Callen's back went rigid.

"It's a trick." Just like the man she'd seen on television sounding just like the president.

"Just sit back and listen. Close your eyes if you're tired."

"*She's all I got and better'n I deserve. These people here, five of 'em aren't worth one of her. I look at her when she's doing her homework and she's bent over her book, and I go in the kitchen and cry. I swear to God, I do. I never liked school, Darren neither, so for us she's like a miracle. She wasn't never meant for Darren'n me.*"

Callen heard her mother laugh.

"*Stork made a mistake, huh?*" A pause.

"*She tells me what she's learning and it ties my gut up. I know a lot of stuff about this country's bad, but, most of what the Brethren say, it's just crap. I never liked that Edgar Barrett and his daughter's worse."*

In the background Callen heard her own voice saying something she couldn't quite hear. She knew then that the tapes were not a hoax or impersonation. They must have been made at the thrift shop. She was listening to her mother's voice, her real voice, her real laugh.

"I'll tell you this, Andy's got her eye on Callie. Wants her 'cause her own kids are retards. She took her over to Shasta City so she could introduce her to someone important. I don't know about that stuff; they never tell me anything. Darren's the same. Him and his secrets. I don't know what they talk about down in the basement, but Callen prob'ly does. She's all the time down there listening."

Another pause, a long one.

"I need to get her away from here. She's gonna finish up like Andy if she stays much longer."

A tear slid down Callen's cheek and onto her upper lip, and she didn't bother to wipe it away. She didn't even care that she was crying in front of a mud.

"Your mother cared for you more than her own life. She knew that if you got stuck with the Brethren, you'd get caught up in their craziness. It's all on tapes. Barbara wanted to leave Codyville, but your father didn't. She begged him to leave the Brethren, and he called her a race traitor."

The brain worm squirmed dizzying circles in Callen's thoughts, and her sobs deepened until they racked her whole body. Tara's earrings flashed gold and ruby-red. She shut her eyes against the brightness, folded her arms on the desk and laid her head down. If she fell asleep at that moment and never woke up, it would be just fine with her.

After a time she stopped thinking about anything special; her mind drifted and then without warning it seemed to click into another gear and she was remembering.

As she knelt beside the blanket basket, Barbara had smelled of sweat, and sweat gleamed on her palm when she held out the tablet.

"Take it. Hurry now and hunker down, burrow deep like a little mouse."

Callen wasn't sleepy, and she didn't want the pill. "If you close the top, I won't be able to breathe."

"Look here, there's lots of spaces in the wicker. Whatever happens, don't make a sound. You're a baby mouse and there's a wolf outside. Not a squeak, little mouse, until I come and get you."

"What wolf?" Barbara had talked to her as if she were very little. "There's no wolves in Siskiyou."

"Never mind, just do as I say." Her mother sounded impatient. "Just close your eyes and swallow the little pill."

She took the pill but did not swallow it. She put it in her mouth and held it under her tongue until Barbara dropped the basket lid.

Callen's thoughts skipped forward, skimming the surface of her memories. If she remembered the next part, she would die.

Her lids sprang open. She was clear-eyed as a bird diving.

The present moment jumped into focus. Tara sat across the desk, watching her.

"What happened? Was I asleep?"

Tara shook her head.

"You hypnotized me."

"You closed your eyes. You were remembering."

"No way."

"Take a deep breath."

"I don't want to take a deep breath."

"Go on, Callen, breathe in and let it out slowly."

"You can't keep me here." She spun around. Two doors, four doors, seeing double.

"Sit down, put your head between your knees." Tara's cool palm touched the back of her neck. "Keep breathing, honey. You'll be okay."

No, she wouldn't; that was bull crap. She would never be okay. Her mother was dead and dead was forever. You couldn't ever get away from dead.

She jumped to her feet, screaming.

"Take your hands off me, don't touch me, don't even breathe on me! I don't care what you say. I don't care what happened. You're still a mud nigger, and I'll never help you or ZOG or anyone. I hate you. I'm a soldier of the True Word, and I hate you all!" Her hand closed on the stapler, and she drew her arm back.

At that moment Eli roared through the door and rescued her.

twenty-six

E LI COULDN'T get out of San Diego fast enough.
He should have listened to Isabelle; he never should
have entrusted Callen to the FBI and its methods.

Cutting through downtown near the stadium he nearly
sideswiped a bus stopped on Market Street. He picked up
the Martin Luther King Freeway going east; and by the time
the Silverado sped under the 805, his knees felt solid again
and he was breathing normally, but there was an unpleasant
brackish taste in his mouth.

She sat beside him, staring straight ahead. Her small chin
stuck out like a rock fortress.

The cars ahead slowed, and Eli drummed his fingers on
the steering wheel and made whistling sounds between his
teeth. A nerve jackhammered behind his ear.

"I did you a favor back there. I didn't have to bust you
out."

"I was doing okay."

"Bullshit, you were going to throw that stapler. What'd she say that made you so mad?"

No answer, no thank-you either. He didn't really expect gratitude, but it would have been a nice surprise. He flipped his phone and pressed the house code. Isabelle picked up on the first ring.

"I'm bringing her home." There were hours ahead for explanations. "I'll fill you in . . . I can't hear . . . Izzy, this phone's running out of juice. Just to tell you, I'm stopping at the Crossroads. Anything you need?"

The phone was dead.

In the lane ahead, a battered VW van with vintage black-and-orange California plates crawled along, farting dark exhaust from its tailpipe. Two little kids peered out the rear window at him, making loony faces. Eli banged his hand on the horn and waited for the van to move over. When it didn't, he sped up until the truck's front bumper almost touched the van's rear plate. Now the kids were yelling at him.

Callen pulled her feet onto the seat.

Eli slammed his horn again, kept it blaring. The van slowed from fifty to forty to thirty-five. In the fast lane.

"Stupid fucker."

Eli lifted his foot from the gas pedal and dropped back far enough to swerve into the next lane. Pressing hard on the gas, he roared beside and ahead of the VW, then cut in front and slammed on his brakes.

"Hey!" Callen cried.

The van swung hard to the right into the second lane. Eli

stuck his hand out the window and flipped the bird. His palm had left a sweat print on the steering wheel. He took a long slug from the water bottle in the console. Not stopping to breathe, just swallowing and swallowing.

"You coulda got us killed."

He turned off the freeway at Avocado Avenue, took a left across the overpass, and a couple of blocks later at the top of a hill he turned right into a rambling, redwood shopping complex, no longer new but well maintained with fresh asphalt in the parking lot and bright white lines marking the spaces. Nosing into the filtered shade of a eucalyptus planted in a cement box, he cut the ignition. Nerves twanging, he sat with his hands on the steering wheel and watched the tree's spear-shaped leaves catch the light and shimmer in the breeze.

"You'll have to come in the market with me."

She looked at him as if he were insane.

"If you stay, I'm taking the keys."

"So? I'm too young to drive."

"I don't for a second think that would stop you, Callen."

"You're going to lock me in?" She slumped against the door, chewed a fingernail and stared sullenly ahead. "Go ahead. You did it before."

"Cars don't work like bedroom doors."

She looked around the parking lot. "Do you think they followed us here?"

"The FBI? Maybe. They'll be everywhere by tonight."

The day before, he had seen a dozen rows of cars and

trucks and motorcycles out on the dry lake bed, the first line of vehicles nosed up against the shoreline within a few meters of the trail. With the suddenness of mushrooms after rain, vendors' stalls and stands had risen up and down Bone Lake's main street. Tomorrow security guards hired by the race promoters would be patrolling on foot and horseback, settling disputes between drivers, shoppers and sellers. In the past these rent-a-cops had been sufficient to ensure an orderly weekend.

"I've got to say something to you, Callen."

She groaned and slid down on the seat, propping her feet on the dash.

"I wish people would just stop telling me things."

"First off, I shouldn't have taken you to Horne. I'm sorry I did it. It was a mistake, but after what you did, the call . . ." He would not explain how anger had bloodied his mind. She had lived with Darren; she knew the irrationality of rage as well as he did. "Maybe it doesn't seem like it, but Isabelle and I want you to be happy."

"I *was* happy. With the Brethren."

"Agent Horne told me about the tape."

Her face turned red and her eyes brimmed. "Just go in the store and forget—"

"I can never forget about you."

"Why not? You forgot my father."

He winced, and by a leap he did not pause to examine, her words took him back to Singapore, where he had walked through Tiger Balm Gardens and thought how Darren would enjoy the monkeys playing in the branches of the Morton Bay fig trees. On long leave in Australia he'd flown to the Northern Territory to hike the Olga Mountains and camp within sight of the great rock Uluru. Surely that was the most beautiful word in any language. He wanted to say it aloud to his little brother and hear his small voice copying him. In Rio Eli stayed awake three nights and days, drunk on the music of Mardi Gras and the beautiful women he kissed, ashamed to be enjoying himself when he knew his brother was alone with Wanda. There were long stretches of time when he didn't think of Darren and his heart lifted, but in the lifting he remembered him again.

Remembering was all he seemed to do these days. If he hadn't been excavating the past, he would not have forgotten Callen's drawing.

He stared over her head at a woman and child loading groceries into the trunk of a sedan. The small boy used two hands to lift a milk jug off the bottom of the grocery cart. Eli felt the mother wanting to step forward and rescue the jug, but she restrained her impatience and let the boy come close enough to hand it to her. She took it from him carefully and put it in the car. Eli couldn't hear what she said, but the boy smiled and went back to the cart puffed up with confidence. It was the ordinariness of the incident that stung.

"From the day I left Great Falls, I've tried to forget your father, tried not to remember where I came from and how we lived. Since you came, I hardly think about anything else."

"If you missed him so much—"

"Family stories are the worst, Callen, because they're so full of contradictions. In a family, two opposite things can be true at the same time. I loved your father, but he frightened me. I wanted him with me, but I never wanted to see him again." He didn't know why he was telling her this, but he had to.

"No one's afraid of a little kid."

"I was afraid of what could happen *because* of him."

"That's totally bogus."

"Bogus but true." He tried to smile. "See what I mean about opposites?"

"You acted like he was dead. Your own brother."

"Yes. You're right. I don't deny it."

But he needed to explain.

⤙

He told her that George Browne had taken nothing with him when he abandoned the family. They had the mortgage on the duplex, and in the beginning it was a decent place on a decent street; and the rent from next door kept them alive.

"But there was never enough money, so when I was nine years old I went down the street and asked the guy who owned the used-car lot if I could have a job washing his cars."

"It's against the law for kids to work."

"The boss was a good guy. He paid me cash."

Every week Eli gave his mother half what he earned, knowing she would turn it into wine and vodka. The renters on the other side paid their rent to him in cash, and part of that he also gave to his mother. Shortly after Browne left, Norgaard moved in and Darren was born. Nothing much changed except there was less money to go around.

"When I was fourteen the boss started me working in the office, a trailer at the back of the lot." He had a key and sometimes took his girlfriends there to drink beer and make out. "I was good with numbers so I kept the books."

Days he went to school; afternoons he worked at the car lot, and at night he swept and mopped the floors and polished the oak pews of a Lutheran church a mile from home.

Over time Eli had felt a growing restlessness, something sitting on his chest, compressing his lungs. He came to believe that only at sea, where the sky was at its widest—the middle of an ocean a thousand miles from Great Falls— would he be able to breathe again. He had always wanted to write stories; at sea he might be able to do it.

His grades weren't good. His teachers fussed and said they were disappointed in him. They all said he had potential, but they did not press him. In those days Great Falls was a small town, and most teachers knew the circumstances of their students' lives.

Eli sat in the Silverado, in the heart of his memory, remembering Darren, silver-blond hair and tubby, with eyes too close together, his two front teeth half broken after he'd run into the kitchen counter. Snaggletooth, Eli had called him. And Maggot. Because that was the way brothers talked to the little brothers who looked up to them.

While Eli worked, Darren had played on the floor of the

trailer, taking things apart and putting them together again. The owner of the car lot said he had a knack for machines. Sometimes on Sunday afternoons there was time to watch a pickup basketball game or cheer in the Little League bleachers. Darren's hand was dry and spidery in Eli's. If he allowed himself, he could still feel how small it was.

"Callen, you say you were happy up in Codyville. What I want you to understand is that when I was your age, I'd never been happy. Oh, maybe for a few minutes or an hour every so often, but not *happy* happy."

He hoped he didn't sound soppy. He was just telling her the truth. He was not sure why he was doing it right there and then. It was as if he'd opened his mouth to say one thing and a thousand had come out. And the oddest thing was, he didn't mind telling her his story. It seemed she had a right to know it.

"I couldn't breathe when I thought about staying in Great Falls with Ma and Darren and Darren's old man, Norgaard. He was on disability, and all he and Ma did was sit around and drink and yell at each other. All day, every day. I collected rent and I paid the bills. I put my mother on an allowance, and she and Norgaard hated me for it."

The only time he'd ever gotten pass-out drunk was when he was fifteen. Norgaard was in Billings doing some kind of odd job. His mother had disappeared, as she did from time to time. She'd met a man, partied and probably thought she'd found her one true love. On this occasion she had gone out for drinks on Friday night and did not come back until the middle of the next week. She returned with her nose and right arm broken. It had taken all of Eli's rainy-day money to pay the doctor in the emergency room, and afterward she fell asleep on the couch, zonked on pain killers, covered with a red, white and blue comforter someone had crocheted years before. Darren had been in bed for hours when Eli started drinking wine. At the bottom of the bottle he switched to vodka.

He'd had a vision of the future that night. It had been as clear and sober as the Holiness Tabernacle across the street from the duplex.

"I knew if I didn't get out of Great Falls, I was going to end up a mean drunk like my mother."

Callen fiddled with the frayed-out knee of her jeans.

"Your father was the only thing keeping me there, but after a while, even he wasn't enough."

"If you loved him, you would have sacrificed."

"Love didn't have anything to do with it." The corner of Eli's brain capable of eloquence and clarity sank into paralysis, and in the Silverado neither he nor Callen spoke for a long time.

He jerked the keys from the ignition. He had to get away from her. "Stay put."

He could not be sure she would, but if it was in her mind to run off, being in the store with him would not stop her.

"Do you promise?"

She rolled her eyes. "I guess."

twenty-seven

THE MOMENT Eli disappeared into the supermarket,
Callen scrambled out of the car. She knew about priori-
ties, and what she had to do now was more important than
any lie.

The Crossroads was a midsized suburban mall anchored
by a bank at one end and a Starbucks at the other. In the middle were a drugstore and a Vons supermarket separated from
the anchors and each other by small shops: a mom-and-pop
Mexican restaurant, a nail salon, a veterinarian and a Subway.
The mall's name—the Crossroads—was meant to sound important, as if life-changing events took place there; but Callen
was neither impressed nor intimidated.

At the south end of Yreka there were several malls bigger
than the Crossroads. Buddy called them the pickin' fields because drivers felt so comfortable shopping there that they left
their windows down and their car doors unlocked. Being a
girl and young, Callen had never gone on raids to the picking

fields and even if the boys had asked her, Barbara would have forbidden it.

"They aren't Aryan patriots," she once told Darren. "They're garden-variety criminals." But Darren agreed with Sarge that the American sheeple had grown lazy and took their comfort and security for granted. For this they deserved to be ripped off.

Crouching and darting between parked cars, Callen made her way to the bank end of the Crossroads, trying to remember what Buddy had told her about robbing cars in daylight. Some had alarms, but she did not know how to determine which were armed and which not. She peered inside a black Escalade, the biggest and fanciest car around, and saw a pile of nickels, dimes and quarters in the front seat divider. The driver's side was locked but not the passenger's. She touched the door handle and pressed down. Instantly an ear-piercing alarm went off, and it seemed as if everyone in the mall stopped and looked in Callen's direction. Doubled over at the waist, she sneaked off, but three cars beyond the screaming Cadillac she made herself stand up and walk calmly away.

A man ran out of the bank and pointed his remote at the SUV. Instantly the alarm shut off. She felt his eyes scanning the parking lot, checking her out. But she was not afraid. She knew how she looked to him: just an ordinary kid in jeans and a T-shirt, meandering along.

Buddy had a slogan: If the cat don't run, the dog don't chase.

Circling around the far edge of the lot to the Starbucks, she kept her eyes on the entrance to the market. Near a garden strip planted with purple lantana separating the parking lot from the street, she found an unlocked Honda Prelude with a handful of change in plain sight. It was too old and beat up to have an alarm, she hoped. The passenger door opened with a noisy crank, and she dropped to a crouch, waiting several breaths before she reached across the driver's seat and scooped up the coins and shoved them into the pocket of her jeans.

An old-fashioned, gray metal phone booth stood to the right of a Coke machine outside the entrance to a Longs Drugs, between the supermarket and Sophie's Nail Salon. The booth stank of sugar and pee and beer, and the floor was sticky under the soles of Callen's cross-trainers. The bottom half was solid, though, and she could duck out of sight if she had to.

She dropped the stolen coins in the slot, all she had and probably much more than needed, but she didn't have time to count. She keyed in the safe house number, and as it began to ring, she squatted out of sight of the shoppers going about their business. The rings went on forever. She thought about what she would say when the man answered. *Don't come to Bone Lake, there's FBI all over the place.* At some point she began to count the rings. *Come get me at the Crossroads. I'll wait for you there.* She was up to fifteen rings when they stopped. Her stomach cramped with frustration. Sarge and Andy had each promised there would always be someone to answer the safe house phone. Unless the Brethren had left the safe house and were already on the highway heading for Bone Lake.

Or maybe she had misdialed. To call again she would need more money, and she was running out of time. She stood to hang up the receiver, and there was Eli walking out of the market toward her. He stopped, surprise and then anger on his face. A plastic shopping bag swung in his fist and banged against his leg as he ran toward her. She lit out of the phone booth, jerked sideways between two motorcycles and ran across the parking lot, dodging cars and cement planters and a train of metal shopping cars until she came to Avocado Avenue. Without looking back she turned right, up the gravel shoulder of the four-lane road. A long block later, she turned right again into a residential street where the houses were small and set back on large lots. There wasn't a tree or fence or shrub to hide behind. She glanced behind her and saw Eli standing still, watching her. He would come back in the car, but he wouldn't find her.

She turned left at the next corner and then right. Where the street came to a dead end, beyond a concrete barricade and a reflective stop sign, a littered cement culvert twenty feet wide ran between the barricade and the bank end of the Crossroads parking lot. She scrambled down the cement slope into the culvert and took off running again, away from the parking lot and Avocado, deeper into the neighborhood. The ditch curved behind the bank and after several hundred yards terminated at the mouth of a huge pipe. She felt safe enough to rest and catch her breath.

To one side of the pipe a path led up and out of sight. Callen assumed this would take her back into the grid of streets where by now Eli must be driving up and down. He might have called the police, more likely the FBI.

She didn't dare rest for too long. When she was running, her thoughts had jumped around like popcorn kernels in a hot pan, avoiding memories of her mother's voice and her laugh or what she had had to say about Andy. She hadn't thought about what had happened in Tara's office. But something *had* happened. She had begun to remember.

Her stomach growled, and the sun, high in a cloudless sky, burned down on the back of her neck.

The mouth of the pipe was big enough for her to walk into without bending over. She peered inside and saw no light at the end. It might go on for a mile and was obviously her best route to freedom; but images of rats and snakes and spiders crowded in on her, and she itched all over. She heard Buddy calling her a pussy and shoved her hands into her pockets to keep from raking her skull and arms with her nails. She filled her lungs with air, exhaled, breathed deep again and stepped into the pipe. No way was she a pussy.

After a few feet, the hot, still air smelled of grease and urine and rottenness. Dead things. To her right she saw a pile of filthy blankets and a few steps farther the remains of a campfire. She pulled the bottom of her T-shirt up over her nose and mouth. Thirty steps into the oily shadows her foot touched something soft and moist, and she uttered a sharp scream that echoed down the length of the pipe. She breathed through her mouth and took another few steps. Her stomach heaved, and she dashed for fresh air.

twenty-eight

A MAN in a Gulls' sweatshirt and cutoff sweatpants, the elastic waist slung beneath his belly, came out of his front door and stood on the stoop eyeing the Silverado as Eli cruised past for the third time. Wearing rubber flip-flops, he walked across his lawn and stood at the curb, watching Eli stop the truck at the barricade. Eli didn't blame the man for being vigilant about strangers in his neighborhood. He sat in the hot car looking across the culvert at the back of the shopping center, debating his next move.

He pulled out his cell phone and keyed in Billy Horne's private line. He'd have some explaining to do, but he didn't have another plan. Every moment Callen was on her own, the harder it would be to find her. He had forgotten: no power. Cursing, he threw the useless phone over his shoulder into the back of the truck, heard it hit the window and fall into the well behind the backseat.

He straightened his back and got out of the truck, leaving

the door open and beeping its displeasure. He peered up and down the culvert. To the right it passed under the busy four lanes of Avocado Avenue. In the other direction it turned and disappeared behind the bank.

"Help you?" Rolls of fat and muscle lay across the shoulders and back of the man in the Gulls' shirt, and his neck was as thick around as a dinner plate. "Seen you drivin' around. Lookin' for something?"

"A girl around eleven years old. Red hair." The Gulls' man nodded. "You've seen her?"

"Maybe. What's she to you?" Military-style dark glasses concealed the man's eyes. "Why's she runnin'? What's she afraid of?"

He was maybe a busybody, maybe a Good Samaritan, maybe a pervert. Most likely just an out-of-work man with too much time on his hands and nothing but crap on television. Eli told himself to be patient, but it was hard not to vent his frustration on the stranger. The day was hot, and he was beating himself up for leaving Callen alone, for losing her in the network of streets, for calling Horne, for failing to keep his cell charged.

"I asked you a question. Why's she afraid?"

"I didn't say she was. She's my niece and—"

"I got a niece; she don't run from me."

Eli shoved past the man, got into the truck and backed into a squealing three-point.

"You come back this way," the man yelled, "I'm gonna call the cops."

"Fuck you," Eli said and floored it.

Callen stood for a moment, dizzied by the sudden heat and brightness of the sun on the cement. Sick to her stomach. The yards backing onto the culvert had fences. From behind the slats of one, a fat yellow cat contemplated her.

Sarge said a person always had options, but every day she realized there was a lot he did not know. He had never been questioned by the FBI or lived with muds like Isabelle and Ixsky and Cholly. Negroes were a whole lot smarter and better looking than he said; Tara proved that. Andy would call Eli a race traitor for marrying Isabelle and polluting the racial purity of America; but they were happy together in a way Callen's own mother and father had never been, and together they did great work saving animals. Tara had said things were bad in Callen's house, and she was right. It had been a house without friendship or laughter. Were it not for her mother, Callen would not have known what love was.

But Sarge was right; she did have options. She could make herself climb back into the drainage pipe and walk until she came out the other end. She could try again to lose herself in the neighborhood, or she could return to the shopping center and stand in front of Vons waiting to be found. One thing she knew about Eli: He would not give up on her.

In the neighborhood she might find a place to stay, a vacant house or one being built. If she found a house with no one home, she could climb in a window and maybe find a cupboard full of food or discover piles of twenty-dollar bills in a closet.

She wasn't an idiot. She knew when an option was really a daydream. There would be no money in a closet, and she would be lucky if she found as much as a shed to hide in. The longer she was on the street, the more likely it was that some-one would offer to help her, and that option was scarier than exploring to the end of the gross-out drainpipe. Andy said that most men in sheeple society were sex freaks created by the mixing of the races.

Like most of what Andy had told her, it probably wasn't true.

If she went back to Pasatiempo with Eli, the conse-quences would be dire. The Brethren would kill Eli and Is-abelle and burn down the ranch, and then they would kill her as they had killed her parents.

She was not going to think about that. But she did.

Tara had spoken her opinions with the kind of conviction that came from a sense of power outside Callen's experience. Andy and Sarge and Darren talked big, but she saw there was a difference. They were showing off and maybe trying to con-vince themselves they were the toughest. Tara didn't have to convince anyone. She had said that Barbara was dead, and Callen believed her.

The marmalade cat slithered under the fence and came down into the culvert with its tail high and quivering. A foot from Callen it stopped and arched its back like a Halloween cat. It tiptoed closer and stopped again. Callen held out her hand, palm first, and the cat extended its head and sniffed her fingers with its twitchy nose.

At Pasatiempo a dozen cats lived in the barn and sheds. Eli called them working cats because they earned their keep killing rodents around the barns and storerooms.

The only thing she really wanted was to go back to the ranch, but she didn't dare. It was too dangerous for everyone.

The marmalade purred, pacing in and out against Callen's legs. She crouched in stillness until her legs ached; she struggled to her feet, startling the cat, which leaped up to the strip of weeds between the culvert and the backyards.

Even a cat had a place to go, somewhere it felt safe.

⌐

The dinky frame houses on the streets north of the Crossroads had carports or detached single-car garages set far back on big, flat lots bare of trees. For all Eli could tell, the Gulls' man was the only person home in the neighborhood. The rest were at work, and the children were in school. He wondered who these people were, what kind of jobs they had and how much debt they carried to afford the expensive trucks and motor homes and boats parked in the gravel driveways and along the street. He knew nothing about people who lived in neighborhoods like this one; and for the first time it struck him that his ignorance was an insult to them. These were his readers, yet he had never wanted to know them.

If he continued driving around the neighborhood, someone behind a kitchen curtain would eventually call the police, and he would waste time in explanations the officer probably wouldn't believe. Eventually he went back to the Crossroads and pulled into a parking space near the phone booth. He had seen her drop the receiver when they locked eyes, so he knew she had not finished her call. She might come back to try again. He glanced at his watch and decided to give her thirty minutes. After that he'd call Horne from the pay phone.

He moved the Silverado and had just taken the key from the ignition when Callen strode out of Longs Drugs, fierce as a warrior maiden with a mop of untidy red hair, a box of saltines in one hand and a two-liter water bottle in the other. He didn't want to know where she'd found the money for her purchases.

She moved quickly, not pausing at the phone, mousing along the edge of the building in the shadows of the deep overhang. He exited the Silverado and went after her. She turned the corner and went behind the bank. Eli followed. He scanned the area and saw her seated on a cement bumper facing the culvert. Almost hidden by a Dumpster and a bright red Cape honeysuckle growing wild, she was tearing open the saltines; she shoved one into her mouth and took a long drag off the water bottle.

"Callen." She jumped; he sprinted and grabbed her arm as she was about to run down the side of the culvert. The plastic water bottle dropped from her grasp and split open on the cement.

"Don't run; I'm not going to hurt you."

He wanted them to walk across the parking lot like civilized people, but she wasn't going to let that happen. She twisted and dug in her heels, yelling at him to leave her alone. He had to drag, carry and shove her back to the truck.

"Hold on just a minute."

Eli turned and saw the Gulls' man a few feet away beside an old Mustang convertible, top down and its driver's side door open.

"Let her go."

"Stay out of this, pal."

"I ain't your pal, and I bet she ain't your niece." The man had the look of an aging vet, nostalgic for some action. He asked Callen. "How 'bout you, honey? He your uncle?"

She didn't answer.

Gulls' man pulled out a cell phone and held it up like a badge. "You let her go, or I'm callin' the cops. Count of three." He was enjoying himself, feeling important.

If Eli let go of Callen and decked this guy, she would take off again. And he might not come out on the right side of the fight. Gulls' man looked like a brawler who'd welcome the chance to throw a punch.

He stepped toward Callen. He had a map of purple veins on his cheeks. He held out his hand. "Come on, sweetheart. You're safe with me. I'll take care of you."

twenty-nine

CALLEN'S BODY froze against Eli's, and he knew her thinking had gone into overdrive. He relaxed enough to breathe normally. She wasn't stupid, this girl.

She handed the Gulls' man the box of saltines.

"It's okay. He's my uncle."

Inside the truck again, Eli locked the door; the instant he did, the rage and fear melted out of him. He tipped his seat back and closed his eyes. A cap of pain had spread from the twanging nerve behind his ear up the side of his head and down his neck. This headache was going to take a whole bottle of aspirin. If it was a headache. It could be an aneurysm. Jesus, he might be having a stroke. Callen was killing him.

He dug around in the glove compartment for a bottle of Tylenol. He shook four tablets onto his palm and then two more and swallowed them dry.

She was talking fast. "I waited in the car for you and then I had to go to the bathroom so I went down to that coffee place and when I came back your car was gone."

"Don't bullshit me, Callen. You called them again."

"Who?"

"I saw you in the phone booth."

"How do you know who I was calling?"

"Goddammit, I want to protect you. Why won't you let me?"

"I can take care of myself," she said, though with less assurance than he'd heard at other times. "I didn't go anywhere except to Starbucks, to use the bathroom."

Like the government she claimed to hate, she spun the same stories over and over and believed he would eventually accept her version of the truth even when it contradicted his own direct experience. If she said the lie often enough and with sufficient conviction, she would even convince herself it was true. It was a kind of self-induced brainwashing.

The parking lot was busy with automobiles going in and out. Men and women and children shoved rattling shopping carts past Eli's truck. He had the same thought he'd had when he was driving around looking for Callen. Who were these men and women talking on their cell phones, scolding their children, buying coffee, deli salads and twelve-packs of soda? Within his own limitations Eli didn't know much more about his fellow humans than Callen did. He did not blame Callen for being misguided; she'd been indoctrinated by the True Word Brethren. He had no excuse.

Maybe these were vital and creative people living in the midst of profound and challenging life dramas. That man struggling to hold on to a little boy's hand and at the same time put his ATM card back in his wallet might be a monster of villainy only posing as a stressed-out suburban father. And the thick-necked Good Samaritan in the Gulls' shirt still watching the Silverado from his Mustang might have been a hero in Vietnam whom other soldiers were proud to follow.

Even harder for Eli to believe was the possibility that he and the Gulls' man shared the same values. But Eli would never know because he'd left such men behind in the merchant marine, and for almost twenty years he had lived on his ranch, writing books and avoiding contact with strangers. For years he had been a semisociable hermit, a good neighbor, an occasional face on the street in Bone Lake. He studied psychology and knew, in theory, how people worked; there was no need to get out and mix among them. Isolation worked for him, had made him rich.

This was more or less what Billy Horne had said to him.

All Eli needed to write his books was the Internet, Amazon, all the movies ever made and—most of all—an intimate knowledge of what it meant to be afraid. Fear and its companion, rage, were his specialties, and he rendered them with literally breathtaking accuracy.

He was disgusted. He didn't have writers' block. He was just bored, dead bored, with chronicling terror.

"Are we going to sit here all day?"

"Would you like to?"

She brushed her hair out of her eyes and glared at him. "Is there something wrong with you? Why would I—"

"I'm going to say this to you once, Callen. Only once."

She groaned.

He wanted this thing with Darren and the Brethren and the FBI settled once and forever. "First off, if you really don't want to come back to the ranch, I'll let you out in the parking lot right now; you can go and do what you have to. I'll even give you enough money to get back up to Siskiyou if you're sure you want to find the Brethren." She watched him dig for his wallet. He offered all he had: three twenties and several fives and ones. "I'll go to the ATM; you can have as much as you need."

Her wide eyes blinked several times, quickly. She shook her head.

"Okay, then I'll take you back to the FBI. You may not like Agent Horne, but I've known him a long time; he's a good man, and he cares what happens to you. Help him identify Mrs. Smith. The sooner you cooperate, the sooner you can start having a real life."

"I'm not a snitch."

He sighed, feeling very old.

"That leaves you with one other way to go. With me. We'll face whatever comes. You, me and Isabelle together. And we'll keep the FBI out of it if we can."

She folded her arms across her chest.

"Make your choice, Callen. You know what happened the night of the fire even if you say you don't. You know the kind of people the Brethren are, even if you won't admit it. But if you want to keep on lying to yourself and go back to them, I'll help you do it."

↝

Callen sat in the cab of the big truck, and she just let go. As if she had been running for a long time holding hard to a handful of kite strings and finally her hand was too tired and she couldn't do it anymore. She just let go.

First she cried, and then she remembered everything and knew that she had never really forgotten any of it.

From her hiding place in the blanket basket, Callen had heard Andy yelling—and her mother pleading, a most terrible sound—and then two shots. Frightened into paralysis, she stayed in the blanket basket until she smelled smoke, and after a moment she knew the house was burning. Against all reason she waited for Barbara to come for her. Then she knew no one was going to help her out of the basket, and if she did not do it for herself, she would die there. She crawled on her stomach to the ladder. Looking down, she could not see through the smoke to the floor below. She gagged for air, and her eyes watered and stung; but her feet were steady as she descended the ladder. At the bottom she turned and dropped to her stomach, intending to make for the door. Ahead and in front of the couch she saw the soles of two shoes, athletic shoes with the toes facing up. She scuttled forward, holding her chin inches from the floor, breathing only as much as she had to. The soles of the shoes were worn almost smooth. Just a day or two earlier Barbara had said she needed to get another pair at the thrift shop. Her body lay between the couch and the coffee table, and a bright red flower bloomed on the front of her white blouse. At first Callen didn't know what she was looking at. She grabbed her mother's hand and shook it. It was limp, like a flower after a hard frost. She looked at the red blossom again and seeing what it was, she made a sound and choked on the smoke that filled her lungs. She dragged the neck of her sweatshirt over her mouth and nose, and with her eyes streaming from tears and smoke, she put her arms around her mother and laid her head against her.

Then she was lying in a hospital bed with bandages over her eyes and the worst sore throat ever. She did not know where she was or why; everything she'd seen and heard she had forgotten. After a day or two a nurse cut the bandages off her eyes, and she looked into the face of a man with a fat nose and sad eyes. He said his name was Agent Horne.

⟿

Eli asked, "Callen, have you been listening?"

"Don't you want me anymore?"

"What I want is for you to know that you're free and that you have choices."

"If you send me away, you'll get in trouble."

"I'll worry about that when it happens." He said, "I don't blame you for being pissed because I left your father on his own, but there's nothing I can do about it now. Or maybe you don't really care about Darren. The truth is, I'm not sure what you care about. Except your mother—I know you loved her. But you've lived with us since before Christmas, and we've spent hours together; sometimes when we've talked I thought you were happy. But it's clear to me now that you've never wanted to be on the ranch; you've never wanted what Isabelle and I have to offer. So I'm giving you the chance to choose something else. Just go ahead and tell me what you want."

No matter how much money he gave her, she didn't want to go looking all over the state for the Brethren, and she said so.

"You've got two choices then. The FBI or Bone Lake."

In the car next to the Silverado, a dog stuck its nose out a window and yapped at her; seeing it locked up and alone made her cry.

"I want to go home," she sobbed.

"But you can't; you know that."

She wiped her nose with the heel of her hand. "To the ranch."

"My terms, Callen. Mine and Izzy's."

She knew he meant they couldn't waste time arguing, because the Brethren were coming.

"Andy killed my mother and father." She almost couldn't speak the words. They stuck to the roof of her mouth. "I heard her voice, and she was arguing with my mom. I heard the shots."

He looked as if he wanted to interrupt, but he didn't.

"My mother was going to tell the FBI all about them, and we were going to live in another town where they'd never find us."

"Agent Horne told me."

"I thought the Brethren was my family."

Her hands shook and then her teeth chattered, and soon her whole body was trembling and she blubbered like a home-schooled child getting beaten at recess.

"Let's just go back to the ranch and take this one step at a time."

"Mom begged my dad to leave Codyville. He slapped her and made her lip bleed. I started beating on him with a shoe, and then he hit me too."

Eli turned the key in the ignition and pressed too hard against the gas pedal. The big truck revved so loudly that people walking by, pushing shopping carts, stopped and stared.

"Now they're coming to the ranch and they'll try to kill us all and it'll be my fault." She couldn't stop crying. "They're gonna kill me."

"We'll keep you safe."

"The Brethren know how to shoot. They'll come to the ranch—"

"And you won't be there."

"Where will I be?" she sobbed.

He didn't have any idea. "We'll figure something out."

thirty

NOW THAT the time had arrived, Darren was not in a rush to leave the trailer in Palm Springs. What lay ahead made him half sick with excitement when he thought about it, and he thought of nothing else. Setting the bomb in Olympia had been easy because no one expected trouble in the quiet little capital city. And he never had to see the woman he killed. Bone Lake would be face-to-face, and the FBI would be there. Couldn't say for sure, but it made sense. There would be no room for mistakes. He was not sure Andy could handle it.

Things had been better when Edgar Barrett was in charge of the True Word Brethren. Life was calmer before he went to prison and turned it all over to Andy. With Andy in charge there was always something going on. Not that Darren didn't like action, because he did; he was good at making bombs, one of the best. But he missed those old days. Edgar had been like a father to him.

He spread a map of Southern California on the table in the trailer kitchen, and using a magnifying glass, he finally found Bone Lake, a smaller dot than Codyville had been and so close to the border it might as well be a Mexican town. Using a bright yellow highlighter he had bought for the occasion, he plotted the route he would take through Indio and over the mountains. It was the long way around. Andy said he couldn't be too careful. Too much depended on getting this operation right. She had done some research and knew there was a big race event in Bone Lake on Saturday. She said this was good news. The town would be overrun by visitors, and the Brethren would fit in easily.

"Dress like a tree hugger," she told him. "There'll be feds all over the place, so watch your step. Get a new phone, and let me know when you get there."

"What if you're not there?"

"I'm here already."

Darren left the trailer in Palm Springs; he walked out the door taking nothing with him but a new phone, his knife and Beretta Cougar, his wallet and sunglasses. At a turnoff near Interstate 10 he tossed the old phone in a culvert where it would never be found. The ride between Palm Springs and Indio was long and hot with more eighteen-wheelers on the road than cars. In Indio he bought water and cruised the malls until he found a Target, where he bought a backpack, khaki shorts and a T-shirt with a tree on it. In the same shopping center there was a Barnes & Noble bookstore, and he went in, though he'd never been in a bookstore in his life.

The place was full of people talking and reading in easy chairs. The party atmosphere disconcerted him. He had expected something more like a library. He asked a girl wearing an employee badge if she had ever heard of Eli Browne.

"Are you kidding?" she asked, laughing, and went into a twitter about what a great writer he was. She dragged Darren down to the end of the store to a shelf crammed with nothing but Eli's books. Darren first thought there must be a mistake; but he looked at the photo on the back cover, and there was his brother's face. After so many years, seeing it almost knocked him over.

He got to the Salton Sea on Friday afternoon and stopped at a big general store for something to eat. The store was a warehouse, one huge room with a thirty-foot ceiling. On all the walls, shelves ran up to the roof and were crammed with food and clothing, kitchen and hardware and automotive supplies. If a person lived in Salton City, he'd never have to shop anywhere else. That gave him a good feeling about the town. It seemed a self-reliant place.

He bought a tuna on white wrapped in cellophane and a bottle of beer to wash down a pill. It was the middle of the afternoon and he wasn't sleepy, but he guessed he would be after he ate. The pill was insurance. He knew he was taking too many pills, but he needed to be alert. He would stop taking them when this assignment was over. He looked at the map and saw that he was still two and a half or three hours from Bone Lake. Andy had told him to arrive late so no one would notice him.

With a heavy foot, he drove west through a stark land-scape of eroded sand and rock along a dead straight two-lane road, empty for miles ahead and behind, to Borrego Springs and then over the Laguna Mountains by way of Yaqui Pass and the Julian Grade.

He drove into the lowering sun and was half blind by the time he turned off 94 onto the county road to Bone Lake. The sun rested on the rim of the mountains and cast long shadows that filled the canyons and ravines. The air sharp-ened and Darren rolled up the window. He looked around him at the valley surrounded by barren mountains covered in rock and scrub, and he tried to figure out why his successful brother didn't live somewhere better than this.

The road narrowed to one lane, and traffic crawled bumper to bumper. The line of slow-and-go cars gave Darren the jitters. On the shoulder a sign indicated there was bridge work ahead; someone or other regretted the inconvenience.

A signalman—signal*person*—with most of her mud dark hair tied up and stuck under a hardhat held up a stop sign and he obeyed her, though he would as soon have run her down. Up ahead high-intensity lights illuminated the bridge. After about five minutes a lead truck came from the direction of the town with a string of vehicles behind it. In the middle of nowhere and far from anywhere that mattered, the traffic surprised Darren. Nervousness began to build in him like a kettle that had gone from calm in Salton City to simmer to near boiling now that he was near his destination. He was sick of waiting; he'd been goddamn waiting for months. He banged the steering wheel with the flat of his hand. If he had a new truck he could depend on, he would drive off the road, go overland and give his brother the fucking surprise of his lame-ass life.

After more waiting, the lead truck returned, kicking up dust on the shoulder, and the traffic into town followed at a crawl. On the bridge, under the lights, Darren felt like a specimen. The workers in their orange uniforms and hard-hats glanced at him as he inched across the bridge.

Why the hell were they just standing there watching the traffic and smoking. No one in America put in a good day's, or night's, work anymore.

On the far side of the bridge another orange-gold sign ordered drivers to proceed slowly. Occasional headlight sweeps revealed horses grazing in a field, watching the traffic. There were more high-intensity white lights, though Darren still saw no one working. He passed a side road marked by three mailboxes, no street sign and not a house to be seen anywhere in the landscape of rocks, scrub and bedraggled trees.

The lead truck pulled onto the shoulder, and the road opened to two lanes again. A big sign announced that Caltrans thanked Darren for his patience.

Fuck you.

He reached under the front seat and brought out his Cougar and laid it on the seat beside him. Andy would tell him to put it away, but Andy wasn't there. He laid his palm on the cool steel; automatically his pointer finger found the trigger and curled around it. The Cougar was a special weapon for a special man in a very special war.

He turned at a sign announcing camping spots available. A man in an orange vest identified as "Security" took his last ten dollars and directed him out on a flat expanse, which he realized after a moment was a dry lake bed. To the left and extending all along what must have once been the shoreline there was some kind of excavation going on behind cyclone fencing. Tents had been set up, and people milled around under more white lights, writing on clipboards or talking to each other. Wasting time. Nudging the truck into a place in a line of parked cars, Darren noted a sign identifying this as an archaeological dig, a joint project of San Diego State University and the Kumeyaay Nation.

Darren hated skins. They liked to say America had been their country before the white man took it. A ZOG lie. God gave America to the Aryan race way back at the beginning of time. The Garden of Eden was somewhere in America. Indians were just another kind of mud.

thirty-one

ARLIER THE same day Eli and Callen had arrived home to find the house in turmoil and Isabelle hot as a hornet.

"They walked in, shoved this piece of paper—"

A search warrant.

"I was in the ranch office, and I heard these cars . . . How many were there, Ixsky? Four? Five?"

"Start at the beginning, Iz."

"I am. Just listen to me. Ixsky rang the dinner bell, and I came running and they just—"

"Did they find it?"

"What? Do you know what they came for?"

Callen came around the front of the truck and Isabelle grabbed her and hugged her. "I'm so happy you're back, Callen. Don't ever go away again."

Eli repeated, "Did they find it?"

"They tore up our bedrooms, your office—"

"Did they go into Callen's room?"

"What about my room?"

"They were everywhere. Do you know what they were after, Eli?"

"Who?" Callen asked. "The Brethren?"

"All the kitchen, great room," Ixsky growled. "Everything is a mess now."

"They went out to the ranch office and the infirmary. They even ransacked the tack room."

"Who?" Callen asked again.

"The FBI," Isabelle said and hugged her tighter. "What were they after, Eli?"

Without answering, he took the veranda steps two at a time and stormed into the great room. The wantonness of the confusion left by the agents made him catch his breath. Drawers and cupboards had been torn open and rummaged through; books had been dragged from the shelves on both sides of the fireplace. The couch and chair cushions lay scattered on the floor. He strode to the phone and jerked the receiver off the hook and dialed Billy Horne's private line. It was answered immediately.

Eli's voice trembled with outrage. "What the hell did you think you were doing?"

"I'm sorry, Eli, I really am."

"I would have given it to you if I'd had it. Did you think I was lying? Whose side do you think I'm on, Billy?"

"After you left, the way you just . . . I couldn't take any chances."

"Is this what you do to your friends?"

"I told you. In my office. This can't be about friendship anymore. We want that drawing, Eli."

Eli hung up.

"Ixsky, when you were in Callen's room this morning, did you see a piece of paper with a drawing on it? A woman's face?"

She shrugged. "I dump the trash every morning."

And Cholly burned it.

⌐

Callen's room was in shambles with everything pulled from the shelves and drawers, the blanket and sheets in a pile beside the bed, her closet floor covered with mounds of clothing. Muttering, Eli pulled the nails from the windows and opened them wide while Callen watched. He pushed a window up and rested his hands on the sill, his elbows straight. He could not waste precious time being angry with the FBI.

Isabelle had stopped asking what the FBI was after and gone into the bedroom across the hall, presumably trying to make some order of the mess left by the federal agents. Probably to keep from raging at him. He would not blame her if she did. Ixsky was cleaning up the kitchen and great room.

The sacred privacy of his home had been invaded, his wife shoved aside while the house was ransacked. He stepped into the hall and picked up the phone. Again his call was answered on the first ring.

"I don't want to see you or people on my property."

"I have a job to do, Eli. We talked about—"

"I don't care what we talked about. You can come here with the National Guard if you want, and I'll set Cholly and the hands at the bottom of the road with rifles. That's it, Billy."

"The law gives me the right—"

"This is still America, Billy. I've still got the right to defend my home and family."

"We're on the same side, Eli."

"Sometimes there are three sides."

"I want you all to come in. Now. Just load up the car and drive down to the county road. Let my people take it from there."

He dropped the receiver and let it hang.

In Callen's room, Eli avoided looking at her. He pulled out the desk chair and sat backward on it. He stank with tension, but a bath would come later.

"They were after the picture you drew. Of the woman with the Iron Cross."

"How do you know about that?"

"I was in your room."

"You promised this was a house where everyone's privacy was respected."

"Just tell me where it is, and we can debate privacy later. Right now I need that picture."

"You can't have it. The night you locked me in I tore it up. I tore up a bunch of stuff. Ixsky must have taken it out this morning."

He could see she was glad to have outwitted the federal agents. And him.

"Who was that woman, Callen? She looked familiar to me. What else do you know about her?"

"Nothing." Her expression turned inward, shutting him out.

"You've got to draw another picture."

They sat—she on her mattress, he at the desk—and looked at each other.

Her eyes filled with tears again. "I don't know what to do."

Just twenty-four hours earlier she could not have admitted that.

"That's part of being grown-up, honey. The older you get, the more complicated life is. Hardly anything's black or white. There's lots of gray. But this thing with Mrs. Smith—"

"When you took me to the FBI? Did it seem right?"

"It did, Callen."

"Then why didn't you leave me there? I don't understand how something can be right and then change to wrong. In just a few hours."

They didn't have time for this conversation, but he must make time because clearly these questions were important to her. He thought carefully how to answer.

"I know the Brethren taught you that right and wrong are black and white, and you can always tell the difference between the choices. But the Brethren were lying to you." He was unaccustomed to talking about deep subjects. "I took you to Horne because this time yesterday I thought it was the best way to protect you. And I want to protect you. That's my bottom line. But while we were there, I realized that you needed to be protected from the FBI as well as the Brethren."

"I thought you trusted the FBI."

"And I do, more or less. But they don't see you as a person. To them you're someone with information they need. Ultimately I thought you'd be safest here with Izzy and me."

"I still don't get it."

"Callen, we'd like you to help the FBI investigation, but that's not our first priority. Number one, we want you to grow up healthy and happy, without all the Brethren crap."

"In the parking lot you gave me a choice."

"Unless you chose your own destiny it doesn't matter what the rest of us do. But I admit it, I hoped you'd choose Pasatiempo. I think we can keep you safe here. If I gave you to Horne, I'd be powerless."

"So you're saying some things are more good than others."

He nodded.

"And some bad things are worse than others. Right?"

He smiled, amused that she could say it better than he could. "And now I've got to go find Izzy. Straighten things out with her. If I don't do that, it'll be the baddest of the bad."

"What did Ixsky mean when she said I'm not as white as I think?"

The conversation was eating up precious moments when he and Isabelle should be planning how to protect Callen and the ranch. But she might as well know the whole truth now. This had been a day of truth.

"Do you really think there's anyone in the world with pure Aryan blood? I bet if you went back far enough, you'd find out some ancestor of Hitler's was Jewish."

"I'm Norwegian, German, Dutch and a little bit of Irish."

He shook his head. "You're way more than that, Callen. I have my mother's birth certificate in my office. I can find it for you if you need proof."

"Proof of what?"

"Your grandmother, my mother, was a Native American."

She laughed but not the way he ever wanted her to.

"She was born on a reservation somewhere. Nevada, I think."

"That's so stupid!" Callen cried, leaping at him, yelling into his face. "Look at my hair! Did you ever in a million years see a red-haired Indian?"

Callen lay on her back on the mattress, held a hand mirror over her face and stared, trying to see an Indian. She wanted to believe it was a lie, but there was no reason for Eli to make it up. If it wasn't a lie, it had to be the truth. Callen was as much a mud as Ixsky.

She threw down the mirror.

Why would he say she was an Indian if it wasn't true?

She retrieved the mirror from the bedclothes still piled at

the foot of the bed. Turning her head slightly, she looked at her profile. Her nose wasn't big, and her skin was fair like her father's. Darren didn't look a bit like an Indian, but Eli . . .

She went to her desk, and in the middle of the mess the agents had left she found a pencil and a pad of drawing paper. She sat on the bed and rapidly sketched a picture of her uncle on a horse, his hair long and straight, a headband around his forehead with a feather stuck in it. She tried to show him holding a bow and arrow, but she couldn't get the arms right, so she started again and just drew his face and shoulders.

She had seen the old photos of Indians taken back when they were still wild. Eli looked just like one of them.

Darren and Eli had the same squaw mother. Indian. Native American. In the Brethren she had known the name of every kind of person. Out among the sheeple she had to learn a new language.

Maybe Wanda wasn't her real grandmother. Maybe Norgaard had had an Aryan wife and a baby son named Darren, and his wife had died; and so he'd married Wanda to get over his grief and to have a babysitter for his little blond son.

She lay back and closed her eyes. That was as likely as finding a stash of twenty-dollar bills in an abandoned house. It was easier to cry than pretend she didn't feel completely miserable.

Her life could be divided into sections of before and after. There was before and after she lived in Codyville, before and after the fire, before and after she sat in Agent Tara's office and started to remember. Until then the truth had been like a snake that wouldn't budge off the path in front of her, and she had been going around in circles to avoid what was right there shaking its rattles at her. Now she remembered everything and felt much worse.

And now there was before and after she found out she was a redskin mud.

She cried some more and then she sat up and wiped her eyes on her forearm and looked out the window at the mountains. All Eli's geological explanations had come down to pretty much the same thing. These were old mountains, worn away to their bare bones. She was eroding too. Whoever she was before she came to Pasatiempo, she wasn't that person anymore. Her mother and father were dead forever and now she'd lost even her pure Aryan blood. She looked in the mirror again and though she appeared to be the same Callen as she'd been an hour earlier, she knew she was a stranger.

thirty-two

DARREN CALLED Andy on his cell when he got to Bone Lake, but reception was poor and finally died out completely. If they could not coordinate, he would take the initiative. He was comfortable with that, though he knew Andy wouldn't be.

For an hour Darren wandered among the crowds on Bone Lake's only street. He picked up a brochure that told him about the Ore-Mex Race, its history and why it was a big deal. He took a free map showing the dry lake and the end of the trail as well as some of the roads in the area; nothing gave him a clue as to where Eli lived. He stood for a long time sorting through piles of T-shirts that cost as much as a full dinner, listening to snatches of conversations about the race. The Kenyan and the Eritrean were within fifteen minutes of each other, and the New Zealander looked like he was fading. It made Darren sick to think an Aryan couldn't compete against black Africans.

He shoved his shoulder against the doors under a red-and-blue neon sign that said BONE LAKE MOTEL AND CAFÉ. The place was crowded and noisy, lots of yelling between the three waitresses and the cook. He took a seat at the counter.

"Help you?" asked a waitress in a blue tank top. Her name tag said she was Jenna.

"How you doing, Jenna? Looks like they're keepin' you busy." Darren ordered a Coke and fries.

When she brought him his order, he tried to sound casual as he said, "Hey, I wonder if you know my pal, Eli Browne?"

"Everyone knows Eli."

"He come in here?"

She blew a strand of pinkish-blond hair out of her eyes. "And you are?"

Darren grinned. "I *are* an old friend of his, Larry Butterfield." He extended his hand across the counter, and after a moment Jenna shook it. She was typically suspicious; under their friendliness waitresses were always wary. Darren liked the challenge. Jenna was a country girl about his age, pretty but fading fast, her best years behind her. Girls like Jenna told him he looked like Elvis or James Dean, and they didn't mind the grease under his nails. He didn't have to speak like a hotshot writer to get them listening.

"How do you know Eli?" she asked.

"Back in Montana. We were friends in high school." Darren had dogged Eli and Larry Butterfield on summer nights when they'd cruised for girls in Larry's blue Chevy convertible. "Long time ago."

"You here for the race?"

"Oh yeah."

"You don't look like a runner."

He pretended to take offense. "Don't judge a book by its cover."

She pointed to the tiny Iron Cross tattooed along his cheekbone, under his eyes. "What's that?"

He touched the mark. "Got it when my mom died."

"Did it hurt?"

Stupid question. "The worst, but hey, it keeps her memory green, you know what I mean?"

"It's a Nazi thing."

"When I got it, I didn't know. I mighta chose something else." He made a disgusted face. "Those guys are crazy." She would believe him.

Jenna gassed up his Coke and went away to clear a table and take another order. Reflecting on her image in the long mirror behind the counter, he admired the swing of her hips and the flirty tilt and tip of her chin. It was a long time since he'd been with a woman who knew she was female. All last year Barbara had been like ice to him. He thought of what she had done, her treason, and it was hard to keep a pleasant expression on his face.

He'd gotten his temper from Wanda, and it was the only thing he thanked her for. Even Andy was afraid of him when he got the heat up. His anger could be explosive, but mostly it spread like oil on water and covered a lot of territory before he lit a flame to it. It went deep as well as wide. It included

Barbara and Eli and ZOG and Andy, and there was room for plenty more.

He dug in his jacket pocket and pulled out the vial of pills, considered taking one and thought better of it.

Jenna leaned against the back of the counter and crossed her arms over her chest, but not before Darren caught a glimpse of her hard nipples. A sure sign she liked him. He thought about standing behind her, slipping his hand into the front of her blue tank top, pinching those hot little berries.

"You sick?" she asked.

"Vitamins. Man's gotta stay healthy. For the important things, you know?" Innuendo filled the space between them. Jenna blushed.

"You gonna see Eli?"

"Maybe." He took a sip of soda. "You guys need some decent signs in this town. I looked for his place on the way in, but half the roads aren't marked. Then I went and lost the paper I wrote his address on."

Her eyes narrowed slightly.

"All that digging out on the lake surprised me."

"It's always going on."

"They ever find arrowheads? Me and Eli used to go after arrowheads. They got 'em all over Montana."

"How long since you saw Eli?"

"I've been in Iraq. Before that we used to meet in San Francisco. Place got a little queer for me, if you know what I mean."

Jenna looked away, scanning the busy café. Darren was patient.

"How'd you know he was here?" Jenna asked.

"I wrote to the company that publishes his books."

"They told you where he lives?"

"Yeah. And, man, was I surprised when they right out gave it to me." The back of Darren's neck prickled. He picked up his cola and took a long drink. "It was a girl told me. I figure she was new to the job or a temporary and didn't know better. Probably caught hell for it."

"He's real uptight about his privacy."

Darren laughed, confident again. "Wouldn't you be if you were him?"

"How'd you lose it?"

"What?"

"The address."

"My wife says I'd lose my head if it wasn't attached."

The mention of a wife seemed to settle Jenna's indecision.

"Plus my memory's worse since I got back from Iraq."

She looked at him as if he were a war hero.

"You drove by it when you came into town," she said. "Some kids stole the sign last month. Wild Horse Road, right about where Caltrans is doing that work on the bridge." She made a face and leaned forward, giving Darren a glimpse of cleavage. "You know, that bridge's been fixin' to fall in the culvert for at least five years, and now all of a sudden, on the busiest weekend of the year, they decide to fix it."

"That's the government for you." He remembered the mailboxes lined up like three school kids waiting for a bus.

"You go about half a mile up the road, and you gotta keep your eyes out for the sign. Says Pasatiempo—that's the name of his ranch. Eli doesn't like attention."

Darren grinned. "Well, he's gonna get some."

thirty-three

BACK ON the busy street the night was festive and noisy. Darren walked against the flow of pedestrian traffic, knocking shoulders and pleased to feel the irritation in the people. Not one of them knew who he was. Not one of them guessed how powerful he was.

He let that thought entertain him until he found himself back on the edge of town, facing the dry lake and ready to go. He hunted among the rows of parked vehicles until he found his truck. He spread a map on the hood and by the light of his flashlight found Wild Horse Road. Though it would be rough walking, it appeared he could get there overland. The moon was not yet up, but the night was very clear and bright, and he was the best outdoorsman in the Brethren since old man Barrett got sent away.

He took off across open ground, and because he knew the stars, he kept a steady northward direction. The ground was uneven, tunneled by ground squirrels and cobbled with rocks and stones. It was hard going at night and without a trail to follow. Most guys couldn't do it. Though there were patches of open ground, more was covered by dense, low growing plants with thick, twisting branches and sharp, sometimes barbed, foliage. He encountered clumps of cactus and more rocks, piles of rocks everywhere, some as big as cars. He thought of what lay ahead and had just the proportion of angry energy and nerves and excitement to keep him on his toes.

He wasn't going to kill Callen, but he knew it had to be done. He would let Andy take her, let the blood be on her hands. When he felt himself recoil from this idea, he reminded himself what Edgar Barrett had once told him. Lives would be lost in the race war, but it was God's will that the Aryan race triumph. When Edgar Barrett was taken up by God, Darren had cried like a child, and he didn't care who saw him doing it. He had been proud to cry for the man who had been more of a father to him than his own.

The sky looked like a black cloth on which someone had spilled a shaker of salt. There was nothing between Darren and his Maker. The air was so clean and clear he felt God's eyes on him, approving.

Eventually he reached a gravel road. To his left, on the other side of a hill, he saw the glow of the Caltrans lights. By their relative positions he judged this had to be Wild Horse Road. Staying south of the road, he followed it until he came to a driveway on the other side. It disappeared over a rise, a rich man's long, paved private road. On either side of the drive oleander bushes gave off the smell of something rotting. He stayed away from them, hiding behind several boulders that lay close together, forming a kind of semicircle of protection.

Andy had told him the feds would be watching the ranch, as if he couldn't figure that out for himself. He saw no one but knew overconfidence might prove fatal. Not all federal agents were city dudes. Some might be as canny outdoors as he was.

There was no traffic on the narrow road, and after a time it bored Darren to sit with nothing to look at; the quiet made his skin creep and put all his senses on alert because when he listened, the quiet wasn't really quiet at all. There were a lot of country sounds around him: the clicking and chirping of night insects rustling in the chaparral, which might be snakes or small animals. Several coyotes passed a few yards from him, their long bodies supple as water and their cold eyes glowing in the starlight. Long after midnight he thought he heard a throaty growl and held his breath, hand on his gun. He was cold and dug in his pack for gloves and a stocking cap. He ate a couple of Granola bars and an apple. It was boring, all this waiting, but he knew it came with the job. Patience was key to the success of a mission. Edgar had told him that.

The face of his watch glowed a sickly aquarium blue-green. Soon it would be daylight. A layer of overcast drifted in from the west, a scrim of fog obscured the stars, and it seemed darker at five in the morning than it had at midnight. He took the fog as a sign from God, a helping hand.

He darted across Wild Horse Road and halfway up the hill to one side of the driveway. He was on his brother's property heading for the house, and the ground seemed to vibrate beneath the soles of his shoes. The power of the moment stunned him, and to enjoy it, he paused behind a boulder. Soon he would stand toe-to-toe with Eli, no longer the needy little boy, a grown man now and chosen by God. If someone had to die, it would be God's will.

Bent low at the waist like a commando, he darted between boulders, every sense alert. He had his pack on his back, his binocs around his neck, the Cougar in his belt and his knife in his boot. He was ready for anything, a soldier in country. Ahead lay a village full of race traitors and muds.

The fog vanished as suddenly as it blew in, and the sky to the east was streaked with cream and yellow by the time Darren topped the hill overlooking the ranch. He dropped to his belly behind a rock and focused his binoculars. Below him lay a huge spread, a kingdom unto itself. The size of the place unnerved him, and for the first time he doubted he would be able to pull off the mission. There was too much he didn't know.

He wished he knew more about Callen's situation. Eli would not be alone with her. He might be married or even have children of his own. And a big ranch like this didn't run itself. There would be muds all over the place—illegals, he was almost positive—and they'd have guns because they were all criminals or they would have stayed in Mexico. His excitement torqued. He wouldn't mind offing a few muds in the name of God Almighty.

Two men slouched around the side of the barn leading six horses, which they tied to posts. A third and fourth man crouched beside the horses and checked their feet and legs. They lugged saddles from the barn and laid them over the animals. A figure Darren judged to be a woman emerged from the ranch house, went directly to a horse and, putting her feet in the stirrups, swung into the saddle.

Fresh doubt disturbed Darren's concentration. What if a whole bunch of them got on horses and rode into the hills. What was he supposed to do? He thought of calling Andy but decided not to. The reception would be crappy, and he didn't know enough yet to assess the real situation. Edgar Barrett would tell him to be patient. Another figure, smaller than any of the others, ran out of the house and went straight to the horses.

Callen.

He fumbled to withdraw his cell phone from his shirt pocket while keeping his attention fixed on the group of figures as he dialed Andy. His index finger hovered over the glowing send button.

Maybe it wasn't Callen. It could be a young boy; maybe Eli had a son. He knew the Brethren were coming, and it made sense that he would get his family to safety. He watched the figure adjust the horse's stirrups and tighten its girth, every movement made with complete confidence. He knew for a fact that his daughter had never been on a horse in her life. She could not have become so familiar with saddles and horses in just six months. The figure put a foot in the stirrups and swung into the saddle. He tried to imagine his stubborn daughter taking riding lessons from sheeple and muds. It was even more unlikely that Eli was such a fool he'd let her ride. He might as well give her car keys and tell her to take off.

Back and forth the arguments ping-ponged in Darren's skull until he could not bear the uncertainty anymore and decided it absolutely wasn't Callen sitting straight in the saddle. He had to be right because God was on the Aryan side. He put the cell phone back in his pocket.

It was a relief when the riders disappeared, whoever they were. He rolled over on his back and closed his eyes, repeating the Fourteen Words in his mind until his pulse calmed and he was in control of himself again. He refocused his binoculars on the house and saw the shadow of a figure moving in the lighted upstairs room. He wondered if it was his daughter up early. Maybe she sensed him out among the rocks with his binoculars trained on her window.

An early morning stillness lay over the ranch; and as Darren scanned the terrain, he saw nothing out of the ordinary. He thought it was strange, this absence of FBI, but he trusted his eyesight. If the agents weren't posted on the property, they might be inside. He had to know and would make his move soon. For a moment, he watched the lighted upstairs window and thought about Callen.

Darren believed he was a man who faced facts squarely. He knew his daughter had been contaminated. Compromised was Andy's word, but to him it was more like she'd been rolling in filth for six months. Television and radio and newspapers—books too, he supposed—had dirtied her mind with ZOG propaganda. She had heard the idle conversation of muds and race traitors. No matter how she had tried to fight it, her mind was fouled. None of the Brethren would ever trust her.

If it came to it, he wondered if he could shoot his own blood child. Unless he got word to Andy, he might have to do that. His hand closed around the butt of his gun, and he imagined the press of the trigger against the pad of his index finger. He didn't want to do it, but he knew God would forgive him.

thirty-four

I T WAS Saturday, race day.

Myrrh was in the kitchen loading the dishwasher when Callen and Isabelle arrived. They had set out on horseback at early dawn, riding to Sunny Hills by a rarely used trail that skirted Jubal Spry's property and circled the hill behind the resort.

"About time you got here," Myrrh said. "I'd almost given up on you." She handed Isabelle a cup of coffee and poured a glass of orange juice for Callen. "Have a muffin," she said, pushing a plate under Callen's nose. "Thanks for helping out, sparrow."

"Are you going to pay me?"

Myrrh laughed.

"Callen—"

"No, Isabelle, if I expect her to work, she has a right to fair wages. How's five bucks an hour sound?"

"Good," Callen said, surprised by Myrrh's generosity, adding as an afterthought, "Thank you."

As Myrrh and Isabelle talked, Callen ate two muffins and upon Myrrh's urging, poured herself a glass of milk. They talked about her. Isabelle said Callen would be safe at Sunny Hills because no one would think to look for her at a nudist resort. She was not to leave under any circumstances, nor was she to have direct contact with the guests. Her work would be in the kitchen helping with meals and cleanup.

Myrrh said, "If anyone asks, you're my granddaughter down from San Francisco."

When it came to grandmothers, Callen could not win.

"And stay out of the rooms," Isabelle said. "Don't get too curious or someone'll notice you."

"You already told me all this."

"But I'm not sure you know how serious this is." Isabelle's dark eyebrows almost met in the middle when she worried. "You understand it's not like an adventure in a book or a movie where everything automatically turns out right? Until this is over you can't leave the resort, not for anything."

"What if something happens to you?"

"Just stay with Myrrh." She hugged Callen. "I'll be in touch as soon as it's over."

At the back door Isabelle turned around. "Nothing's going to happen to me, Callen."

As Isabelle stepped out into the garden, Callen's imagination leaped ahead, projecting calamity. She did not want to be alone and angry with the world anymore, but if something bad happened to Isabelle, she would have no alternative. It would be like losing Barbara twice over.

She dashed across the kitchen and outside, coming to a breathless stop in front of Isabelle.

"Promise you'll come back."

Isabelle's warm, strong embrace held her, but she made no promises, Callen noticed that.

The Brethren did not believe in appliances more complicated than stoves and refrigerators because they fostered dependency on the Zionist economy. But how hard could it be to load a dishwasher? She'd seen Ixsky do it. Callen went to work and when she finished, Myrrh stood back, surveying the inside of the appliance, hands on her hips.

"Interesting. You have a creative style, and I want to say I've always been a sucker for imagination. There's soap on the shelf. Fill her up and turn her on. This is the dial; just turn it to here."

The machine clicked and growled, and a second later Callen heard the swish of water.

"Good girl. You saved me ten minutes doing that."

Myrrh did not seem like a bad person, but she had an irritating way of talking. Perhaps in time Callen would get used to it. Strange to think into her future and see people like Myrrh and Ixsky being part of it.

"You know how to make corn bread, I hope. No? Never mind. I assume you can read a recipe, and if you can't, you'll start learning today." Myrrh shuffled through a box of cards with recipes scribbled on them.

Like a hammer to the head, the memory of Barbara's cooking hit Callen, and suddenly all her senses were awake. The moment of hope she had felt in Isabelle's arms vanished, and there was only longing in its place. She remembered macaroni and cheese with the top crunchy and brown, creamy chocolate pudding on her tongue, and sweet potato chips deep fried in Crisco and bacon grease. Wild cherry fudge so dense and sugary it crunched when she bit into it. Callen could live a thousand million years and search the universe, but she would never taste her mother's good food again. Not one mouthful.

Dead was forever.

She pressed the heels of her hands against her eyelids and leaned against the dishwasher; its warm, chugging reality was all that held her upright.

"Here it is," Myrrh cried with a note of triumph, holding up an index card. "Hope you can read my scrawl. The nuns gave up on me." She clipped the card to a plastic book stand. "You'll need the big ceramic bowl. It's over in that cupboard. This recipe makes a triple quantity."

From the depths of the house came the sound of a clock, chiming the quarter hour. "Good Lord in Heaven, who stole the morning?" She laid the recipe card in front of Callen and patted it. "Your job is to make corn bread for supper, after the race is done. Look around, and you'll find what you need; if you don't, you can improvise." She flashed a smile. "Izzy says you're a clever sparrow, and she's as good a judge of people as there is."

Callen watched Myrrh steam out of the kitchen.

She had never in her life made corn bread. She had eaten plenty, so she knew the finished bread was supposed to be yellow and crumbly, crusty on the top like a dry cake. Between the large bowl before her and the completed product lay a mystery. She read over the recipe three times before she began to poke through the kitchen cupboards to find the listed ingredients. That part was easy. She gathered the ingredients and measured them into the bowl. She couldn't find a square iron pan like the one Barbara used. She could ask Myrrh, but she didn't know where she'd gone. She heard voices and music coming from the pool area. She might be out there with her guests, but Callen wasn't going to look. There was a big difference between spying on nudies on her belly under the oleander bushes and seeing them just outside the window, practically face-to-face.

She dug deeper in the recesses of Myrrh's cupboards and found an aluminum pan that was the wrong shape but would have to do. The directions in the recipe said the batter should have lumps, but Callen thought that must be a mistake. No one would want lumpy corn bread, so she beat it until her arm ached and it was smooth as melted butter. She tipped the bowl and watched the batter ribbon into the pan. She slid the pan into the oven and after experimenting with dials and buttons, found a way to turn on the heat.

Outside a man was singing to the music of a guitar.

The corn bread cooked, and good smells filled the kitchen. Callen cleaned up the mess she'd made, washing the dishes by hand as she stood at the sink and listened to the man singing about Scotch and soda while the guitarist played a lot of fancy notes. Callen wondered what kind of faces these men had. They might be the sodomites she'd seen the day before; or maybe it was just one man, singing and playing. All she had to do was open the blind over the sink a crack. Three or four inches would be enough.

Carefully she parted two slats of the blind. She didn't see the man playing the guitar or the people singing with him. All she saw, sprawled naked on a terry-cloth-covered chaise, one leg cocked up, one arm stretched behind her head, her eyes closed and her lips parted in a sweet smile, was Andy.

thirty-five

CALLEN DROPPED to a crouch.

Andy. Buddy's mother, Dor's wife, Edgar Barrett's daughter. Andy naked on a chaise at Sunny Hills Natural Resort.

Callen sat on the floor, pressed into a corner of the kitchen with her scabby knees up to her chin, hugging her legs. Seeing Andy naked beside Myrrh's swimming pool at ten in the morning was the final proof she needed that everything Eli and Isabelle and even the FBI had told her was true.

She had to get word to Isabelle and Eli, but she had been forbidden to leave Sunny Hills under any circumstances. Isabelle had been precise about that. She could phone the ranch, but that would alert the FBI; and Eli had told her they would do what was necessary without involving the FBI.

She didn't want to tell Myrrh. Myrrh was too strange to be any help.

The oven bell rang, and glad for something to do, she took the corn bread out of the oven. It was flat and too brown around the edges, but this was not the time to worry about what she'd done wrong.

She turned off the oven and walked through the arch into the dining room and across the shuttered common room to where it opened into a foyer. Against one wall was the rolltop desk where Myrrh had said she kept the registration book. Callen riffled through the disorder under the accordion top and eventually found an official-looking leather-bound book. It wasn't the register. It was a journal of some kind written in Myrrh's handwriting, a diary like Eli had nagged Callen to keep. Irritated, Callen tossed it aside and kept looking. The registration book turned out to be an ordinary chartreuse spiral notebook with a strip of masking tape across the cover to identify it. Callen thumbed to the last entry and read down the list of names. There was no mention of a guest named Andy DeWitt or Barrett.

She scanned the registered names again. Second from the bottom: Andrea Smith. Andrea. Andy and Mrs. Smith.

It was too much of a coincidence.

She bit down on her lower lip, considering her next move. Sarge said a soldier had to be one step ahead of the enemy. Just knowing that Andy was at Sunny Hills was not enough. Callen had to know what she was planning.

She went back to the kitchen and out the back door. Hurrying behind the house, she passed the vegetable garden and washhouse. Her heartbeat fired and charged ahead. She ran breathlessly up the slope to the cottage where Andrea Smith was registered.

Sunlight burned through a screen of eucalyptus trees onto the dusty yard in front of the cottage, mentholating the hot, dry air. On the porch Callen felt the heat through the soles of her shoes and across the back of her neck. She tried the cottage door, and it was locked. She should have taken more time at Myrrh's desk and found the key. She had been too eager, not thinking clearly.

She stepped off the porch and hurried around to the back of the cottage where a dangerous-looking cactus garden had been planted below two sash windows. She recognized the paddles of the prickly pear and steered clear on a path around them. Halfway to the window she stopped, sensing she was not alone. She turned, and there was Andy standing only a few feet away, bare legged and wearing an oversized white T-shirt. Callen stepped back, not thinking, and scraped her calf on a prickly pear. A drop of blood dripped down the back of her leg.

"Hello, Callen. Cat got your tongue?"

thirty-six

ANDY WAS blond and fair skinned with light eyes and lashes that were almost white. Callen had heard someone say she had the face of an angel, but no heavenly angel had her whining, buzz-saw voice. In another life a long time ago, Barbara had told Callen that Andy's beauty lied, but her voice gave her away.

"I would have thought you'd be surprised to see me." Andy's expression was bland. "Why aren't you surprised, Callen? I'm very surprised to see *you*. Come here and give me a hug."

Callen would rather have embraced a prickly pear, but she did it anyway. Against her she felt the soft flesh of Andy's naked breasts. She pulled back quickly, her cheeks burning. She couldn't think of anything except how Andy looked without her clothes on; and she was pretty sure Andy knew this and was laughing at her, relishing her embarrassment. She smiled, her eyes alight with shards of glass. Callen's brain went crazy with chatter, like when Eli used the remote to bang through the television channels. She was losing control; in another second she would do something ridiculous, and Andy would take advantage of her lapse. Callen tried to count her breaths the way Sarge had taught her. In out, one; in out, two. It didn't help.

"I expected to find you at your uncle's ranch. Not right here, practically on my own front porch." She would kill them all and set fire to the ranch, and even the horses would die unless Callen did the right thing, right now.

"I have a job." Sarge had taught them: When you lie, keep your lies as close to the truth as possible. "In the kitchen."

"When did you see me?"

"Just now. I looked out the window."

"You saw me, but you didn't say a word."

"I figured you were hiding out, and you wouldn't want me to let on it was you." She felt better when she was talking, but if she went on too long or said too much too fast, Andy would know she was terrified and use her fear against her. Sarge had explained all this. "I looked in the registration book and didn't see your name; only I thought maybe you'd used a fake one, so I thought I'd come out here and check if Andrea Smith was you before I said anything."

Sarge said liars couldn't look you in the eye, but Callen raised her eyes and proved him wrong.

"I asked myself what Sarge would do."

"Didn't you know my name was Andrea?" Andy's eyes

were large and blue and innocent. "I'm surprised you didn't know that."

Those eyes had been the last to see Barbara and Darren alive. The knowledge of this should have made Callen more frightened; instead, it steeled her.

The sound of her own voice, steady and calm, gave her courage. "I guess you decided to ignore my second message, huh?"

"Second message?"

"I said you shouldn't come because the FBI and everyone's all over town. They're around my uncle's house too. And inside. About twenty of them." Andy might not believe there were that many, but she couldn't take the number back. "Didn't you get the message? I called yesterday." Callen knew that in a game of chicken against Andy, she barely had a chance. But she was in the game now and had to play on with convincing lies, eye contact, a calm voice and no hesitation.

"Does the FBI know you're up here then, not at your uncle's house?"

"I'm s'posed to be hiding out. Eli didn't think you'd find me here."

"Poor Callen."

She almost ran when Andy's hand stroked her shoulder.

"You must have been very lonely so far from your family and friends."

"They wanted me to tell them everything about the

Brethren." She had to pretend that she was glad to see Andy. That was the hardest part.

They walked to the front of the cottage, and Andy unlocked the door, stepped aside and gestured Callen in. "And did you?" She asked the question as if it barely mattered.

Through the gaping door Callen saw a room in dark shadow. She wanted to stay outside where she could feel the sun burning the back of her neck, but she was sure Andy had brought guns; and if Callen knew how many, she would be able to tell Eli and Isabelle something useful. If she ever saw them again. If Andy didn't kill her right then.

The cottage was furnished in dark wood in a square, plain style. A double bed, still unmade, was at one end of the room under a large window. Two other windows faced the cactus garden. On another wall there was a pair of closed doors, probably a bathroom and a closet. Two suitcases lay on a daybed. Andy didn't need two big suitcases.

"Is Sarge staying here too? Is Dor?"

"Who've you talked to? What did you tell them about the Brethren?"

"I never told anyone anything." She didn't blink. "I'm not a race traitor."

Andy pursed her lips and studied Callen. Abruptly, as if she'd decided something, she walked to the dresser and poured a glass of water from a carafe. She handed it to Callen.

"You seem awfully nervous, Callen. Have a drink of water. It's so warm in this part of the world; how do the sheeple stand it? What's it called? Bone Lake?" She shuddered. "What a name."

"They said my mom's dead."

"They told you that?" Andy laughed and quickly apologized. "It's not funny, not at all, but is that really what they told you?"

"They thought I'd rat."

"And you didn't."

" 'Course not."

"I wouldn't blame you if you told them *something*. The fire was terrible. You didn't see it?"

"I was in the woods coming back from reading to Old Lady Schmidt. I got scared and hid." The mind could be so tricky. Callen told the lie and half believed it. In spite of everything her sensible, logical mind knew and despite what her own reluctant memory had told her, a spark flared in the wishful tinder of Callen's mind. "Can I see my mom?"

"Well, of course you can. She's waiting for you up in Codyville."

Andy should have known better than to say it. Her lie cut right through Callen's wishes. The Brethren would not have stayed in Codyville. Anyone who had studied the Manifesto knew that.

"The FBI told me you all left Codyville after the fire."

"Why would we do that? My Dor's the best handyman in town. He's got a good business going. Codyville's our home. It was terrible about your house burning, of course, but the

Brethren got together and built a new one. Your family's started over and everyone's fine and healthy. We've been half crazy trying to find you."

For a few minutes Andy talked about daily life in Codyville, and Callen wanted very much to believe. It was as if she were sliding down a muddy slope into a blackness she tried to believe was white.

"Will I see my dad?"

"He's here with me today, Callen."

Another lie.

"And Sarge and Dor and—"

"Remember what the Manifesto says: Two people can handle most jobs better than a crowd."

"The FBI—"

"The Feebs, Callen. The Feebs. How do you think they earned that name?" Andy smiled again—so many smiles—and her eyes could not have been rounder.

"The woman who runs this place—"

"Myrrh." She wondered if Myrrh had gone to the kitchen, found her gone, and seen the mess she'd made of the corn bread recipe. And if she went into the foyer, she would know that Callen had been nosing in the rolltop desk and had not taken the time to close the top. She would think she was a liar and a cheat.

"What does Myrrh know?"

"She's friends with Eli and Isabelle."

"Isabelle?"

"Eli's wife. My aunt."

"I see. You've got a whole family, huh? And Eli, is he like your dad?"

Callen shook her head.

"Your uncle's a very rich man, I guess. A big success." Andy's mouth smiled. "Pretty good life, huh? Maybe you'd like to stay?"

It was a trick question, and Callen didn't know the right answer. What if she stayed with Eli, and her mother really was in Codyville waiting for her? She wasn't, she couldn't be, but *what if?*

"I want to see my mother."

"Then what we have to do is get out before you're missed. We've already used up valuable time. I'll put on some clothes, and then we'll be gone." Andy's mouth seemed stuck in the smile position. "Isn't it lucky we saw each other? I really didn't know how I was going to find you, Callen. I assumed you'd be at your uncle's ranch, but I didn't know where that was; so what was I supposed to do? Walk in and drag you out by the scruff? It's so much better this way, so much simpler. You came to me. I'm just so glad to see you, Callen. Life hasn't been the same without you. My goodness, what a party we're going to have for you."

Callen had seen Barbara on the floor with a red blossom on her chest. There was no *what if.*

A hectic gust of wind scraped the eucalyptus trees across the roof of the guesthouse.

Callen blurted, "I left my diary in the kitchen. It's full of stuff about the Brethren."

"Diary?"

"I was careful. I kept it in my backpack. I never left it around."

Andy's eyes sliced Callen the way a knife peels back the skin of an orange. "That was a very stupid thing to do."

Ixsky's breakfast of beans and eggs bubbled in her stomach.

"You wouldn't be shitting me, would you? You wouldn't be trying to get out of here, find a telephone maybe? Call your new friends?"

Everyone knew that Andy Barrett DeWitt was most dangerous when she started swearing.

"I wrote about you and my mom and dad because . . . I wasn't so lonely then. I kept trying to call you but the FBI bugs the phones and I was hardly ever alone and then finally I got a chance." She looked at Andy. "You've never been alone and with muds all around. I really missed the Brethren, it helped to write."

"Did you write about Mrs. Smith?"

"I barely even remember Mrs. Smith."

"There's not a word about her in the diary?"

"I just want to go home and see my mother, Andy."

"I asked you a question."

"I might have drawn her picture, maybe. I don't remember. But I never would have written her name, and even if I did, it's not her real name; and there are a billion Smiths in this country. We can forget about the diary. The stuff I wrote was just to keep me from missing you guys so much. I didn't write anything important." She was talking too fast, and she was going to throw up if this didn't work.

Andy wasn't beautiful. At this moment she looked like an insect.

"You have five minutes."

As Callen stepped past her, Andy laid a hand on her shoulder. "Don't make me come after you." Her hand was heavy, as if she held a revolver in it. "I don't want to hurt any-one, but you know I will if I must. There's too much at stake here, Callen."

Liar. You want to murder me right now.

Callen took another step and as she did, her stomach surged and up came everything. At Andy's feet she vomited up tortillas and eggs and beans the color of dried blood.

"Jesus," Andy cried, jumping back. "What's the matter with you?"

Callen's throat stung and her eyes watered. She mumbled, "Mud food," and threw up again.

Andy looked at the mess on the pale blue carpet, at Callen and in the next moment burst into a full-throated laugh.

"You are incorrigible and I admit I have missed you." She handed her a towel from the dresser and watched, still smiling and chuckling to herself, as Callen wiped her mouth. "Go. You've got five minutes."

thirty-seven

Eli FOUND Cholly shoveling gravel into the ruts and pot-
holes in the dirt alley separating the barn from the vegetable and flower gardens. Over the heads of daisies and
tomato plants, red, white and blue flags marked the route of
the Ore-Mex Trail.

"This isn't your job, Cholly."

"Gotta work," Cholly said. "Feels like trouble."

Eli understood. "Are the men off the property?"

"Last of 'em left this morning with Isabelle and Callen."
Cholly lobbed gravel into a ten-inch furrow. "Isabelle got
back a half hour ago."

"Good."

"The men, they wanted to stay, Boss. You been good to
them; they say they owe you."

"They don't owe me anything. They earn their keep." He
laid his arm across Cholly's shoulder. "You go too, amigo.

Ixsky's gone up to help Myrrh, and you don't have to get messed up in this either."

Cholly shook his head. "Like I tol' Isabelle, I'm tellin' you; you gonna need help."

Eli did not disagree. The situation in which they had landed was so alien to his experience, he almost believed that someone had misread the evidence regarding the Brethren, and in the next five minutes or five hours it would be revealed that the group was no more dangerous than a troop of disgruntled Boy Scouts. Things like this didn't happen . . . But there he was wrong.

Every day ordinary men and women and their families found themselves in terrifying situations. Their nightmares became the murders and beatings and shoot-outs of the nightly news, and from there, the plots of his novels. He'd written books about people to whom the unthinkable happened, as if he had even a small notion of what it meant to fear for your home and those you loved.

After this weekend, if he survived it, he was through writing books to frighten people. There was too much real terror in the world already.

⌐

Isabelle was in the tack room cleaning up the last of the FBI's mess. It was something to do until the trouble began. Eli put his arms around her and held her close. Whatever happened, he wanted to remember how her body felt against his. He felt the pressure of tears against the roof of his mouth and let her go.

"I told her we'd come and get her when it was safe." Her calm amazed him. "She didn't fight me, Eli. She's ours now, not theirs."

"Maybe. I hope so. But that's not the point."

"It's the whole point."

"It's time for you to go too."

"Go?"

She was going to be difficult.

"I'm not going anywhere. I'm surprised you can even ask me to. This is my ranch; I've lived here all my life, and I'm not letting anyone run me off." She shoved her hip against an open cupboard door, its slam an explanation point. "Unless you come with me."

"I have to do this. If he comes, I have to be here." To protect the ranch. To see Darren. His right hand made a fist so tight the fingers cramped.

"Eli, guilt isn't an exclusive club. We all have things we regret doing and not doing. When you left Darren—"

"I left him twice."

"And so you're the worst person in the world, and you have to stick around and die to prove it? Is that how bad you are? Too bad to live?" She touched his face. "This guilt about Darren . . . it's held you hostage for as long as I've known you."

There was a saying Eli recalled from the psychobabbling eighties: Understanding is the booby prize.

"I've always thought that you write scary books because the fear you make up in your imagination is so much easier to take than the real stuff. If you focus on serial killers and child molesters, you don't have to think about what kind of man abandons his brother."

Hearing the truth spoken in the voice he loved more than any other, Eli almost walked away.

"You tell me you want to write a straight-out, serious book about a man and his life. You can't do that, Eli. You're like the people in your books: trapped in a nightmare."

And tied up by guilt, she could have added that. Isabelle was right, and he had resolved not to run from the truth anymore.

"I know I have to let it go, and I'm ready. But if Darren comes for Callen, I have to be here. Seeing him again . . . It's the last step."

thirty-eight

DURING THE night, moving from the cover of one large boulder to another, Darren had worked himself to within fifty feet of the house. Since the departure of the group on horseback, he had seen no one. He remembered the small figure swinging confidently into the saddle and felt a flutter of doubt behind his ribs. Callen could not have been taught horseback riding unless she cooperated, and he knew his little fighter better than that. She was his daughter all the way and would not have cooperated with anyone. It pleased him to think of his daughter, a captive patriot standing firm in the principles of the True Word Brethren as he would have. But the silence around the ranch still bothered him, and to settle his mind he returned to the Fourteen Words, his lips moving as he spoke the oath in his mind.

He twitched and jerked, jabbing the small of his back against a rock. He had dozed off for a few moments but not for long; he didn't think the shadows had moved. He ate his last PowerBar and swallowed a pill with the last of his water; then he prayed again, thanking God for the cover provided by the huge rocks scattered everywhere, placed just so to enable him to approach the ranch unseen. He knew the Almighty would not have led him to the ranch and set out protection for him if Callen was not there.

Andy had warned there would be feds staked out on the property, but during the night he had seen no one. Coyotes had skulked at the corner of his vision, and though he thought he had heard another growl, it was only wind and shadows playing with his imagination.

Andy and Darren had kept their plan to take Callen as flexible as possible, but they had anticipated being in constant cell phone communication. They had counted on a good connection, which was something he was sure Edgar Barrett would not have done. He had warned Darren against relying on technology. He and Andy had planned to surprise Eli together. Right now Andy was somewhere waiting for his call, getting madder by the minute.

Maybe it was just as well he didn't have to talk to her. He was not sure what he'd tell her. The house and the ranch were so much bigger than either of them had supposed. Callen could be locked in the barn somewhere or back behind a hill surrounded by armed muds. She might not be on the property at all. Getting her away would be the smart thing to do. Shit, they could be in Europe. China even.

He had to get into the house to figure out what was happening. Until he knew, he and Andy were walking through a field of land mines. In the house there would be a regular phone. Maybe it would give him a clear line to Andy.

Until they talked, he was on his own.

⟶

He had a view of the house's back door, which opened onto a porch that seemed to go all the way around to the front. He could see part of a barn with an open door and a big truck.

Maybe he'd steal it.

A big man in jeans and boots stepped from the barn with a woman walking beside him. Darren had not seen them enter the barn and realized that they had probably gone in when he dozed off. Had he missed anything else? To guarantee he didn't fall asleep again, he slipped another pill into his mouth and focused his binoculars, recognizing his brother immediately. He looked strong and moved with confidence, like a man who knew what he was doing and knew that he was good at it. His tanned skin had lines around the mouth, and behind his dark glasses there were probably crow's feet cornering his eyes.

Eli was the spit of their mother, a 'skin through and through.

The couple disappeared from sight, and Darren took the opportunity to dart closer to the house. The Feebs might be inside, gunned up and waiting to ambush him. He might not live another three minutes. But he didn't think they were around, and where the law was concerned he trusted his intuition. What did worry him was working without a plan.

Edgar would tell him to stop and think the situation through. He didn't have time to stop. The FBI could be right over the hill, loading up.

He had to get into the house.

He darted from behind an Indian hawthorn bush up onto the porch. Beside a screen door he pressed his back against the house, his Cougar out and ready. An old shepherd dog came around the porch and stood a few feet away from him, staring and barking. Its eyes had the flat bluish look of cataracts. He relaxed a little.

A woman's voice inside the house told the dog she was coming and to pipe down. Darren heard the click of a dead bolt, and she opened the door, giving him a glimpse of blue-black hair.

"Come inside, Zack. It's dangerous—"

Darren grabbed her from behind and clamped his hand over her mouth.

thirty-nine

CALLEN SAT on the tree house floor trying to figure out her next move. She knew what she *should* do, which was to go to the house and warn Isabelle and Eli. She had left Sunny Hill with the intention of doing that, but by now Andy knew she'd been tricked. Callen was hot and furious, and she had never been so scared in her whole life. It would take a herd of rattlesnakes to drive her back to the house.

From a metal box secured with a combination lock, she took a Ziploc bag of trail mix. The raisins and berries were juicy, but the nuts and cereal tasted stale as dirt. She lay back on the floor of the tree house and stared up into the oak tree.

She was back where she'd been the day before, examining her options. Except that now the threat was real. Callen had tricked Andy, who would now be coming after her.

She could go find the FBI, but she didn't trust them. And besides, she didn't have a clue where they were or how they looked. Wandering around Bone Lake would waste precious time.

She had money in her bedroom, maybe fifty dollars, but Andy and whoever she'd brought with her were probably watching the house.

One time when she and Eli were in Jamul, she had seen a church. She could hitch a ride to Jamul, and if she sat in the church and refused to go outside, even the police could not walk in and arrest her. Being safe in a church was some kind of religious law that everyone in the world had to follow. The preacher would ask her name; and she could pretend to have amnesia. Did people with amnesia forget basic things like how to open a door or flush a toilet? Would she have to stand in the police station and pee her pants to convince them she'd lost her memory? Maybe amnesiacs even forgot how to talk, how to breathe. She didn't know cat scat about amnesia.

A gust of dusty wind brought down a flurry of dry oak leaves that clicked like dice thrown down on the tree house floor. She dragged a sweatshirt out of a plastic storage box and pulled it on, thinking as she did so that it was cool for April. Maybe this was that global warming thing Eli had told her about, and from now on all the seasons would be mixed up; it might even start snowing in Bone Lake. Andy said ZOG scientists made it up to scare people.

Clouds dulled the morning's blue sky, the kind of high, thin clouds Eli called cirrus. He loved words—for clouds and plants and rocks; everything had a word to go with it, and Eli knew them all. He probably knew all about amnesia, and if he didn't, he'd find a book and help her look it up.

If she ran away, she'd never read all the books on the great room shelves.

It would be good if she could live in the tree house and sneak into the house at night to snitch books. This thought was a great relief after imagining herself killed by Andy or standing in a puddle of pee pretending to have amnesia. She spent time considering where and how she would get supplies and what she could do to make the tree house more comfortable. She might steal a tarp to make a roof. She thought of herself snuggled inside the down sleeping bag she would steal from someone camped out to study the Kumeyaay artifacts at Bone Lake. She would make instant cocoa and read books by candlelight.

A blue Steller's jay startled her as it swooped through the clearing between the oaks, making a loud scratchy noise telling Callen to stop daydreaming. The Brethren would never stop looking for her. They had to find her because she could identify Mrs. Smith and ruin all their plans.

She'd steal a horse—she'd steal Sweet Pea—and ride over the border into Mexico. She would take Bear too. This was a real plan, not a daydream. She knew immediately that it would work.

Sweet Pea's corral was far from the house and barn, so she'd be easy to take. She'd have to be careful getting Bear, but he knew her and would cooperate if she took her time.

The ranch office was across from his corral, and just a few days ago she had seen Isabelle give Cholly money from the tin cash box in the big desk. There had been a lot of green in that box.

The plan was coming together as if it was meant to happen.

She filled her pockets and her backpack with a few things she might need, like the energy bars she had nicked from the pantry and the knife she'd taken from Jubal Spry's tool shack. The revolver fitted snugly at the waistband of her jeans and gave her confidence even if it wasn't real.

On a rise overlooking the ranch, she crouched behind a lemonade berry bush and surveyed the scene. Below her, where it crossed the ranch property, the Ore-Mex Trail was lined with signs and patriotic flags flapping in the wind. There were no runners in sight—it was still too early—but a crowd of kids in bright green Ore-Mex T-shirts sat on folding chairs at the water stop. Myrrh had said the winner would cross the finish line sometime in the afternoon.

The barn and stables appeared deserted, and there was no sign of a second vehicle in the ranch yard. Andy was too smart to park in the open. She would have left her car down the driveway and crept up on the house. The door to the ranch office was closed, but Eli and Isabelle were trusting and never locked it during the day.

She made her way down the hill, slipping on the scree, dashing from rock to bush where the ground was flat. She crossed the trail and reached the first of the corrals. A pair of miniature horses came to the fence and looked at her with their large and oddly human eyes. They were dusty, their manes knotted, and she felt them wanting her to groom them. Beyond their corral was Rotten Robert, who had bitten her hard when she'd tried to feed him a carrot. In the next enclosure Tina had a limp from some kind of fungus in her hoof; beside her, Kansas was sweet and tricky.

In the next corral Bear was down, lying on his right side, taking his regular afternoon sunbath. As she approached, she said his name softly and saw his ears prick and turn in her direction. She said his name again, and this time he lifted his head and rolled his eyes around to see her.

"Yo, Bear."

His ears moved but that was all.

"Bear? You okay?"

She opened the corral gate and went in. A pair of barn dogs appeared from somewhere and barked at her, lost interest and wandered off.

She gave Bear a gentle nudge with the toe of her shoe. "Hey, lazy, time to get up. You'll grow roots." She tugged smartly on his halter, but he barely stirred. She realized he was not taking a sunbath. "What is it, what's the matter?" She laid her hand on his forehead as if checking for a fever. He groaned.

A horse lying down, groaning and not able to get up easily: She'd read about this. The book said the first thing was to get it up and walking. Even a healthy horse should not stay down too long.

She looked around for ranch hands to help her, but of course they were in the mountains hiding until it was safe to come back to work.

He wore a rope halter; she tugged on this, and he seemed to want to oblige. He groaned and rolled his eyes and shifted his weight a little, then laid his head down, groaning again.

"Now," Callen half whispered fiercely. "You have to get up now."

The only horse sickness Callen could think of was colic, but what she knew about it was almost nothing, although she thought it might be similar to her own stomach pains—though much worse. The book said if a horse was healthy, a person could rest her ear against its stomach and hear strong, gurgling gut sounds. She heard a few sounds in Bear, but not many and definitely not loud. Colic could kill the youngest, strongest, healthiest horse if not attended to, and Bear was neither strong nor healthy. He needed a vet.

There was a phone in the office, a plain old black wall phone, and beside it a list of emergency telephone numbers, including the veterinarian's. Overhead the sun had moved beyond its zenith. She needed to raid the cash box and get off the ranch quickly. She'd have to ride Sweet Pea hard if she wanted to put distance between herself and the Brethren. Bear was sick; she couldn't take him with her.

But she couldn't leave him down. Things were crazy at the ranch, and by the time someone noticed him, he'd be dead. Digging in her heels, she dragged on the halter rope. He was young and bony but still heavier than anything she'd ever tried to move. She got behind him and strained to raise his rump, but she might as well have tried to move a gunny-sack full of bones.

She knelt in the dirt and pressed her face into his long neck. "Don't die," she whispered. "I'll get help. I'll do it."

forty

FOR TWO or three seconds Eli was mesmerized by the sight of his brother suddenly there in the great room, his gun pressed into Isabelle's side. Darren had been in his late teens the last time Eli had seen him, five feet eight or nine and scrawny, with a soft, pouty mouth and a saddle blanket of rusty freckles across his nose and cheeks. Almost twenty years later, his face hadn't changed much, but it was obvious he'd spent a lot of time lifting weights, and his arms and neck were covered with black ink jailhouse tattoos. Most noticeable was a nickel-sized Iron Cross on his cheekbone below his left eye. His weight lifter's body stretched the fabric of his camp shirt over his shoulders and across his back, and the rolled sleeves revealed biceps like softballs shoved under skin blackened by ink.

The sight of Darren standing in the great room with a gun jammed into Isabelle's life organs was a reality no amount of planning and anticipation could have prepared him for. Several seconds passed as he struggled against his emotions, the predictable ones like rage and fear and love as well as some he had not expected, some that blindsided him: anguish, pity.

"Put the gun away. You don't need that."

"You always did think I was a dumb shit, Eli. If I put my gun down, that beaner over there," he gestured toward Cholly, who stood to one side of the front door with his head down and his arms folded across his chest, "he's gonna make some jerk-off move, and you'll jump in and then where'll I be?"

Behind Eli on a magnetic rack attached to the wall there were a dozen knives. He could grab one of them.

"Darren, we can work this out. We're brothers—"

"Shut the fuck up and do what I say."

Eli looked hard at Isabelle, hoping she could read his thoughts. She must not fight or move.

"Darren, she's never done anything to hurt you."

"Except breathe." He pointed at the two long couches that faced each other before the fireplace. "Sit at the end by the fireplace, mud woman. And I wanna be able to see your hands."

At Darren's direction Eli sat at the far end of one couch, Isabelle at the other. Cholly sat on the second couch, facing them.

"Where's the phone?"

Eli pointed to the wall near the laundry room door.

Darren backed toward it and lifted the receiver. He hung up almost immediately. "It's got a bug on it, right? You want me to call out so the feds'll know I'm here."

Chewing his lip, he paced and played his gun between his hands. He removed a cell phone from his shirt pocket and opened and quickly closed it. He chewed his lip and glanced from his watch to the clock on the wall near the foot of the stairs.

Something's wrong, Eli thought. Despite his bravado, Darren was unsure of himself.

"Where's Callen?"

"Gone," Isabelle said. This was the answer they had planned to give.

"Did I ask you, bitch?"

"She ran away," Eli said.

"You're a fuckin' liar."

A drop of sweat ran down Eli's side. "Could we open a window," he asked. "Or turn on the air?"

Darren looked at him as if he did not understand.

"I'm just saying it'd be more comfortable—"

"I don't give a rat's fat fanny if you're comfortable or not."

Anger burst from Darren like the flare of a safety match, and Eli knew his brother was waiting for an excuse to kill them.

"You never cared if I was comfortable before. You want me to believe you been worrying about me for the last—how long is it? Fifteen, twenty years? You'd sooner I was dead. Right? Like Mom. You know how she passed? Drunk, with her nose in her own puke."

Eli was not surprised, but it hurt to hear it and that *did* surprise him.

"Big rich writer." He spat on the hardwood floor. "Me and Mom, we coulda starved for all you cared."

"I came back for you."

Darren's honking laughter scaled a half octave and filled the great room. "Jesus, you were lame, talking like you'd been all over the world and we were supposed to be impressed. You coulda begged me, but I'd still never of gone with you."

"Darren, what I did, leaving you—twice—I've been sorry for it all my life." Eli moved to the edge of the leather cushion, resting his forearms on his knees. "But if you're here now, because of that—"

"Shit, I forgot about that a long time ago. You're just another race traitor to me, big bro. No better'n these muds." Darren stood behind Cholly and placed the barrel of his gun to his head. "Bang-bang."

Isabelle sobbed, and he laughed and stepped away.

In the midst of fear and incredible, immobilizing tension, Eli had a moment of clarity. He understood what Isabelle had been clear about all along. Over the course of Darren's life there had been hundreds of occasions when he chose to be angry, to hate and to kill. And it was those choices that had made him who he was now. Eli was willing to live with regret and a portion of guilt, but from that moment he gave up responsibility for the man his brother had become.

A cell phone vibrated noisily. Darren dug in his shirt pocket and fumbled with the flip top.

"At the ranch," he said after a moment. "I said, 'the

ranch . . .' I know you did, I know, but—Wild Horse Road."
Darren shook the phone and slammed it down on the breakfast bar. "Piece of crap."

Darren looked at Eli and grinned broadly. "Trouble's
coming now. You can about count on it."

forty-one

IN THE ranch office Callen dialed the number of Dr. Blank, the veterinarian. He answered on the second ring.

"It's Bear. He's down, and I think he's got colic."

"Wait a minute, who's this?"

"Callen. At Pasatiempo."

"Put Isabelle or Eli on the phone."

"I can't. They're not here."

There was a dry, thoughtful pause on Dr. Blank's end, and for a second Callen thought she'd lost him.

"You've got to come. He's going to die."

"What's happening up there? Where is everyone? At the race?"

"It's just me."

"Well, get him up, walk him. Cholly—"

"He's not here either."

She had begun to cry again. "I can't get him up, and his gut sounds—he doesn't have any."

She heard him mutter disgustedly.

"Just come, just come right away," she begged. "You've got to come before it's too late."

She hung up the phone and opened the desk drawer and pulled out the flat metal strong box. She was crying hard now, not even trying to stop. The box held a checkbook and a scattering of change, less than a dollar. Callen stared into the empty space and, suddenly furious, threw the box across the office, where it hit the printer and bounced to the floor.

She had to have money, and the longer she stuck around Pasatiempo, the more likely it was that Andy or someone else would find her. She had to leave Bear and trust that Dr. Blank would get to him in time.

In his corral she knelt in the soft dirt beside his head. "I called the doc. He's on his way." Again she pressed her ear against his side and listened for sounds. Not much, not enough. The harder she listened, the less sure she was of what she was hearing. Maybe just the faint gurgle of her hope. She moved her hands over his hard, taut belly, hoping her touch might relax him and loosen whatever had tied up his insides. Had she given him too much mash, or was it the wrong kind of food altogether, or should she have mixed a thinner gruel? Or thicker? Had he drunk enough water? She tried to lift his head into her lap. He looked at her through a veil of dark eyelashes.

Help him, and I promise I'll be good, God. I'll be the best girl in the world.

Good like the Brethren or good like Barbara or Eli and Isabelle? She didn't know, but she would find out and she would be it. Sobs bruised her throat, and her tears wet the colt's forelock. His eyes rolled and he sighed.

"Hang on, Bear, hang on."

With a cool wind swirling dust and grit up around her and mixing in muddy streaks on her wet face, she picked up her pack and left the corral.

forty-two

THE SOUND of barking dogs penetrated Zacky's deafness. He had been asleep on the kitchen floor and got up to pad over to Isabelle. He laid his head on her knee.

Darren said, "Get rid of the dog."

"He can't hurt you," Isabelle said. "Half his teeth are gone."

Darren grunted.

"Anyway, he's a watchdog and there's something wrong outside. Let me go check. We've had a lion around. Sometimes they come in close."

"Jesus." Darren looked at his watch.

"Let me go—please. I've got a pair of miniature horses. They can't defend—"

"You're not going anywhere, mud."

"They might be barking at the runners. If the officials have to stop the race, someone'll come and—"

"I'll be your hostage," Eli said. "If she's not back—"

"Sit down and tell me where Callen is."

"We lied to you. We really sent her to Arizona." Isabelle said it exactly as they'd planned, even to the lie. "After she called the second time."

"Fucking—"

At that moment a white Toyota 4Runner sped into the yard and slammed to a stop in front of the house. A woman got out and ran across the gravel, leaving the door open. Eli felt the band of the panic button tighten on his wrist.

"Now the shit's gonna hit the fan," Darren said. "You guys don't know trouble till you know Andy."

If Eli pressed the button now, and Billy Horne and his agents roared up the road with their weapons drawn, Andy and Darren would take them hostage. A siege and a shoot-out would be inevitable. Anyone familiar with recent history knew that. Eli could not take the chance.

Andy Barrett wore jeans, a flannel shirt and heavy boots. Thick silver blond hair dropped straight as rain to her shoulders. She looked like a Wagnerian heroine, a tall solid woman with hands the size of a man's.

She kicked Eli's ankle with the metal toe of her boot. "You're the uncle? The writer? Where is she?"

"Arizona."

"You're a frigging liar. She was up at the nudie place. I talked to her."

Eli's heart sank. Sunny Hills had seemed like the last place on earth one of the True Word Brethren would hide out. Too late he remembered Billy telling him not to underestimate them.

"Where is she now?" Andy stepped between the couches and kneed Zacky away from Isabelle. Grabbing the dog by the collar, she lifted his front legs off the ground, resting her gun against his throat. Isabelle surged forward. Andy dropped Zacky and hit her across the jaw with the butt of her .45. Isabelle fell back, stunned, Zacky whimpering at her feet.

Eli jumped to his feet. Darren stopped him, grabbing his wrist.

"What's this?" Darren held Eli's arm up. "Andy, you ever seen a watch like this?"

⬅

Callen approached the house from the side, detouring behind Ixsky and Cholly's bungalow to avoid crossing the yard. A white 4Runner she did not recognize was parked in front of the house. It might be Andy's, or maybe the FBI was in the house waiting in ambush. It didn't matter who it was, she was going into the house because the cash box in the ranch office was empty; she and Sweet Pea wouldn't last a week in Mexico without money. At the foot of the pepper tree she looked up and was relieved to see that her bedroom window was open, just as she had left it. The screen was easy to slip out, and she'd climbed the tree a dozen times. She dug her shoes into the rough barked trunk and groped her way up to the first limb. In less than a minute she was standing in her bedroom.

She tiptoed to the door and opened it a crack, looking up and down the hall, making sure she had the upstairs to herself. She wondered what was going on below in the great room; but she had no time to investigate.

From the bookcase she withdrew the one-volume *Columbia Encyclopedia* she had hollowed out to make a bank her uncle would never discover.

She slipped off her backpack and sat on the bed to count her money. It felt so good to get the weight off her shoulders, she decided she could do without it. All she really needed was the knife she had sharpened to a scalpel's edge and the homemade revolver. If she got in trouble across the border, she might need weapons. At a distance the gun would discourage unwanted visitors. Up close she could use the knife if she had to.

There was not as much in the bank as she'd remembered, maybe thirty dollars and a lot of change. She hoped she could feed herself on the small amount and that she would find grass for Sweet Pea. She shoved the bills and coins into a pocket and the gun and knife into her jacket and walked to the window. She was about to scoot out and onto the limb of the pepper tree when she heard Isabelle scream. She froze where she stood.

She couldn't leave without knowing if Isabelle was okay.

She opened the bedroom door and took a big step across the creaky hardwood floor onto the thick, runner carpet that stretched from one end of the hall to the stairs going down to the great room.

At the head of the stairs she stopped and drew the gun from her pocket. She held it as her father had taught her to hold a real gun, in her right hand, arm slightly bent and supported by her left. Even so, her hand was shaking by the time she got to the landing. She heard arguing and recognized Andy's voice. And Eli's. And Darren's. She dropped her gun and it clattered down the stairs, breaking into several pieces.

forty-three

DOWN ON the county road Billy Horne sat behind the wheel of a late-model domestic sedan parked at a wide spot opposite the turnoff for Wild Horse Road.

Maybe the Brethren were already in Bone Lake, maybe holed up at the motel like ordinary race fans. They might be up at the ranch right now, and any minute he'd hear the panic button go off and the waiting would be over. There would only be two or three of them, four at the outside. The Brethren kept their operations small. It was in the Manifesto.

Billy had read the Manifesto online. The Brethren's social and political philosophy was on the Web, available to anyone; but the actual Manifesto, the group's leadership structure, names and faces and long-term plans, how they networked with other cadres and with supporters who lived in the mainstream—all that remained a mystery.

Mrs. Smith was a mystery.

A few minutes earlier he'd sent two agents cross-country on foot to take up a position where they could see the ranch. They had orders not to get too close without an order from him. It was critical that the FBI hold back as long as it could.

Without Callen's insider information, the government had no case against the Brethren. They could not prove they had murdered Singh and Barbara. Without Callen, the most Andy or anyone else might get was a year in the county jail for trespassing, a little more for flashing their guns around. In jail, where Edgar Barrett was a neo-Nazi hero, they would be celebrities. Horne's men had orders to do nothing until the Brethren had done some damage with real time behind it.

He had been working this case for a long time, and he wanted to be done with it. It stuck in his throat like a bit of rancid beef, strangling the humanity out of him.

He had put Eli and his family in terrible, unconscionable danger. It would be his fault, his alone, if the job went south. Even if, in the end, he discovered the true identity of Mrs. Smith and she was apprehended and brought to justice, he would not forgive himself. Superiors would tell him that the war against terrorism involved losses that were unavoidable. He would tell them that Edgar Barrett had said the same thing about the war against ZOG.

In this business the good guys and the bad were often no more than opposite sides of the same coin.

◄━

Traffic was still heavy into Bone Lake, but no one had turned up on Wild Horse Road since early that morning when they had stopped a mean old guy with three pit bulls in the truck bed. Jubal Spry was hot as Mexican chili about the race and the traffic and pretty much everything in the world including lions. Billy had concluded he was too crazy to worry about.

By midafternoon the wind was blowing, and the sun was mustard colored behind a haze of gritty air. He didn't envy the Ore-Mex runners breathing half oxygen, half dust.

"Hey, Bill."

The sound of his partner's voice startled him.

"Heads up."

A white truck with a pair of large lockboxes on the back slowed to make the turn up Wild Horse Road. The lettering on the door of the truck read BONE LAKE VETERINARY SERVICES with a name and telephone number.

Billy burped the siren and swung his arm out the window to set the light on the roof. The truck drove fifty feet up the road and pulled to the shoulder. Billy nosed onto the shoulder just in front of it. He got out of the Ford and walked back.

"Exit your vehicle, please."

"What's this all about?" The man in the driver's seat wore a Padres' baseball cap and a pair of wire-rimmed glasses that magnified his pale eyes.

"Exit your vehicle, please, sir."

He stepped out, rubbing his palms on the top of his chinos. "Are you a cop? Security?"

Horne flashed his ID.

The man looked impressed "What're you guys doing here?"

"Now you show us yours."

Eager to cooperate, the driver pulled out his wallet and removed his California driver's license and several other cards as well.

Apparently this was Marcus Blank, DVM. Office in Bone Lake.

"I haven't done anything wrong, Officer. Agent." He looked at Horne's partner, who stood to one side observing. "Have I?"

"Just tell us where you're going."

"Sure, no problem." He smiled nervously. "Ranch up the road called me. They've got a horse down."

"Which ranch?"

"Pasatiempo."

Sweat prickled in Horne's armpits.

"Eli and Isabelle aren't in trouble are they?"

"Who called you, Dr. Blank?"

"There's a girl staying with them. She's got a colt down with colic."

"You sure it was the kid?"

"She said Eli and Isabelle were gone—"

"Gone where?"

"What's this all about, Agent? I've never had any trouble with these people. I've known the Brownes for—"

"This kid, you're sure it was her?"

"She sounded like a kid. She told me her name. And she was awfully upset."

It was time to be a good guy, the real thing.

forty-four

DADDY!"
Callen ran across the great room and into her father's arms, knocking him back against the breakfast counter. "They told me you died, but you're alive!"

No one said anything. Callen looked around and the scene in the great room clicked into focus. Cholly sat on one couch with his hands dangling between his legs, apparently half asleep. Isabelle lay against the cushions holding her face in her hands. Eli sat at the end of the couch nearest Callen, and she could feel his tension like an electric current.

"Where's Mom?"

Darren looked at Andy.

"Daddy?"

"She's dead," Eli said.

"But, Daddy—"

"The Brethren killed her. He was part of it."

"Don't listen to him," Andy said. "It's like I told you; she's up in Codyville."

Darren's face had gone a pasty white, and the Iron Cross under his eye seemed larger and darker than before. And he smelled of sweat. The last time he'd gone on assignment he came back smelling the same; he took long showers, but for a week the stink on his skin was like what she smelled now. Nerves, Barbara had said.

"It's true. She's dead, Cal."

"Blame ZOG," Andy spoke too fast. "If the feds had stayed out of our business, your mother'd be alive right now and you'd be home with her in Codyville."

"You said she was in Codyville."

"I didn't want to upset you any more than you already were. I didn't think you were ready for the truth, but you might as well know it. The FBI turned her and then when they'd got what they wanted, they killed her to shut her up. That's how ZOG works."

Eli spoke softly. "Use your head, Callen."

She looked from Andy to her father to Eli and did not know whom to believe, so she decided to believe no one. Whatever the truth was, she would have to figure it out for herself.

A drop of sweat, resting like a diamond, trembled at the center of Darren's Iron Cross tattoo.

"You can't trust anyone except the Brethren." Andy

walked from window to window, closing the blinds and filling the room with deep shadow. "You're a child of Adam, Callen. You're Aryan, like me. We are God's chosen people."

Callen thought about this god who hated everyone but fair-skinned northern Europeans. She wondered why this god had declared that Andy should possess a soul and not Isabelle, her father or Cholly. She thought of Bear and her tree house and all the dozens of books and movies she had read and seen since coming to Pasatiempo. She remembered the first time Isabelle helped her into the saddle and showed her how to hold the reins and Eli's patient lectures about animals and plants and the million words he knew and used and didn't mind explaining. She thought about what made sense and what didn't.

"I'm not an Aryan. I'm a mud."

"Let's get outta here, Andy, get on the road before anything else—"

"What're you talking about?"

"She's crazy," Darren said, out of breath. "Like Barbara."

Callen pressed her palms against her chest, feeling pain behind her ribs as if she were breaking, a hairline crack, extending, splitting, branching, widening. "My grandmother was an Indian."

"Barbara's mother? Why didn't I know that, Darren?"

"My mother," Eli said. "Mine and Darren's."

"You fucking liar!" Snarling, Darren yanked Eli up off the couch and slammed him back against the stone fireplace.

Eli's hand closed around a poker. He turned, bringing his arm up and then down at an angle, striking Darren at the waist and knocking him over. The gun fell from his hand and landed at Cholly's feet. Cholly lurched for it and Andy shot him.

forty-five

CHOLLY LAY across the couch opposite Isabelle. She couldn't see where he'd been hit, but judging by the blood, it seemed to be the right side of his body and fairly high up. Eli had torn off his shirt and was using it to create a makeshift bandage. When he'd done what he could, he sat beside Isabelle and took her hand. No one seemed to care that they were no longer in their assigned seats. Andy's blow had broken Isabelle's jaw, but if she supported her face in her hand, the clouds of pain parted a little and she could think. That's what she had to do: think.

She heard a car.

Andy whispered to Callen to lock the door. She told Eli, "One word, one sound out of you, and I'll kill the mud woman."

Isabelle squeezed her eyes shut and drew her feet up onto the couch, wrapping her arms around her bent legs, supporting her jaw on her knees. She wanted to be quiet, but every breath was a little cry of fear and pain she could not control.

"It's the vet," Callen said.

What was Marcus Blank doing at the ranch a week before his regular appointment?

"I called him."

Andy grabbed Callen and pulled her behind the breakfast bar, catching her neck in the crook of her elbow. "You do what I tell you, you'll get out of here with your red skin on."

"You killed my mother."

"Shut up or I'll break your neck now instead of later."

"I don't like this, Andy, I don't like it," Darren muttered, jerking up and down on his toes. He held his retrieved gun in one hand and rubbed his side with the other. "We can go out the back door; there's plenty cover."

"Shut up and let me think."

"Listen to me, Andy, I know this country. I was here all last night. We can go overland. Hike outta here. Take her with us. She's just a kid."

"And you're a mud."

Callen spoke to Isabelle, her expression miserable. "I called Dr. Blank on account of Bear."

Darren said, "You have bears on this ranch? Bears and mountain lions?"

Andy tightened the pressure against Callen's throat. Isabelle saw her wince and her eyes grow wide.

"You did the right thing," Eli said.

Isabelle knew immediately that the footsteps on the porch did not belong to Marcus Blank. He was an excellent veterinarian but a vain man and inordinately proud of the custom-made, hand-tooled, high-heeled boots he had made in Taos. The man at the door wore city shoes. She risked a look at Eli, but his expressionless face revealed nothing.

"Eli? Isabelle? You in there? You got a problem with your horse?"

The voice was Billy Horne's. He shook the doorknob, waited a moment and then walked away, back down the veranda stairs.

"That's a cop," Darren told Andy. "You better believe me. He doesn't talk like a rancher."

Andy looked at him.

He said, "We gotta move. Fast."

Pulling Callen with her, Andy moved to the window and cracked a slat of blind. "It's a vet truck. There's two men."

"Two cops. Jesus, Andy, what're we waiting for?"

Eli said, "Blank always brings an assistant."

Andy watched the men for another moment. "They've gone behind the barn."

"To see Bear," Callen said.

"Are we going, or are we going to throw down our guns and surrender because if we—"

"You're right," Andy said. "I'm taking Callen."

"What about me?" Darren asked.

Andy looked him up and down. "You're a mud."

"You believe that story?" he asked. "You believe him?" He stepped toward Andy, and Isabelle thought she saw her flinch. "I'm as good a soldier as you. Better. In Olympia—"

"Shut up, Darren."

"And Sacramento—"

"Not another word." Her pistol pointed at Darren's chest.

"You don't scare me." Nevertheless, he took a step back and adopted a more reasoned tone. "So what if I'm a breed? The Manifesto says the Brethren have to be adaptable. It says that's how we survive, by adapting to conditions. What do you care if my old lady was a 'skin? I look pure-blood; no one's going to know unless you tell 'em, and I fight the fight as good as anyone. You know I do. Plus I've got a skill you need, Andy. Don't forget that. There's nobody else can do what I can. Your father called it a talent."

Isabelle watched Andy weigh Darren's argument.

"I'm still taking Callen with me."

"She's my daughter."

"As long as I've got her, they won't shoot me. We'll meet up back at the safe house."

"You're not thinking straight, Andy. Wherever you go, they'll be on your tail." Darren thought a moment. "Here's what you do. Take the woman; keep a gun to her head. You'll still have your hostage. At the same time, I'll take Callen out the back and go overland."

"What about him?"

"We don't need him," Darren said. "Or the beaner. I'll take care of them both."

forty-six

I N   T H E second of silence that followed Darren's words,
Callen heard music.

"What's that?" Andy tightened her arm. Callen saw
stars and knew that if Andy's neck hold squeezed her throat
again, she might pass out. "Where's that music coming
from?"

"The race," Eli said.

Callen recognized "The Stars and Stripes Forever."

"But where's it coming from?"

"The trail runs through the property on the other side of
the barn. Sounds like they might be detouring through the
ranch."

Callen expected Andy to be angry, but the pressure on
her windpipe eased; when she spoke again, she sounded
pleased. "That's good. That'll work. The more confusion, the
better."

Darren stepped to the couch and jerked Isabelle to

her feet. Callen saw her bite down on her lip and sob as he thrust her toward Andy. "Take her," he said. "Give me my daughter."

"No. She's going with me. Like I said, we'll meet up."

Darren's face was terrible when he was angry. Callen remembered how fast he could pull back his arm and hit with the heel of his hand. He shoved Isabelle away, and she fell against the arm of the couch, crying in pain.

"You son of a bitch," Eli dropped to the floor, taking Isabelle in his arms. Cholly groaned.

Andy ignored them. "Trust me on this, Darren. I know what I'm doing."

"You're going to let me swing."

"I'd never do that. You're the soldier I depend on. You think I trust Sarge and Ansel, those doofuses? I need you, like you said. I need your loyalty and your talent, and I don't care about . . . the other thing."

Callen recognized the self-important swagger of Darren's shoulders as he shifted his weight. Now, when he felt sure of himself but was still angry, he was most dangerous.

Andy shoved the muzzle of her gun into Callen's waist and spoke into her ear. "We've only got a couple of seconds to do this, so listen up. You and me are going to walk outside. Maybe the vet or whoever he is, he's watching us, maybe not; it doesn't matter because we're not gonna stick around, and he's not going to do anything so long as I've got this gun. And what you'll do is cooperate all the way. If you don't, at the first sign of trouble—you listening, Darren?—your father's gonna start shooting. First the mud woman and then him, your uncle."

"It'll be a pleasure," Darren said.

"We're going out the door and down the steps, and you're getting into the front seat of that white 4Runner, then down on the floor. If you make a break for it . . ." She jerked Callen's head around so they were looking at each other. In the dim light the blue of her eyes had turned as gray as concrete. "I've got nothing to lose at this point, Callen. You're smart. You get that, right?"

Darren said, "Soon as you're out the door I'll set fire to the place." He took a lighter from his shirt pocket and flicked it. He held it up so Eli and Isabelle could see the flame. "All this wood, it'll go up like a bonfire." He looked at Andy again. "We'll meet up at the safe house, right?"

Andy didn't answer him. She had shoved Callen onto the veranda. A pair of nondescript dogs barreled around the corner of the barn and across the yard and stood at the foot of the stairs, barking at them.

"You know their names? Say their names. Tell 'em to shut up."

"Mamie, Sedge. Shut up."

Callen's voice trembled but not because she was afraid of the dogs. If the FBI rushed them, Darren would shoot Isabelle, and Andy would put a bullet in her side where the gun point bored into her. Eli would go next. She tried to walk, but her knees were jelly. Andy jabbed the gun hard; Callen misstepped and stumbled down the last veranda stair into the dusty yard. Andy wrenched her up by the back of her shirt and pulled her to her feet at the same moment a half dozen cars and vans roared up the driveway and jammed to a stop in the yard, nosed toward the house and the 4Runner. Men and women in blue FBI jackets jumped from the vehicles and took positions, their weapons aimed at Andy and Callen.

A megaphone voice demanded, "Drop your weapon and let the girl go."

"I'll kill her," Andy yelled. "I swear I'll do it."

More softly she said, "They don't know the True Word Brethren, do they? They don't know a soldier of the True Word will give her life for the Fourteen Words."

Not me, Callen thought.

Billy Horne stepped out from the side of the barn with his gun drawn. "There's nowhere to run, Andy. Let the girl go."

"I'll kill you," Andy told Callen. "They'll kill me. We'll all go down together, and they'll never find out what they want to know. Sarge'll take over, and the Brethren will be good as new."

Horne looked behind him, yelled something once and then again. He was still yelling, but Callen couldn't hear his words over the blare of a Sousa march. A square white van with broadcast equipment on the roof came around the corner of the barn accompanied by a phalanx of security officers on mountain bikes. Billy Horne ran along beside, yelling at the driver.

"Now," Andy said and shoved Callen toward the 4Runner. Callen hooked her toe behind her ankle and stumbled again.

As she did, she drew the knife she had brought from the tree house and jammed it with all her strength into the only part of Andy she could get to. The blade went into the back of her knee half way to the hilt and Andy hit the ground screaming.

With the blinds drawn, Isabelle had no idea what was going on in the ranch yard. She glanced at Darren and saw him blink away the sweat stinging his eyes. At any minute he was going to put a bullet through Eli's head. She thought about her father and hoped that heaven was real. And then there was music, a march, and she was too much in pain to understand what was happening.

"They diverted the race," Eli said.

She wanted to laugh and then she heard a scream. Darren looked toward the sound. She staggered to the window. In the second before Darren grabbed her, she saw a crowd streaming into the ranch yard. She saw FBI windbreakers, a van with a satellite dish on its roof. In the middle of this she glimpsed a thin and exhausted and obviously confused black man in sweat-drenched shorts staggering forward. Callen and Andy lay on the ground with FBI agents around them, guns drawn.

Darren grabbed her arm and jabbed his gun into her back. The pain in her jaw screamed and the rancid smell of his sweat filled her head. In the last few minutes his features seemed to have squeezed toward the center of his face, and a clot of foam had gathered at the corner of his mouth. He opened one of the blinds a few inches and looked out, muttering to himself.

More vehicles came from around the barn, sunlight flashing on chrome and glass, creating constellations of light. Blaring noise from the yard filled the great room as security personnel, coaches, fans and hangers-on talked and yelled at the same time. Isabelle counted five media trucks and vans and photographers and video cameras too. The crowd milled about, talking and gesturing and staring at something Isabelle couldn't see.

"Shit," Darren said and bit down hard on his lower lip.

The small black man continued to run painfully forward and out of Isabelle's line of sight.

Eli's voice was low and urgent. "You can see how this is going, Darren. You have one chance. For the next few minutes no one's going to be thinking about you and—"

"I didn't ask—"

"No one'll notice if you sneak out the back."

Darren touched his bleeding lip and looked at the red on his finger as if the blood belonged to someone else.

"Don't go back for your truck. They'll be waiting for you. Just cross behind the house and go south. You can get to Mexico."

"What are you talking about?"

"I'm telling you how to get out of this, Darren. If you go on foot, overland, they'll never find you, not in this wild country."

"Why should I believe—"

"You're my brother, Darren. I'm giving you a chance to start all over."

Outside the yelling and cheering grew louder and more confused.

Darren's breath was labored.

"I've got a thousand dollars in emergency cash I keep in the freezer. It's yours. Go get it and take off."

Darren couldn't seem to understand what his brother was saying.

"Look, I'll get it for you." Eli took a step and Darren squeezed the trigger. Isabelle's ears rang with the shot as she drove her shoulder up under his arm. She heard a whoof of surprise and the sound of his body hitting the breakfast bar. At the next moment she gave up, closed her eyes and passed out.

forty-seven

CALLEN SAT on a stool apart from the visitors in Eli's small hospital room. Isabelle sat on the edge of his bed and she never looked at Horne or at the electronic monitors. Her eyes were fixed on Eli, and Callen saw that she was holding his hand so tightly it would take a team of Clydesdales to part them. The doctor had wired her broken jaw, and her face from forehead to chin and cheek to cheek was turning a ripe, plum-purple. The doctor had pumped her full of painkillers, and cleared her to go home provided she did not talk until he gave her the go-ahead.

Billy Horne stood beside Eli's pillow. Callen listened as he explained the circumstances that had led to the closure of the Ore-Mex Trail the day of the race.

"That old guy, Jubal Spry, was standing in the middle of the trail yelling about mountain lions and pointing his shotgun around. And then your friend, Wim—he was riding in the front van with a couple of race officials—he decided on the spot to detour through Pasatiempo."

"What about the lions?" Eli asked.

"No sign of them. For all we know the old man was hallucinating."

Earlier the doctor had said that Eli's wound was superficial, and he would have an easy recovery. Cholly, knocked out on sedatives and painkillers and separated from Eli by a three-quarter circle of drawn curtain, was having a harder time. He had lost a lot of blood, and the bullet had shattered his collar bone and would require steel pins to hold it together.

Ixsky had no faith in modern medicine and refused to visit the hospital. Callen knew she was in the kitchen at Pasatiempo mixing up her own nauseating Mayan potions, and filling the house with horrible smells.

After her tussle with Andy, Callen's only injury was a scraped knee and a tear in her jeans. Andy and Darren had been taken away in handcuffs. Horne said they would be handed over to Homeland Security and might never see daylight again. Darren had killed a woman in the Olympia bombing, and the government would find a way to make the case against him. She wished her father had died with Barbara in the fire so she would not have to think of him as a murderer. Testifying against him would be the hardest thing she had ever done, but Agent Horne said she must do it. Her testimony was crucial to the case against the Brethren. He wanted her to remember everything she could about what went on in the basement in Codyville and told her to be prepared for attorneys and agents who would ask a thousand questions about the fire and the activities at Patriot Camp.

He had not said anything about Mrs. Smith, but she knew he would.

Half an hour earlier, Ixsky had called from the ranch to say that Dr. Blank had treated Bear, and now he was walking around as if nothing had happened to him. Callen envied him his quick recovery. She would never be happy or light or whole again. A part of her anatomy had shattered like Cholly's collar bone and would never mend. The space left behind was full of pain no medication could take away.

"Callen?" Agent Horne stood a foot from her.

She stared at the vinyl tile floor, preparing herself.

"I'm going to need to talk to you."

"Give her a break, Billy," Eli said from the bed.

"About the woman you met in Shasta City."

"Billy, not now." Eli sounded old and creaky and about ready to give up on the whole idea of talking. "Give her time."

When Callen closed her eyes, she saw Mrs. Smith clearly. The cold eyes and the queenly way she held herself, as if she expected Callen to fall down and kiss her feet. She remembered the pale blue of her eyes, the taut skin around her eyes, and her hair done up in silly ringlets.

Isabelle left Eli and stood by Callen with her arm around her. She smelled like antiseptic, but her body was familiar and comforting. Another time Callen would let herself remember the feel of Barbara's arms around her and the rosemary scent of her hair.

Mrs. Smith's image faded. In its place she saw her mother; she was in heaven. In Callen's imagination heaven was a place of green fields and lakes and blue sky and horses running free while angels strolled about like ordinary people. The people in Callen's heaven did not mind that they were dead. But she knew a daydream when she had one.

When you were dead, you were dead; you didn't smile down on the living. You didn't talk to them.

She had spent her life being trained by the Brethren to make choices based on a set of black-and-white rules and beliefs. The most important of these was the one that said loyalty to the Brethren was the same as loyalty to God. Now Horne wanted her to break through years of indoctrination and ignore the bonds of loyalty that connected her to people she had known all her life. Buddy and Sarge and even Marilu and her lame school and the giggly girls who were afraid of their own shadows. She had studied with these people, feasted with them and learned from them. They had gone to Patriot Camp together. Now she had the power to break up their families, destroy the unity that made the Brethren feel like a family. It was a terrible thing Horne asked of her.

Talk to Horne. Tell him what he wants to know.

She imagined Barbara's voice and her breath on the shell of her ear.

Sighing, she stepped away from Isabelle and stood by herself, facing Horne.

"The woman I met? With Andy? We called her Mrs. Smith. And I don't know anything about her." She wore a necklace, a gold cross like the one on her father's face. "She was just an old lady."

Leave it there, she thought, and walk away into the future and never look back. Forget about Codyville and Patriot Camp and be a new person with a brand new life. She had buried her memories before; why could she not do it again?

Because you can't have a new life without finishing the old one.

In the hospital room the only sounds were the beeping monitors.

"I can draw you a picture of Mrs. Smith. If you want."

Author's Note

Bone Lake, and its characters and events, is a work of fiction. The True Word Brethren is a fictional entity, an amalgam of several so-called Aryan groups including but not limited to Christian Identity. These groups are characterized by an interpretation of Christianity supporting a violent and racist agenda.

The views of the True Word Brethren in no way reflect my own.